DEADLY RANSOM

By Robert Harper

With special thanks to my Wife, Jenny, who persuaded me to complete this book which I started nearly 20 years ago.

Also thanks to Andrea for proof-reading, good humour and helpful suggestions.

CHAPTER 1

AGE. James Jackson considered the word. Was age a question of determining whether one viewed life as a 'still to do' or a 'once did'. Was forty the changing point or fifty or, God forbid, was it thirty when one considered the past, when one stood back and thought about all the once did and maybe looked forward to the still to do. Either way he thought here I am on the wrong side of forty. He smiled, don't be dishonest with yourself, the wrong side of forty-eight. A weighty subject.

He looked at his reflection in the large round bathroom mirror, features softened by condensation. He stared into the mirror his pale blue eyes looking back at him and he allowed them to take in the whole of his reflected face.

His hair, collar length, was silvery grey, though thinning and receding slightly there were no bald patches. His full beard was neatly trimmed, grey except for a few dark brown hairs on his upper lip. He had been grey haired from his early twenties, it had never worried him, the fear of baldness did worry him, but he was not sure why, he just knew he wouldn't like it. He often joked that he went to the barbers on a regular basis, every three months whether he needed to or not. Sometimes he allowed his hair to grow almost long enough for a Poldark ponytail, but he lacked the courage to let it grow the extra inch to make it possible. He stroked his beard with his left hand, pulling the lines from under his eyes, he sighed, his breath on the mirror obscuring his image.

He walked the few steps to the bedroom opening the door slowly and quietly so as not to disturb Karen his wife who was still sleeping. It was nine and the November sun was casting the first light through the window, its rays creeping slowly up the bed towards Karen's face. James looked at her. She looked peaceful and content which pleased him, both of them had had a stressful time recently. His jeans and shirt lay neatly folded on a chair near the window. He dressed quickly. He checked his image in the full-length mirror, his six feet and two hundred pounds filling it. He had noticed recently that he was getting a paunch but by eating sensibly recently his paunch was no longer visible and his jeans were no longer tight. He wasn't an athlete or keep fit fanatic, but he did like to swim a couple of times a week at lunchtime.

He left the bedroom leaving Karen sleeping, went downstairs and made coffee. He sat at the kitchen table looking through the window at the garden and he wished that events had not taken place that had prevented him from his routine autumn tidy up. Nursing his coffee, he sat alone and still.

James managed an oilfield service company. Specialists in the explosive abandonment of oil exploration wells; one of only a handful in the world that performed this service. It was demanding work and he had been committed to it for more than twenty years.

He had enjoyed almost every day of those twenty odd years, potentially dangerous work, he took it seriously but considered it a big boy's game. Where else except in war can a man set off a powerful explosion and get paid for it. The work was not complicated, basic rules and standard calculations made it simple, but most jobs are if you enjoy the work,

The years had brought little new technology; better detonators, and cleaner chemicals with more robust hardware but no real advances. In the early days of his career, he had loved the buzz of jetting around the world, visiting new countries, meeting new people, performing in a professional manner and just doing a good job but as the company grew his management role had tied him to a desk although he still travelled, selling the service, planning the work and infrequently trouble shooting when things went wrong.

A couple of his regular customers still insisted on him being on the job and this kept his hand in and his adrenaline running. He could teach anyone to do the work but not everyone wanted to do it. A job where a mistake could mean termination and termination could mean death.

James had seen much of Africa, most of Europe, both east and west, a great deal of the Middle East and some of South and North America, Canada and acres and acres of the North Sea. He was familiar with the interior layouts of many international airports and more than a few domestic ones. He had once calculated that he had spent a total of eighteen days waiting on connections at Amsterdam Schiphol, an airport he did not rate highly as it seemed to close its food outlets before the last flights left, he thought they operated for the benefit of the employees rather than the flying customers.

His job paid well. Home was a large old farmhouse with seven acres of land on the outskirts of Rothienorman, a small, blink twice and you miss it village, in rural Aberdeenshire some twenty-five miles from his office in Aberdeen. Aberdeen on Scotland's east coast was the reputed quality assured oil capital of the world. A good place to live and work. Dark, harsh winters compensated by long summer daylight, pure air and the friendliness and generosity of the people.

However good the pay, James and Karen spent it on the things that are necessary. Mortgage, heating, food, insurance for peace of mind, pension for the future and the normal outgoings of an ordinary family.

Karen was vivacious, her attractive face framed by a mass of brown hair and the bluest of blue eyes. Several years younger than James she would tease him about his grey hair and his well-worn features, but it was only teasing as she loved him to distraction. Married for nine years, Karen had brought a daughter to the marriage, Molly, and like stepchildren the world over she had mixed emotions about James. Mostly she loved him dearly. The marriage had made James incredibly happy.

James nursed his coffee until it was lukewarm. He then drank it quickly, the milky thickness of it making him feel slightly sick.

His tongue circled his teeth, feeling the coating of tiredness, lingering on the fillings and crevices. He was pleased that despite caps and fillings and a few gaps the teeth he felt were his own. Thankful that he had taken Karen's advice and made regular visits to his dentist, a Mr Henderson, big and burly but compassionate and gentle as a lamb whose most used word was 'sorry'.

James caught his reflection in the windowpane, he watched himself cry. The tears formed and gently and slowly they welled up in his eyes rolling down his cheeks. Pictures in his brain playing back the nightmare of the past two months.

CHAPTER 2

IN September James' warehouse and office at Tullos industrial estate on the south side of Aberdeen had been blown up.

Newspapers, radio, and TV had told the story simply and accurately and it had made the headlines until more important news superseded it. The headline the day after the bombing read: -

EXPLOSION KILLS SEVEN IN SUSPECTED TERROR ATTACK

James knew the seven, their habits and families. What he didn't know was who had done it and why.

It did not seem to him that two months had passed. Time stood still sometimes and raced by at others and some was lost completely.

The day had started with him going to the office early to leave some work for his secretary before leaving for a nine fifteen dental appointment which he had been lucky to get. A cap that had succumbed to an extra hard chomp on a pork chop needed replacing. Sat in the chair in the ultra-modern surgery he thought about visiting the dentist as a boy and the treadle drill that had inflicted misery and suffering on him and started his fear of the profession. Now Mr. Henderson with James' mouth full of modern virtually pain free contraptions and repeatedly saying sorry had gone about his business. Mr. Henderson chatted about golf and holidays, never expecting more than a grunt in response. Then there was a muffled noise, they both sensed the air tremble and the surgery windows vibrated momentarily and rattled. For a second or so neither moved it seemed as though their world was on hold. James' first thought was that it was an explosion. Just as suddenly the world returned to life and the everyday noises of birds and traffic were heard again. The nurse made a comment about low flying aircraft but before James could disagree Mr. Henderson was drilling. Ten minutes later, the work finished, James left the surgery and walked to his car. The air was cool, but the sun shone brightly in a clear blue sky, the kind of day that sets the stark granite architecture of Aberdeen shimmering and earns it the title of the silver city. A beautiful Scottish autumn day.

The sound of sirens, wailing and two tone were clear on the still air. He wondered if the sirens related to the sound of what he was sure had been an explosion. His mind took him back some twenty or more years to a previous blast in Aberdeen which he had heard and which had demolished a large hotel, The Royal Darroch, in a busy suburb to the west of the city. That blast he recalled had killed six and injured many others, many more escaping shocked but uninjured physically.

He started his car and headed towards his office taking North Anderson Drive south towards the River Dee, one of the two rivers, the other the Don, that flow into the North Sea on the North and South side of Aberdeen. Traffic was light, he pulled in twice to allow several ambulances and police cars travelling at high-speed, sirens screaming, to pass. He crossed the Bridge of Dee turning left and following the course of the river towards the sea. At the brow of the hill, he saw and smelt acrid smoke billowing up in black anger ahead. He drove on, still more than a mile from his office, the black smoke filling his vision the closer he got. He picked up his mobile phone which sat on the passenger seat. He called his office, no reply, he pressed redial, again no answer. The traffic on Abbotswell Road some five hundred yards from his office was at a standstill. A police car, lights flashing, was stopped in the centre of the road preventing traffic from moving. Now stopped with window open the fumes of the acrid smoke were strong, stinging the eyes and burning the throat. He spotted a friend's car ahead and got out of his own and walked towards it.

'Hi Geoff, what's happening?'

'How are you? Long time no see' replied Geoff. 'A fire over in Tullos, this smoke is stinking, looks like it's pretty close to your place.'

'Yes, it does, I think I'll double back and see if I can get closer, see you later' said James, turning and running back to his car.

He heard Geoff shout 'Right, hey let's meet next week for lunch and a catch up.'

James managed to three point turn his car and took a round-about route through the industrial estate and came out on Greenwell Road several hundred yards closer to his office but again found his route blocked. He pulled into the Bank of Scotland car park and parked up. He redialled, again just a dead line. He tried the bypass numbers but still just dead. He dialled his secretary's mobile; it went to voice mail. James was worried, his company prided itself on its response twenty-four seven and took its obligation to provide this service very seriously. He could not believe the office was unattended no matter what excitement was going on nearby.

He started to walk towards his office, the road ahead of him became totally blocked with fire engines, ambulances and police cars, the smoke heavy and obscuring the view. The driver of a lorry had climbed onto his cab roof for a better view.

James shouted up to him 'What's happening?'

'Looks like a pretty bad fire at Cut and Pull' he shouted down.

'Are you sure?' asked James.

'No, not sure but that's what it looks like' replied the driver squinting to try to see through the smoke.

James ran. He was a hundred yards away and into the smoke before he could see what looked like the wall of a warehouse, what was left of it was bowed and distorted. Closer he could see it was bowed outwards, the metal sheeting blackened and twisted. Smoke was pouring through a hole where the roof should be and now, he could see flames. Getting closer he could only see devastation. The main road was blocked by cement blocks, blackened sheets and twisted steel.

James' chest tightened, he screamed out 'My God, the explosives!'

He sprinted forward, dodging past a policeman who was directing the emergency services traffic. His sprint became a blind panic run.

He could see the building clearly now, or at least what was left of it. It reminded him of a bombed-out warehouse he had seen in Kuwait after the liberation in 91. No, this was worse he thought.

'I'm part of all this!' he shouted.

In his blind panic run he tripped and fell headlong, his trousers ripping at the knee, his skin grazed and bleeding. Lying face down he tried to regain his senses. He saw a fireman running towards him, looking like an alien in his breathing apparatus. The fireman grabbed him and pulled him to his feet and away from the building. James was confused, his eyes streaming and he tasted the smoke burning his throat.

'What the hell happened?' he shouted at the fireman who was removing his breathing apparatus. James became aware of the roaring of the fire and shouted his question again, louder this time.

'Think a bomb' the fireman shouted back 'you shouldn't be here; you must move back.'

'It's my building, I'm the boss, my people, my building' James shouted struggling to get away from the fireman's restraining hold.

The fireman held his arm firmly and said 'Calm down mate, just calm down. There's been an explosion and we think there are casualties, but we are still checking. Let's go across to the police control unit, okay, are you okay?'

James was far from okay, but he allowed himself to be led by the fireman to the police caravan. James did not have time that day to feel shocked.

The next twelve hours were a total blur for James. He was interviewed by a police superintendent who was directing operations. In less than an hour it was confirmed that all seven employees of the company had been killed in the explosion. Later, James, accompanied by a police sergeant who had been assigned to him, entered what was left of the building.

James was able to provide details of where the various chemicals, detonators and primers were stored; it was difficult to pinpoint them as the building was so damaged but after some time he found and accounted for everything.

Identifying the bodies of his former colleagues had been almost too much to bear. The bodies were all severely damaged, but he knew them so well that he had been able to put names to the mutilated corpses. He knew that his efforts now would make it easier for the relatives to make formal identification later. These shattered bodies of his colleagues had been his friends. His entire work force was gone, there had been no offshore jobs ongoing, so they were all at the workshop maintaining, repairing, and getting ready for the future. A future none of them would now experience. James thought about the business they had built together then realized that his thoughts should be with the families whose happiness had been destroyed in a split second.

He met with the forensic team who, because of the explosives kept on the premises, were being assisted by military police and Royal Marine explosive experts who had helicoptered in from their base at Arbroath within an hour or so of the explosion.

James worried that the explosion had been caused by his own employees and his own explosives but shortly after the arrival of the military team they had found and confirmed that the explosion proof boxes that contained the detonators were intact and still locked and secure. An accident or incident with the chemicals could not be ruled out but James thought this most unlikely.

On that day and subsequent days, James had been impressed with the professionalism and compassion of the police officers. He accompanied them over the next few days to visit the wives, husband, girlfriends and other relatives and friends of his dead colleagues.

His telephone call to the President of Cut and Pull at the Houston head office had been met with disbelief at first but within a few moments he received an assurance that everything possible would be done to support and assist in any way.

So many questions were asked that first day, but most of the questions were the same. Why? How? Who?

The smoke cleared slowly over the site on that first day, but the smell of fire and death were sharp on the senses. They were on James' clothes when he arrived home, driven there by the sergeant who had been assigned to him. James had telephoned Karen several times during the day and early evening, she had wanted to be with him, so grateful and thankful that he had been spared, wishing to share his grief and torment and help him cope but he had insisted she stay at home not wanting her to see the terrible things he had seen that day.

Karen stayed at home, unable to get far from the constantly ringing telephone. Explaining to local, national, and international press that she had no details and that her husband would be home later, and he would have a lot more information on the day's events. At midday, a police superintendent called her and gave her the number of the major incident room so that she could direct any further calls. By early afternoon two police constables were protecting her privacy at the house and keeping the press and radio cars as far away as possible. The first of the press had arrived at the house within an hour or so of the explosion and by early evening SKY TV and BBC TV trucks were parked in the lane leading to the house. It seemed like the whole world wanted to speak to the man who was being dubbed Mr. Lucky.

The lane leading to the house became blocked and the police good naturedly sorted out the confusion and Karen had provided teas and coffee.

Karen's closest neighbours Elizabeth and Peter visited in the late afternoon bringing much needed supplies of milk but more importantly, friendly faces. They watched the early evening news and saw for the first-time pictures of the devastation. Karen needed all their support when James was shown on the screen looking tired and drawn, his face grey and his shoulders slumped.

'He looks terrible, so tired,' said Karen.

Peter put his arm around her 'he's had a tough day, the worst in his life'.

Neither Peter nor Karen knew James' secret.

Peter knew Karen would also be grieving for the dead and he stayed with his arm around her until the news moved on.

At nine forty-five that evening James arrived home. The police cleared a path through the press and got him into the house. Peter came out of the house several minutes later and asked the pack of journalists to be patient, informing them that James would come out and answer questions in fifteen minutes. This news settled them, and they busied themselves ensuring their equipment was working properly and hoping that they would meet their respective deadlines.

James didn't smoke or drink, the cigarettes had gone ten years before and the alcohol was a lifetime ago. Tonight, he craved the calming nicotine and the burning alcohol. If he had been alone, he might well have succumbed to the temptation but he wasn't alone and thanked God for that.

Karen's arms encircled him, and her warmth and soft touch reminded him of how much he loved this woman, and he knew her strength would help him through this terrible time.

A few minutes after ten, as promised, he gave the press their interview which went out live on national TV and radio. James was amazed at how insensitive and stupid some of the questions were and he was on a short fuse when he brought the questions to an end by reading a prepared statement paying tribute to his dead colleagues and to the emergency services who were still at the scene.

He finished by saying 'the police are treating these deaths as suspicious. I understand this to mean that an explosive device was placed and detonated by a person or persons who the police are now seeking. I am asking on behalf of the bereaved families if you have any information that could assist the police then please contact them immediately. My company is offering a reward of fifty thousand pounds for information that leads to the arrest and conviction of those responsible. Thank you.'

As soon as the interview was over the reporters drifted away and the two police officers cleared away those who thought there was more to come. Peter and Elizabeth left shortly afterwards with Molly who they had agreed to look after for a few days until things calmed down. Karen and James were alone in the house. The phone continued to ring. The kettle stayed on. Karen's parents called offering sympathy and any help required. Friends and business associates called and with sympathy and support. Senior management from companies who were in competition with Cut and Pull called and offered sympathy, support and any assistance that might be required. Without exception everyone who called was shocked that such a thing could have happened.

The following days were lost in a blur of seemingly endless investigation that was being carried out by the civilian and military police, insurance adjusters, Cut and Pull's security and loss investigators. The corporate security advisor came over from the States. A bit late James thought. Four days after the explosion it was confirmed by the police that the blast appeared to have been caused by an unsophisticated possibly gelignite-based device. James was relieved to have it confirmed that the explosion was nothing to do with the explosive materials stored on the premises. James had always operated the company in strict accordance with the legal requirements of working with explosives and was a stickler for correct safe procedure, never allowing his employees to take short cuts. He had always known in his heart that his staff were not to blame but he felt so much better having it confirmed.

Five days after the explosion the first of the funerals was held and by day seven James and Karen had attended the funeral service of every one of his colleagues. The strain on them both was almost too much, and the local doctor had stopped by the house to make sure they were coping.

Fourteen days after the explosion the City of Aberdeen came to a standstill as the memorial service took place. Dignitaries and worthies emerged from the woodwork and the Langstane Kirk was filled to overflowing. It was a moving service and James was impressed by the dignity and courage shown by those personally affected by the tragedy. James, a Tory voter all his life, was most moved by the few moments he and the families spent with Prime Minister Blair whose kind and thoughtful words did much to comfort and lift the spirits. James met again the police sergeant who had been assigned to him on the day of the explosion. He looked different out of uniform and it took James a moment or two to recognize him and James apologized for not acknowledging him sooner. They spent a few minutes talking and James was shocked but delighted when the sergeant in a whisper, emphasizing it was confidential, told him that three Irishmen had been arrested in

London. They had purchased tickets for a long-distance Aberdeen to London coach that had departed thirty minutes before the blast.

'We've got the IRA bastards James' the sergeant said, smiling.

CHAPTER 3

JAMES nursed his coffee. The mug's heat on his hands barely noticeable. He sat alone in the kitchen. He watched the November sun cast patterns over the lawn. He was listless. Restless and ill at ease with life.

After the traumas of the funerals and memorial service James and Karen had a few days at home just trying to rest and relax and spending time with Molly who had been a real comfort to them both. She had been strong and supportive in a way that was beyond her years. The three of them had visited the twenty or so people who had been working near the building when the explosion occurred and who had suffered injuries of varying degrees; thankfully the most severely injured were now off the danger list. James knew most of them, at least by sight, and he felt a bond with them knowing that his own life had probably been spared by an unplanned dental appointment.

He sat, his coffee going cold; the faces of his dead friends clear in his mind's eye. His eyes misted with tears.

Karen woke and found the space in the bed beside her cold

and empty. She went downstairs to look for James. She was worried about him. She knew how stressed he was. He had talked about how if he had been at his desk, he could maybe have stopped the explosion and he felt guilty and responsible. Karen had told him this was crazy thinking and rather than feel guilty he should be pleased that he had survived.

Karen found him in the kitchen, and she moved behind him placing her hands on his shoulders, pressing her body to his back.

'Come on James' she said softly 'this isn't like you, get your mind together and let's get on with our lives, the newspapers called you the luckiest man alive, make use of that luck, you can't bring anyone back, it wasn't your fault. Come on please I love you so much and I cannot bear to see you like this'.

The words that she had been storing up poured out of her, she slumped down at James' feet and sobbed. James looked out of the window, far into the distance, lost in his own thoughts and thinking hard about Karen's words. He sat still for several minutes. Karen's quiet sobbing and the clock ticking the only sounds he heard.

He turned in the chair and looked down at her. He broke the silence 'Karen you are right' his voice was soft, 'it's just that.....' he could not finish as Karen threw herself into his arms and they wiped the tears from each other's faces. He led her up the stairs to their bedroom and they sought the solace of each other's body. They made love, the tensions and strains releasing from them. Then, they slept as they had not slept in weeks. Waking, hours later, they arranged for Molly to spend a few days with friends, then went back to bed, made love again and slept till the following morning.

They sat together in front of the open wood fire in the lounge and pondered their future.

James had been thinking about the company and what future there was for it and for him. He had been given leave for as long as he needed but he had worked a few days with the lawyers and accountants trying to make some sense of the mess of paperwork that was salvaged from the building, as well as and more importantly making sure that all the pensions and payments due to his dead colleagues' families were paid or in hand. He had visited his customers and without exception they told him that whenever he was up and running, they would use his services. He had been very moved by the support he had received from them.

'Karen', he said, 'what would you think if I decided not to go back to work. I have a real problem thinking about starting up again with new people. I'm not sure I will be able to do it. The challenge doesn't hold any excitement for me, it all seems to have been a waste of time building the business up into something good only for it to be snatched away in a moment's madness'.

'Whatever you want is okay with me' she replied, 'I only want you to be happy'.

Discussing the idea some more they made the decision and James picked up the telephone and dialled the States. He spoke first with Mary Jane, secretary to Barry Hendrich the company president. He told her what had been happening since they had last spoken a few days previously and assuring her that both he and Karen were well. After a few minutes chat she put him through to Barry. Barry, with regret, accepted James' decision to stop working and told him that he would do nothing about it for ninety days and he would continue to honour James' contract. This, he suggested would give James the time to consider his future and selfishly would ensure that James was around to continue to handle the various legal issues that would continue to need settling.

Barry and James had known each other for years and the conversation was easy.

Barry said 'Let me sum up our conversation James. We have known each other long enough for me to know you have thought this through, but it would sure help us out if you would agree to stay on the payroll until all the legals are out of the way and this sad business is finalized, however and whenever that might happen. We will continue to pay you and try to change your mind about leaving, is that a deal?'

James agreed, he had no intention of leaving the company he loved in the lurch and was incredibly pleased with Barry's attitude and his generous offer.

'Let's stay in touch every few days' said Barry.

'No problem, I'll be around the house if you need me for anything urgent, thanks for being understanding, I really appreciate it, thank you' said James smiling.

The call ended. James told Karen what had been agreed. For the first time James thought about the financial implications of not having a job and was thankful that Barry had made the offer. They sat and made a list of their assets and obligations and after a while with the pencil and paper he pushed it away from him.

'What are you smiling about' Karen asked him.

Instead of his usual 'nothing' he looked at her and gently pressed his forehead against hers, he took her hands and held them in his own, gently caressing them.

'Do you realize my darling that in a few months we could be broke, no more pay cheques but, no more call outs at midnight, no more leaving early and getting home late, no more messed up weekends. It's not all bad, the going might get tough but at least I'm alive.'

He cried then, his grief and torment, hatred of those that had killed his friends spilling over. His tears wet his cheeks and his beard. Karen removed his glasses and kissed his eyes, tasting the salt of his tears. She let him cry whispering to him that she loved him.

The rest of the day was a blur to them both. Molly came home from school and found them both sleeping in front of the fire, she crept across the room and gently kissed James' forehead. Her kiss barely brushing the skin. She left them to sleep. Molly was fully aware of the strain they had both been under.

It was late afternoon and dark when James woke. He went to the bathroom, showered, and changed into clean jeans and a fresh white shirt. He went back downstairs, his eyes still a little puffy but feeling and looking a new man. That evening they relaxed and tried to regain a normal family life.

The next morning when James woke, he could not have known that his life was about to change for the second time.

James watched the rain flooding the lawn. It had rained a lot in the past few days and James who had been intending to tidy the garden which had been neglected since the explosion was at a loose end. He picked up the newspaper, something he had not done in the past couple of months. The explosion was old news and no longer made headlines. Turning the pages and doing no more than glancing at the stories he saw a story on page three:

SUSPECTED ABERDEEN BOMBERS RELEASED – POLICE SAY NO EVIDENCE AGAINST THEM.

He read the story, the three Irishmen had been released the previous day, the alibis they had furnished standing up to investigation. Apparently, they had been leaving Aberdeen after a hill walking holiday and while they had been living in the hills for several weeks, they had been in contact with a few people who had been located and confirmed their story. The report went on to say the police were appealing for any information regarding the explosion and advising that the reward was still on offer.

James couldn't believe it. He had convinced himself the men were guilty, and he was waiting on a trial date followed by a long sentence. The sergeant had been so convinced.

Molly came into the kitchen, almost sixteen, her body well developed, with short brown hair matching her brown eyes as bright and sparkling as her personality. Not a brilliant scholar she made up for it with an easy going and forgiving nature and a huge amount of common sense. Like James she was a Scorpio and needed to have the last word in any argument. She was pretty and much tougher than she looked.

'Give me a cuddle' she demanded.

James smiled and turned towards her. He was aware that he didn't give his stepdaughter enough physical attention. He did love her dearly, though, and enjoyed her company and her humour. He wrapped her in his arms and patted her bottom, she echoed her mother with,

'Don't pat me like a horse'.

James smiled, squeezed her, and then released her.

'Aren't you getting bored being home all day, when are you going back to work?' she asked.

'I'm not' he replied.

'You've been home a lot lately' Molly said.

'Yes.' James replied 'Hey! Has your mother put you up to having this conversation with me'?

'Mum is worried about you, she thinks you are okay on the outside but still confused and hurting on the inside, she thinks you feel guilty because you were out of the office when the explosion went off'.

'What do you think?' James asked.

'I think you were dead lucky, all my friends at school think its dead brilliant you weren't killed' Molly said, smiling.

'Yea, I think its dead brilliant too' James said, leaning forward and kissing her cheek, 'I get the message'.

Kettles, the Yorkshire terrier, came yapping and jumping into the kitchen ready for her walk. She had never been so fit, her little body muscled and her energy levels high. James had been taking her for a long walk every day since he had been at home. He looked out the window. The rain had stopped. He picked up his Barbour jacket and Kettles began to yap dementedly knowing a walk was imminent.

'Taking the dog for a walk!' he shouted to Karen who was upstairs making curtains in her workroom at the back of the house. Molly stood on the back doorstep and saw them off.

'Don't get wet!' she shouted as James and Kettles went up the lane. He waved to her.

James and Kettles made their way up the hill. The grass was slippery and walking was difficult and tiring. The dog running around his feet, James stopped and breathed deeply. He looked down at the dog, yapping and jumping. A dog happy with life.

James looked down the hill towards the house which was nestled in a fold at the bottom of the hill, and at the head of the valley which stretched beyond. The farming land, fallow or ploughed brown, stretched for miles in the distance merging into the Grampian hills not yet covered with winter snow. In the far distance the peak of Bennachie was just visible, the highest point in the area. Bennachie looked purple and majestic as the sun's rays reached it through a gap in the rain clouds. Solid and dependable, thought James.

A bright flash attracted his attention, the earth jumping by his right foot. And then CRACK! His brain told him it was a rifle shot. Then told him, that's ridiculous, then instinct kicked in and told him to get moving. Brain, action, move legs, run, God, shit, the sheer surprise that anyone would shoot at him scrambled his brain. In what seemed like minutes but in fact was a split-second James bent, picked up the dog and ran zig zagging to his right and a fold in the ground. CRACK! CRACK! the earth spurting up slightly ahead of him. He made the fold and the stream that ran through it. He jumped and landed in the stream the dog tumbling from his arms and she yelped as she hit the cold water.

'No noise' James commanded as he rescued the dog from the water. He could hear nothing but his own heartbeat and the sounds of nature. The stream, the ground water running through the grass, the rustle of the whin bushes at the edge of the stream. His eyes and ears strained. His heart pounding, filling his chest making breathing difficult.

James was frightened. Being shot at was a new experience. He didn't like it.

The house was a good three hundred yards downhill to his left. He saw a pick-up moving in the lane before he heard another CRACK! and the sound of the engine. It was heading for the house. His feet slipping on the sodden bank he pulled himself out of the stream and slipping and sliding he ran towards the house, the dog no longer at his heels.

He kept his eyes on the pick-up, as it neared the house a rain squall swept through blurring his vision. The squall cleared and he could see Molly being dragged into the pick-up screaming and struggling. Karen was trying to hold onto her but as he watched she was knocked to the ground and lay still. James could just see one man dragging Molly as he continued his run towards the house still several hundred yards away.

This is not happening, he thought, as he saw the pick-up now moving away from the house, he heard himself screaming 'NO!'.

He changed course and ran towards the bend in the lane that was nearest to him trying to cut off the pick-up's escape. He leapt the fence and landed in the lane reaching out for the tail gate of the pick-up his fingers failing to grip the rain slippery paintwork. He could not hold on and he went sprawling on the ground, watching the truck disappear down the lane in a shower of spray. He got up and ran after it but it was pointless and he could only watch as his step daughter was carried away.

James turned and ran up the lane towards the house. Karen lay at the back door her lip and eye cut and her head bleeding.

'What the fuck is going on? Jesus Christ, Karen, Karen what's happening Karen, are you okay?'

She looked blank eyed at him. He ran past her into the house and picked up the telephone, fingers shaking and fumbling he dialled 999. He asked for ambulance and police, impatiently he gave his address and then threw down the phone and went to Karen. She was now half sitting against the back doorstep, her blood mixing with the rain and staining her white blouse.

James tried to make her comfortable and going back into the house pulled an antique quilt that was used as a cover over an old settee, carried it outside and wrapped her in it trying to keep her warm, dry and comfortable. She was crying now, confused and in pain.

'Oh Karen, what the fucks going on? Who was he? What's happening?' James asked not expecting her to know, or to answer, simply confused and in panic.

He went back into the house and called 999 again, he explained to the operator that he had already called for an ambulance and the police but now he needed urgently to speak to the police. The operator put him through.

'Incident room, Sergeant Dawson, how can I help you? The trained calm of the policeman helped to reassure James,

'Sergeant, my daughter has just been forced into a pick-up and my wife assaulted. I need help urgently. Please help me.'

The sergeant had many years' experience and obtained from James all the relevant details and the address, names, ages, of Molly and Karen, details of the abduction and the pick-up type and colour and the direction it was heading when last seen. As they spoke James could hear the sirens of the ambulance wailing in the distance. James told the sergeant he must go to check on his wife and the sergeant advised that the police car would be there a couple of minutes after the ambulance.

James went to Karen, he held her in his arms waiting for the ambulance. The sirens' wail was much closer now and he reassured her that help was on the way, but it still seemed an age before it arrived and the medics took over. Karen was more shocked than hurt. The medics checked her over and patched up her cuts and checked her head wound. She refused to go to hospital and when the medics heard James explain to the police constable what had happened, they called the local doctor who agreed to come by as soon as possible.

Kettles walked slowly across the path towards James, her trusting eyes searching him out. James saw her, bedraggled, soaking wet and with what looked like blood coming from her ear. One of the ambulance crew gave her a quick once over and saw that the blood from her ear came from a small perfectly round hole and a graze along her skull. He pointed this out to James.

'He shot my fucking dog!' exclaimed James. 'Jesus, what's going on?'

He gave Kettles to Karen who held the dog close keeping her warm.

The doctor arrived and checked Karen and, realizing the seriousness of what had happened, decided that he had better not give her too strong a medication as he was sure she would need and want to be as coherent as possible when talking to the police. He made sure she was comfortable then drew the police sergeant, who had arrived at the scene a few minutes after himself, to one side.

'Sergeant, I know you will want to speak to Mrs. Jackson but please be very gentle with her she has taken a bad blow to the head and is a little concussed. I will return later and if her condition has deteriorated then I will have no alternate than to admit her to hospital, is that clear'.

'Yes Sir,' replied the sergeant, 'fully understood.'

The doctor told Karen that he would return later and gave the same information to James who was now telling the police sergeant all that had occurred. The shots, the assault on Karen and the abduction of Molly. It took the sergeant just a few moments to realize that he needed to consult with more senior officers. This was a lot more serious than the poaching, sheep stealing and cannabis growing that were still considered major crimes in Aberdeenshire.

A detective chief inspector arrived within an hour. From the information that Karen was able to give to the sergeant a search had already been instigated for the white Toyota pick-up. Karen had been alert enough to look at the number plate but she could only remember H71. On the national computer this was traced to a pick-up not reported stolen and enquiries discovered that the owner, who was tracked to a vacation complex in the USA, had left it parked at Glasgow airport some days before   The Detective Chief Inspector introduced himself as Euan Sinclair, he began by talking to James and Karen together and when he had the general outline, he spoke to them separately. He realized that this was the same family who had been involved with the recent Aberdeen explosion. He was compassionate but forceful enough to get a more detailed story from Karen.

Later in the afternoon the Doctor called back and gave Karen a quick but thorough examination and was pleased to see that she was composed and calm and apart from her cuts and a slight headache was in good health.

Their stories told the DCI all he could hope to know from the first gunshot to the disappearing pick-up. Following James' second 999 call, police cars had been alerted to look out for a white Toyota pick-up with one male driver and possibly a female passenger. Any vehicle answering the description was to be stopped and held until they could be eliminated. Around eight vehicles answering the description were being held in various parts of Grampian region, irate drivers waiting to be cleared to go about their business. Officers were sent to interview the property owners closest to Karen and James' house in this fairly isolated rural community.   A community which was alert to strangers and where rural theft from farms and outbuildings was not unusual.

With daylight rapidly failing a forensic team was deployed to search for the bullets, the task made somewhat easier by the wet, long grass still tracing the route taken by James. A search later in the evening by metal detector revealed three bullets which were sent to Aberdeen for identification.

DCI Sinclair briefed his team. He felt that it was likely that this had been well planned and that Molly had been taken for a reason. With the use of the gun, he felt that this wasn't a chance abduction by a paedophile so he reasoned that they would possibly be hearing from the abductor. His gut feeling was this was a well-organized kidnap and until he knew any different that was his strategy.

The team were joined by Sergeant Tom McLeod from Edinburgh who had been in Aberdeen attending a training course on survival techniques at the Robert Gordons Institute. He was the only fully trained police hostage negotiator in Scotland and was available so close purely by chance. The DCI, with Tom's input, made several calls putting into place the necessary actions for an operational plan for this kind of incident.

It would not be long before hundreds of officers were involved.

Two young policemen were left at the entrance to the lane leading to the house ensuring only those approved and authorized would get through to the crime scene. Tom stayed in the house supervising the telephone and recording devices waiting to see if there would be contact from the abductor.

For two days there was nothing. Country wide enquiries

were made regarding the Toyota but there was no sign of it, Molly, or the unidentified driver. The trail had gone cold very quickly, this was a worry.

Tom, James, and Karen were trying to stay as calm as possible. For Tom it was a lot easier than for James and Karen, his training had been sophisticated and thorough and he was well used to long hours of inactivity followed by short bursts of adrenalin filled action. He told them about his experiences and his successes, trying to keep their spirits up and their minds focused. They both liked him and connected with him. For James, used to giving orders and not taking them, this was a new experience and he forced himself to have faith in Tom's knowledge.

It was two and in the early morning hours the house was quiet. The embers of the log fire still glowing in the grate. Tom was drinking a small glass of whisky, James was with him, his coffee half drunk and cold in a mug on the table. They had been talking, waiting for something, anything, to happen all evening and were about to go to bed. Karen had gone up earlier, recovering well from her injuries, her eye was black and the lump on her head still sore, her lip scabbed, nothing that a few more days would not take care of. Mentally she was strong, positive that her daughter would be returned to her. She hadn't slept at all since the kidnap but at ten she had gone to bed exhausted and had fallen to sleep almost immediately.

Tom stood up, his whisky finished, he stretched, his body stiff from inactivity.

'Well James it doesn't look like we are going to get a call tonight, let's turn in, you must be knackered.'

'Yes, I suppose I am, but how can I sleep for worrying about Molly, I just feel so helpless' James replied.

'We aren't helpless. While we sleep there are several hundred officers searching and lots more going back over old cases trying to piece some clues together, we are working, we will get results. Go and rest, you need to be fresh and strong for Karen's sake' Tom said, trying to give James some encouragement.

'As usual Tom, you're right. Good night.'

'Good Night, Sir' responded Tom, settling down into the large soft leather sofa in the lounge where he was close to the telephone.

James undressed and slid silently into bed beside Karen who stirred for a moment before falling back into a deep sleep.

The old house cooling down, creaked and moaned as its occupants slept.

The phone rang. The strident tone waking Tom instantly, he swung his long legs from the settee and gathered his thoughts. He allowed the phone to ring; he heard the sound of James running down the stairs. He waited for James to enter the room and Tom indicated to James by putting his fingers to his lips that he must be quiet. The phone had rung five times. Tom lifted the receiver. He took a firm grip to ensure he did not drop it. He said nothing. He checked to ensure the tape recorder connected to the phone had switched on automatically. The tape whirled almost silently. James was sure he could hear his own heart beating. Time seemed to stand still. In reality two seconds had passed since Tom had picked up the handset.

'I have the girl' the voice was distorted and electronic, undulating and high pitched.

Karen entered the room and James whispered for her to be quiet. She held his arm tightly. All three of them stared at the phone willing the speaker to say more. There was silence.

'We want proof,' said Tom.

Silence again. Then a faint click. Then 'Mummy' a voice frightened and confused. It was Molly's voice, not calling to, but calling for, her mother. Another click. Silence again.

'Proof enough' said the electronic voice 'that was recorded this morning, that's all the proof you get.'

James and Karen both nodded when Tom looked at them. The nod to indicate it was Molly's voice. The colour drained from their faces, their bodies shaking.

'Okay,' said Tom in his calm and gentle voice.

The metallic voice spoke again 'Good, now I need you to listen.'

At the telephone exchange the tracking and tracing devices searched for the number and location of the phone that metallic voice was using. The experts knew that time was not on their side. All things might be possible in Hollywood but in real life it was more complicated and usually disappointing.

'I know you are the police, with the shots being fired it was obvious you would be called in, but it doesn't matter, it will make no difference. Tell that bastard James Jackson that he must die to ensure the girl is released. His death is the only thing that will ensure this girl lives. I'll call again sometime, and the password will be "an eye for an eye"'.

'Please repeat that,' said Tom, but the phone line was already dead. The call had lasted less than thirty seconds. Five seconds later it rang again.

Tom answered it with a curt 'McLeod'.

He listened and nodded several times. He replaced the receiver.

'The exchange didn't have enough time to trace the call which is a pity but at least we have contact,' he said, adding 'it's only the beginning' trying to give Karen and James confidence and reassurance.

He ran the tape playing it from start to finish.

'What have I done that he wants me dead?' asked James sounding shocked and frightened.

Karen clung to him. They both looked towards Tom McLeod for an answer. He couldn't give them one.

'I don't know, we don't know who this man is, but we will. It's early days. Molly is alive and that's great news. We will find her.'

CHAPTER 4

ARTHUR Summerskill was a quiet man. In his mid-thirties he worked in the drawing office of a small engineering company in Northampton. He had worked for the same company since leaving technical college at nineteen. Arthur's father had worked there for thirty years when Arthur joined. His father was now retired spending time on his allotment and tending his pigeons. Like his father, Arthur was a man of little ambition. He did not aspire to a fancy job or great wealth. He was content, careful with his money. He had few friends, not because he didn't like people, he simply didn't need them. Arthur's life centred around his wife Annette and their twin three-year-old daughters Susan and Sandra. Home was a small, beautifully decorated and maintained terrace house with a tidy, productive garden.

He had met Annette in the works canteen when he was twenty-one and she was seventeen. He knew from the moment he saw her that she was the woman who would share his life. Four years later they were married, both still virgins and proud that they had saved themselves for each other.

Annette and Arthur were well suited. Each liked what the other liked whether it was music, literature, or the countryside. When they had viewed their house before buying, they both knew immediately that this was the house for them. They liked the same clothes; they shared the same opinions on many diverse subjects. There was truly little they did not agree on and as a result there were very few arguments. They worked together and had delayed starting a family while they saved for their own home. Once they were settled in their house, they had tried for a baby but after several miscarriages it seemed that this joy would be denied them. It was seven years before the twins arrived. It seemed like a miracle and they had both been delighted.

Arthur had never been mean with money but he spent it wisely ensuring the house was well maintained and the family comfortable. Christmas, birthdays, and special occasions were always well celebrated and each year they had a two-week holiday away. The holiday each year since they were married was always the last two weeks of August when the factory closed for maintenance. It was spent in a caravan on a small family run site just south of Skegness on the Lincolnshire coast. When the twins arrived, the destination was the same, the only change the caravan they booked for the two weeks was larger. Arthur was proud of his three-year-old Morris Traveller and he had spent the last few days lovingly polishing and servicing it ready for the annual journey to Skegness.

They were really looking forward to this year's holiday. The twins, at three, were old enough to really appreciate the beach and had been kitted out with buckets and spades and new holiday clothes. Annette and Arthur loaded up the car checking and double checking that everything was packed and loaded. The car fully loaded, and the twins settled into the back seat. They were ready for the off.

The weather was good. Bright and sunny. The whole of the summer of 1968 had been hot and dry, they hoped it would continue for the next two weeks.

The Traveller was running really well and they listened to Radio One, singing along to the Beatles and to Ohio Express who were number one. The twins sat quietly listening to the music and their parents singing.

They stopped at one that afternoon at Harrington Hall, fifteen or so miles from Skegness. They stopped here every year and picnicked. In previous years they had often picnicked in the heaviest of rain but this year it was hot, sunny and dry. They laid out the chequered tablecloth on the sun scorched grass.

Annette busied herself, setting out the plastic knives, forks and plates while Arthur got out the cardboard box which contained the food and the especially important primus stove. The sandwiches were wrapped in greaseproof paper to keep them fresh. The twins had both been sleeping when they arrived at the picnic site, so they left them in the car until they had everything arranged before gently waking them and settling them onto the dry grass. The food was delicious, and Arthur had the primus working without too much fiddling and they were all happy and content drinking tea and orange juice, eating and resting in the sunshine.

Annette had decided when she left the doctors surgery two

days before the holiday that the picnic would be a good time to tell Arthur that the twins were going to be having a new brother or sister in seven months or so.

Arthur had sensed during the journey that there was something about Annette that he had not seen for some time but he could not decide what it was that was different about her. He noticed that she seemed very happy her skin had a glow and her long brown hair shone. He thought she looked the picture of health and as beautiful as the day he had first seen her.

He was pleased she looked so well. He had been worried about her. The twins were a lot of work and were very active but in the past year they had had lots of minor illness, flu and chesty coughs then measles, then colds and sore throats. It had been never-ending visits to the doctors and sleepless nights for Annette who had nursed them both with unselfish care but as a result she had been tired. He knew she needed this holiday.

Annette passed Arthur a cucumber and sugar sandwich, his favourite. He munched it, enjoying it and the fact that once again she had remembered to make them especially for him.

'I have some news for you.' Annette said smiling and laughing nervously.

'Good news I hope?' said Arthur.

'Yes, well I think it is,' Annette responded, 'I hope you think that my being pregnant is good news and makes you happy.' she blurted out, nervous and unsure of how he would respond.

She need not have worried. Arthur dropped his sandwich tried to speak but his mouth wouldn't work. The sandwich, half chewed in his mouth as a broad grin split his face. She could tell he was happy.

Arthur cleared his mouth of food and got his breath back. He kissed her, he kissed the twins, he kissed her again. Arthur was very happy, oblivious of the other picnic parties going on around them.

'Happy, oh yes happy, I'm the happiest man in the world' he said.

They enjoyed the rest of the picnic very much. Arthur got the details and heard about the visit to the doctors. The twins were happy catching the sheer joy being shown by their parents.

The picnic finished they relaxed in the sun for a while before re-packing the car and continuing their journey.

'This is going to be a great holiday' Arthur said to them all.

CHAPTER 5

THE Ford Consul sped through the village of Burgh le Marsh travelling from Skegness. The young driver ignoring the speed limit his attention wandering from the road to the exposed breasts of the young blond-haired woman beside him.

He had met her three months ago, backstage at the Salon Pavilion Theatre Skegness. He was the comic compere for the end of pier summer season show, she was a chorus line dancer. He had fancied her as soon as he had seen her at the auditions. A week later he had spent an evening plying her with vodka and that was the first night he slept with her. They had been in a steady relationship ever since. Being in a steady relationship was not something that he had considered, he was easy going and as an entertainer was used to being the centre of attention and had never had a problem moving from one girl to the next; this was different. For her, he was her first real boyfriend. Her name was Jane. She was slim with long dancers' legs, long blonde hair and the greenest of eyes. They just clicked. They had fallen in love. The sex was great. The summer was hot. Life was good. She had fancied him the moment she saw him. Her first audition coincided with his first rehearsal and while waiting to audition she had watched him. His jokes were funny and she loved his routine. He spoke to her after her audition, which was successful, and she found him both easy going and easy to talk to. He was tall and well-built, and she liked the way he was, clean, dressed well and smelt good. Three months after meeting they were married.

The end of the pier show was her first proper job in show business, she had left drama school two weeks before her audition. Following her successful audition, she met the other girls in the troupe, and they spent the first week at a dance studio learning the routines. Moving to Skegness was going to be the start of her rise to fame.

Jane was shocked at the lust she felt for him, she hadn't had a proper boyfriend before so didn't know what to think about her feelings. She just knew that when they kissed her nipples went hard and her pussy throbbed. She could not get enough of him. She knew she was in love with him the first night they made love.

Jane also loved vodka, it didn't make her nipples go hard but she did love it and needed it. She had a problem with it, she was not sure it was a problem but the people who knew her best knew it was. She had started drinking at drama school as she felt it settled her stage fright; it did, but she needed more of it when she came off stage. A couple of large straight vodkas was her usual nightcap and sometimes her breakfast. The dancing kept her fit and the lack of food kept her trim and it was amazing that her bottle a day drinking had not destroyed her good looks, as it surely would if she continued.

He also loved vodka. In fact, he wasn't particular about the colour of the spirit he drank. His consumption had increased a lot since meeting Jane but if she wanted to drink, he was more than happy to keep her company. They were happy, working hard and doing a good job on the show which was playing to packed audiences.

They were both good for and bad for each other.

Obtaining a special licence, they were married at Skegness Registry Office on the afternoon of Friday, 16th August. The show had gone on as normal and the audience gave them a huge cheer when their wedding was announced at curtain call. The party after had continued till the early hours and they staggered back to their digs very drunk but very happy.

The following day, Saturday, was a day of rest for the show's artists as holiday makers finished their holidays to be replaced by new arrivals. They decided late in the morning to drive to see his parents and break the news of the wedding. The day was hot, and they had a couple of drinks with lunch before setting out. Jane had picked up a bottle of vodka, now it lay half empty nestled for safe keeping at his crotch. He drove one handed, Jane nestled into him on the bench seat, his left arm around her shoulder. He had enjoyed undoing the blouse buttons delighted to find she was not wearing a bra and his left hand cupped her left breast gently caressing it.

Life was good and getting better he thought, the letter offering him a pantomime season in Norwich was in his trouser pocket. His wife was beautiful and sexy. The Ford Consul was in good shape. All was right with the world.

The car was his second love now. He was the third owner; it

was a 62 model. It was low mileage and he kept it well maintained and tuned up. It was white with lots of extra chrome around the headlights and he had put on a set of white wall tyres. The car was a bit flashy, but he felt it suited his image.

Turning left down Burgh Lane he had decided to take the scenic route. Burgh Lane was narrow with little traffic and nice gentle bends. He accelerated, the warm air blowing in the open windows blew her hair into his face. He breathed in deeply, he loved the smell of her.

He took his right hand off the steering wheel momentarily and picked up a packet of Embassy cigarettes, he lit one with his Zippo lighter and inhaled deeply, the warm sun and the vodka had made him feel drowsy and he felt the nicotine hit would counter that.

The rabbit was confused, the myxomatosis distorting its vision and impairing its senses. It ran from the hedgerow trying to escape the gnawing pain in its brain. It never heard or saw the Ford Consul and was dead a split second after being hit by the speeding car.

He didn't see the rabbit. The bump jolted him from his daydream. The cigarette dropped from his mouth and landed inside his shirt burning his skin. He moved his body to avoid the pain and in so doing knocked the vodka bottle to the floor where it lodged beneath the brake pedal a split second before his right foot attempted to depress it. He saw the stop sign for the junction with the B1195 but he couldn't stop the car. He tried to turn right to avoid the cluster of road signs ahead of him. He was going too fast to make it and the car skidded sideways. The speed, her body pressed against him, the cigarette still burning his skin and the bottle below the brake pedal all acted against him.

He remembered nothing of the accident.

The road was quiet. The sound of moaning barely audible above the hissing steam from the burst radiators of the mangled crashed cars.

It was several minutes before another vehicle came upon the scene and the memory of the tangled metal and bloodied bodies haunted the middle-aged driver and his wife for many years.

He was found sitting on the grass verge, the limp body of Jane in his arms. She was dead before the ambulance arrived. Her beautiful face smashed and slashed to ribbons as it had preceded her body through the windscreen of the Ford.

He could remember nothing of the accident itself. His last clear memory before it was of saying 'I do' at the registry office the day before. But he could remember very clearly sitting on the grass verge with Jane limp in his arms. Looking at the wreck that was his own car and the Morris Traveller embedded in the front of it. He could remember seeing the firemen cutting the Morris apart trying to release the woman trapped in the front passenger seat. He could remember, oh so clearly, the bodies of the two children being covered with heavy fireman's coats in the road where they lay having been thrown from the Morris by the force of the collision. Most of all he could feel the hatred of the policemen and firemen who asked him if he had been drinking.

The days after the accident passed in a blur. He had been arrested and released on bail. Somehow, he had taken care of the funeral arrangements for Jane and had met her parents for the first time. They blamed him for her death and there was nothing he could or wanted to say except 'sorry' which he knew was not enough and never would be.

The funeral had been well attended but he stood alone with just his parents for support. He felt desolate and ashamed.

It was more than a year before the case against him was ready to proceed at the Crown Court in Lincoln. He had moved back in with his parents and supported himself by doing odd jobs and labouring when it was available.

The doctors could not agree on what exactly had caused his memory loss for the period leading up to and the accident itself. The shock of the accident. The shock of seeing his wife dead, her face smashed. Physical damage to his brain caused by the accident. Possibly guilt. While they couldn't agree on what caused his memory loss, they did agree that it was real, and the judge accepted this expert testimony.

He stood facing the judge. It was a cold November day, the fourth, three days before his birthday. He had been charged with various motoring offences. The most serious being causing death by dangerous driving. By some technicality and procedural incompetence by the police his alcohol levels had been incorrectly recorded and were inadmissible in court. Since the accident he had been free on bail awaiting the trial, it had been a long and painful wait for him but he knew the pain for Jane's parents and for Arthur and Annette Summerskill was so much greater than his own.

He listened as the judge praised the efforts of the police and fire crews and the skills of the ambulancemen. He heard how they had risked their lives in rescuing Annette from the wreckage always knowing that the petrol tanks were liable to blow and fire could engulf them at any time. The judge praised the driver of the first vehicle on the scene and how his prompt actions had prevented other vehicles from running into the wreckage. Issuing instructions for the emergency services to be called and for attempting with his bare hands to prise away the metal that was trapping Annette.

He listened as the judge said that Annette was making a slow but good recovery from her injuries but how unfortunately she had lost not only her twin girls but also, because of the injuries she sustained, her unborn baby.

Arthur Summerskill sat at the front of the public gallery, as he had done every day since the start of the trial three days before. Arthurs eyes were fixed upon the eyes of the man in the dock.

Arthur had escaped from the crash with only minor injuries, his body intact, his life shattered.

The defence lawyer was young and clever. He reminded the judge and jury that the defendant's own wife had died in the accident, how in fact it may have been her who was driving the car at the time. Despite extensive publicity and police enquiries there had been no witnesses to say that the accused had been the driver. He argued that while the defendant assumed he had been driving, the medically proven loss of memory did not allow him to admit to being the driver. He simply did not know. He emphasised to the judge and jury that the defendant's marriage had taken place just the day before the accident and how Jane and the defendant were looking forward to married life and starting a family and how her death had deeply affected the mental health of the defendant. How, if he had been the driver, then the drinking which was out of character might have played a significant role but more importantly why had the brakes of the Ford, which was maintained in excellent order, not been applied or if applied had not worked. A mystery that many had an opinion on but one that could not be explained to the court's satisfaction.

The judge was old. Over the past few months, he had considered retiring. The latest crime and punishment reports that he had received from the Home Office had finally convinced him that at the end of the year he would retire. He was fed up with the media trying to influence the courts, unhappy with do-gooders and social workers who seemed to be able to write reports that praised even the evillest of wrong doers and which urged light sentences and work in the community. As a judge he had always, he hoped, taken due cognizance of public opinion. He wasn't ready for the liberalism that he felt was changing his role. He wanted to dispense justice the way the majority of ordinary working-class people wanted it. Murderers should hang unless there was an exceptionally good reason to show mercy. Crime in general should be punished and criminals deterred, and long sentences were the way to deter. He was sure that the innocent appearing before him would be found not guilty and the guilty would tremble when they heard he would judge them. He considered himself a man of the people acting for the people.

He listened as always attentively and carefully to the prosecution and defence arguments. There was no doubt that this was a serious matter which had had a profound effect on all those involved. He was sure the defendant was not a bad person and took due regard to the fact that he was now a widower. His wife of one day dead. A punishment surely.

The arguments concluded; he adjourned the court till the following morning when he would sum up to the jury.

The day was bright and sunny. The early November sunshine sending its rays through the high windows of the court room, dancing and playing on the highly polished walnut panelling.

The defendant took his place in the dock. He looked around at the faces in the packed court room. The trial had been well attended every day with the middle aged and elderly men and women who had watched and listened, ghoulish in their interest.

He noticed Arthur, sitting as he had done every day in the same seat. Their eyes met and he could see the hatred in them. He looked away quickly but had felt Arthurs eyes burning into his.

'All rise' the court came to order and the judge entered from his chambers.

He stood, legs unsteady, body trembling. He took a deep breath willing himself to be strong. His hands gripped the wooden rail surrounding the dock, trying to stop his hands from shaking. He knew that he might go to prison. His lawyer had explained to him that it was always a possibility and that he should prepare himself for it. He didn't know how to do that.

The judge commenced his summing up. He spoke for ten minutes, summarised the arguments, advising the jury of the need for them to be convinced beyond any reasonable doubt that the defendant had been the one driving the car. He explained to them that even though the defendant thought he was driving the medical evidence was clear that the memory loss was real and the defendant in fact had no idea if he had been driving. He advised the jury that difficult as it may be, they should put out of their minds the death of the children. The matter was simple, if the defendant was the driver then he was guilty as charged. If the defendant was not the driver then he was an innocent man whose life had been changed as the result of being involved in a tragic accident.

The jury left to consider their verdict. Five hours later they returned to deliver it. The court was packed, with Arthur in his seat and the ghouls in theirs, not wanting to miss the sentencing.

For the defendant the last five hours had been more than he thought he could mentally stand. He had considered running away, he had considered suicide. He wished that he could remember all or any of the details of the accident. He so much wanted to be able to tell the truth but he just could not remember. He was sure he had been driving. He felt guilty. He was ashamed.

He heard the court clerk ask the jury foreman if they had reached a verdict.

He watched the foreman stand and look around at the faces of the other members of the jury before saying in a clear and loud voice.

'Not guilty.'

Arthur felt the anger rising in him. Not guilty, not guilty, he could not believe he had heard the words. There must be some mistake. But no. He had heard the words. The defence lawyer was smiling and shaking hands with that drunken murdering bastard who was fucking smiling. Fucking justice, fucking injustice, the bastards. This fucking judge knew nothing about justice. The anger rose in Arthur. An anger that he did not know he possessed. The anger rose from his stomach, he felt sick, his chest heaved, he was sweating. He stood up his body rigid and erect, his right arm extended, and his forefinger stabbed towards the dock.

'You're a dead man, you drunken, murdering fucker' he spat the words.

The court ushers moved to him but as quickly as he had got up, he sat down, slumped, his body wracked with pain. He cried but through his tears he kept his eyes on the figure still in the dock.

The defendant, now proven innocent gripped the rail in front of him, in one moment all his emotions had erupted, love lost, relief, shame, sorry, frightened, sad, happy, fear.

The police officer touched him on the arm.

'Come on lad, it's all over' he said.

Together they left the court. He spent a few moments with his lawyer and barrister. They were cock a hoop that they had been successful in getting him acquitted. A police inspector interrupted them.

'Excuse me, sirs but there are a lot of media people at the

front entrance, you may wish to address them or leave by a side entrance, that's your decision but if I may, I would like a word in private with you.'

The three of them followed the police inspector to a side room and remained standing while he spoke.

'You will be aware that a threat was made against you in court. The judge has decided that bearing in mind the overwrought condition of the man who made the threat the court will take no action. However, should you be threatened by this gentleman in future you should bring it to our attention immediately. But I wouldn't worry too much about it, if I were you. We hear many threats in this court and nearly all are empty. Any questions?'

They didn't.

'Thank you' they said.

'I can understand how he feels and why he said it, in his eyes I am guilty and maybe in my own eyes I am guilty'.

The inspector shrugged and his lawyer put a comforting arm around his shoulder moving him quickly and quietly out of the office.

His parents were waiting for him at the side door. He didn't have words for them, he felt ashamed, disgusted with himself, that drink, whether his drinking or hers, should have brought so much misery and pain. He noticed how old his mother was looking, the strain and worry had aged her ten years in as many weeks. His father too was looking older and frailer. He put his arms around them and gently squeezed and just as quickly released them, turning he ran off shouting over his shoulder.

'I'll be in touch; I love you both.'

'Be careful James' shouted his father.

'Love you James Jackson, be careful' whispered his mother, quietly sobbing into her husband's shoulder.

CHAPTER 6

Molly was warm. She had just eaten a cheese and pickle sandwich and was finishing a can of cola. She could not see the can, the black bandage that covered her eyes allowed no light in. She sat, her back to the wall wondering if it was Pepsi or Coke.

She put her hand up to the bandage feeling its thickness and the tape that held it in place. There was a hospital smell so she thought it must be surgical tape. He had told her that if she attempted to remove the bandage, he would kill her. She believed him. It was a temptation to try to lift the bandage and relieve the pressure on her head but she stopped herself from doing it, his threats were real she felt sure.

She knew she was dressed in a shell suit. Her feet were bare, and she could feel the rough texture of a carpet. Her ankles were bound together with an electrical tie wrap the end cut off so that she could not accidently tighten it. He had allowed her to bathe and had removed the tie wrap and replaced it when she had finished and was dry and dressed. Her hair was greasy and dirty as he had not removed the bandage and tape to allow her to wash it.

Molly had tried to keep track of the days. She guessed at six days since she was dragged from the house and into the pick-up. Timewise she guessed it was early evening. Estimating the time gap between meals had not been easy. The first two days she had tried to count the seconds but the numbers were very different on both days, so she gave up that plan. She hadn't gone really hungry, but her meals seemed to be irregular. The room was very warm and stuffy and there was silence.

The only sound she heard was the door being unlocked whenever he came into the room to feed, her, check on her, or to take her to the bathroom for a bath or the toilet. The bathroom was exactly seven steps from the door of the room she was held in. They were his steps as he always carried her there sitting her on the edge of the bath to cut loose the tie wrap before allowing her to bathe. He did not cut them off when she just needed the toilet.

She had checked every inch of the room. The single bed mattress was roughly in the middle of the room which she guessed was four by three metres. The carpet covered the whole floor but was not fixed at the edges as she could pick up the carpet in the corner and feel the solid cold floor beneath it. The door was in the corner of the three-metre wall. The electric radiator that kept the room hot was against the four-metre wall and the cable went under the door. There was no window but she thought that a board was fixed to the wall where a window might be, covering it. There were no skirting boards and she hadn't found a light switch or a power point. The walls felt damp to her touch but the air in the room didn't smell damp.

He had said very little. She had glimpsed his nose and eyes for an instant when he had bundled her into the pick-up. She knew it was a pick-up as their neighbour had one but his was blue, this one was white. He had thrown her roughly to the floor in front of the passenger seat and snarled.

'Stay on the floor, don't look at me, shut up, obey me or I will kill you.'

She had obeyed, frightened, not knowing what was happening.

He had stopped at the end of the lane leading from the house and put a coarse smelly sack over her head securing it around her neck with a piece of rope. He secured her hands and feet with tie wraps.

'Move or speak and I will strangle you' he had said, his voice strange and scary.

Molly didn't move or speak.

Lying curled up on the floor of the pick-up she had tried not to cry but knew that she had. Swallowing her sobs, she had thought of nice things and told herself not to call out and she hadn't.

The pick-up had travelled for about an hour she guessed. Mostly on tarmac roads except for the first part down the house lane and a longer slower section of rough track at the end of the journey. Close to the end of the journey she smelt that they were in woods and she had heard birds singing.

He had dumped her on the mattress with the sack over her head and hands and feet bound.

'Shout out or try to escape and I will kill you' the strange electronic sounding voice had said. He had pulled her to her feet and cut the ties that bound her hands and feet.

'I am going to undress you and give you other clothes to wear, I will not hurt you but if you struggle, I will kill you' the strange voice said.

He began to undress her. Molly was terrified, the threat of death not as frightening as being naked before him. At sixteen Molly was a well-developed girl her breasts were large and her waist slim, at five foot two she was already taller than her mother. James and her mother treated her as an adult but nothing they had taught her or she had experienced had prepared her for being stripped and looked at by a man.

He had unbuttoned her blouse, removed her bra, her skirt and pants followed, then her trainers and socks. She stood naked except for the sack over her head. He dressed her in the shell suit with no underwear. She felt the silky texture of the material on her body. His hands did not touch her body in any sexual way. He tie wrapped her ankles and cut the long end flush.

The voice said 'Stand up, keep your eyes tightly closed and your hands down by your side, if you open your eyes or move then I will have to kill you.

'Please don't hurt me' she had said trying hard not to cry.

She stood up and felt a knife cutting the rope that held the sack around her neck. Her eyes were screwed tight shut her hands gripping the pockets of the shell suit. He removed the sack and bound the bandage around her head covering her eyes. It was tight against her skin pulling her hair a little. He taped it in place. She smelt the hospital smell.

'I will leave your hands free but if you attempt to loosen or remove the blindfold or release your ankles, I will kill you. Do you understand? The electronic voice asked.

'Yes' was all she had said, too scared and confused to ask any questions or make any other comment.

'I will be able to hear you and see you at all times, do not shout or call out. Do you understand?'

Again, she answered, 'Yes.'

'You will be warm and I will not hurt you provided you do exactly as I tell you when I tell you. Do you understand?' The voice said.

'Yes,' she replied as he picked her up and carried her to the bathroom.

'When you use the toilet, I will leave you alone with the door closed, the window has been blocked up so do not think you can escape. When you are finished you may call me quietly and I will open the door. If I ask you through the door if everything is okay and you fail to answer I will open the door and come in. Do you understand?'

'Yes' was all she said trying to feel her way around the bathroom, wondering how long she would be blindfolded.

He left her then to wash herself and she managed. Clumsy at first, dropping the soap onto the floor and the towel into the basin but over the past few days her coordination had improved, and she was able to wash, bathe and use the toilet without too much problem.

The meals had been good. Everyday there would be breakfast of cornflakes with milk and a hot drink of tea.

Lunch was always two sandwiches, always cold meat, ham or chicken. On all but one day there had been a hot meal, always boiled potatoes with peas or carrots and sausages or fish fingers or hamburger and once corned beef which she didn't like. Nothing fancy but always hot and tasty. The food came on paper plates with plastic cutlery and the drink in a plastic or paper cup. The coke can she held today was the first drink in a can that he had given her.

She thought about the past few days, six, she thought, since she had arrived here, maybe seven. It had not been too bad. She was still frightened of being captive but wasn't frightened of him. He always carried her gently and she sensed that he wasn't a cruel man or a sex pervert. As long as she obeyed him without question, she felt she would live.

Nothing like this had ever happened to her before. It hadn't happened to anyone she knew. Not being able to go out when she wanted, wash when she wanted, change clothes when she wanted, go to the toilet when she wanted was horrible. She was an independent girl and although nothing in her life had prepared her for this, she felt that as a Scorpio she could handle it and she intended to do all she could to get out of this alive and then get even with this man who was holding her against her will.

Molly heard the door being unlocked and the swish against the carpet as it was opened, she smelt him fresh and clean. He picked her up, she felt his broad shoulders and muscular back as he walked the seven steps to the bathroom. Today she had decided to talk to him. Nervously she cleared her throat with a small cough.

'Would you move your hand up my leg a little please, it's

hurting' she said.

He shifted her weight and moved his hand.

'Thank you' she said smiling into a face she couldn't see.

He grunted.

He put her down in the bathroom. She had dreaded having to ask the next question but she knew it had to be asked and today was the day to ask it.

'May I please have some tampax, my periods are due any day' she whispered it, so embarrassed, she had never had to ask that question of a man before. Her Mum always took care of these things.

She heard him fumbling and then the electronic voice

'Yes, tomorrow, is there anything else you need?'.

She thought for a moment, then replied

'Yes please, may I have some hair shampoo and some deodorant'

'Yes' the voice replied.

When she had finished in the bathroom, she quietly called him. He picked her up took her back to the room with the mattress and laid her down. She heard the swish of the carpet and the door being locked. Then silence.

Molly felt so much better. More confident. She had made contact with him and she felt safer somehow.

CHAPTER 7

ANNETTE lay still to avoid the pain, barely able to move in the hospital bed. Every movement she made was painful, so she willed herself to be still. Every day she knew that her body was getting stronger and the scars and breaks were healing well. Her body slowly mending, her mind not mending at all.

She mourned daily for her twins and for the baby that had been growing inside of her. The accident replayed in her mind over and over again. Her memory was crystal clear. The white car hitting them and of her pain as she lay trapped in the wreckage of the Morris. Her head twisted around and her eyes seeing the body of one of the twins laying twisted and bloody on the road, not knowing where the other one was. Knowing the foetus in her womb had been smashed and squashed by the twisted wreckage that trapped her. Physical pain ignored; the mental pain so real she had screamed for her children not for herself. The firemen had fought for several hours to release her from the wreckage, a doctor on scene bringing her back from death several times. She wished he hadn't.

She looked across at Arthur who had occupied the chair next to the bed almost every day since the day of the accident his own superficial physical injuries long healed. Today was Christmas Day. Arthur had brought her a new nightdress and some perfume. One of the few friends who visited had bought her a tie so that she would have something to give to Arthur. They exchanged gifts but there was no Merry Christmas in word or in thought, they both knew that it couldn't be. They cried together, holding hands, Arthur resting his head on the bed and Annette staring at the ceiling trying to look through it into heaven where their babies played.

Their crying done, they talked. Annette was due to be discharged shortly and they needed to make arrangements for her homecoming. They did their best to ignore the comings and goings of the busy hospital ward on this special day. They didn't want their grief to ruin it for anyone else.

Annette was worried about Arthur. Ever since the trial he had been a changed man. She had never known him hate anyone or hold a grudge against anyone but now he did, and she felt that it was consuming him. Sucking from him the kind and gentle man he had been. Annette told him to forget James Jackson and that they must somehow build a new life together. He had told her that he would never forget, the man had ruined his life and, to all intents and purposes, had taken his life. He went on to say that he would not forget him for one day of his life and would wish him dead every day until I die or he does.

Arthur had buried the children, just himself and his Mum and Dad, Annette's Mum and Dad and Annette's sister Cissy attended. Annette had been too ill to attend and now Arthur

Robert Harper / Deadly Ransom

was making plans for them both to visit the grave as soon as she was out of hospital and able to do so. She hadn't had the chance to say goodbye properly, she hadn't seen the gravestone, just a photograph; and the pain she had felt when looking at the photo was bad enough.

On this Christmas Day they talked of the grave and Arthur's visit to it before coming to the hospital, past Christmases with the twins, James Jackson, Annette's exercise programme, Annette coming home, a convalescence holiday, Arthur going back to work, and all the other things that husbands and wives might imagine they would speak about when one of them is hospitalized and they have lost three children.

Arthur looked at her, she was still the pretty young girl he had met in the works canteen all those years before, but now there were the permanent lines of pain in her face and the white streaks in her hair made him sad and so angry. One man's stupidity has destroyed our happiness he thought for the thousandth time.

The engineering company had been marvellous. They had given Arthur all the time off he wanted on full pay and had put no pressure on him to return to work. Today he told Annette he would go back to work after the New Year and that her sister had offered to come and stay and look after Annette until she was strong enough to look after herself.

Arthur visited Annette every day over the holiday and she could sense he was pleased to be going back to work. The doctor had told her she could leave hospital on the second of January and Arthur delayed his return to work for a few days to get her home and her sister installed.

The first night home Arthur thought they would sleep together in the double bed but both Annette and Cissy said that would be too painful for her, so Arthur had moved into the twins' room, the smell of the twins so real he thought they were with him. He lay alone in the dark, brooding, even now James Jackson was robbing him of holding his wife, smelling her, lying next to her. It seemed to Arthur that the love that had given him so much happiness had been snuffed out by grief.

Never again did he make love to her. They slept together but they did not for the rest of their married lives make love together.

Arthur, non-competitive and unambitious before the accident became even less ambitious, his employers tolerating his plodding ways, allowing others to take on the more technical work, leaving Arthur to the drawing board and the less demanding work. In all other respects he was a model employee. They tolerated him because they knew how he suffered.

In the twenty years that followed Annette's release from hospital she never fully recovered her health. She had no zest for life and no will to live. A simple cold would end in pneumonia, a cut would turn septic, her body had lost its ability to fight infection. The diagnosis of the cancer had not been a shock to them. The speed at which it spread to the rest of her organs was both frightening and shocking. The chemo and radiotherapy made her extremely sick, her hair fell out, she wanted to die, to join her babies. She gave up; dying a painless death, drugged and unaware.

Arthur leant on the open coffin. He looked into Annette's

face, the only woman he had ever loved. He looked carefully seeing no change in the face of the girl he had married all those years ago. He carefully adjusted the silver necklace she wore, and he brushed a stray wisp of hair from her face with his hand, gently and lovingly allowing his hand to brush her skin, cold in death.

His face was over hers and his tears fell on her. He thought of the good times they had shared early in the marriage before the accident and of the bad times after. The lack of communication, the lack of laughter in their home, no longer a home, just bricks and mortar, a house.

He knew she would forgive him the twenty years of wedded unhappiness if he could carry out the threat he had made to the person who had caused it.

He sniffed, wiping away the tears from his eyes. Standing upright he took her hand in his, he looked at her face, in a strong voice full of emotion, anger, and frustration he spoke to her.

'I swear to you that James Jackson is going to pay in full for the misery he has caused to you, I will be your avenger.'

Annette's funeral was held on a Tuesday. A bright day. A day full of sunshine and birdsong. The kind of day that Annette had enjoyed with the twins. A good day to lay her to rest.

The funeral was a simple, private affair. Arthur and Annette had been content in each other's company and had little social life, the circle of friends was small. Cissy attended but both sets of parents had sadly passed away. Those that could, went to the funeral. A couple of Arthur's work mates attended and several of the neighbours.

The service over, Arthur had to be helped to the car such was his grief. He made no attempt to invite people back to the house for a drink and sandwiches. He was tired, bitter and wanted the day to end.

The house was empty and cold. They had not spent money or effort in maintaining it since the accident. The interest had gone. Arthur looked around at their possessions accumulated over some thirty-five years of marriage, nothing more than could have been loaded into a small removals lorry in a couple of hours.

Arthur changed out of his suit and put on his corduroy trousers and his wool cardigan. The house felt cold and damp. He lit the coal fire, but its warmth didn't reach him. He was lonely now, he put the television on, not watching or listening to it. His mind churning and jumping, thinking about her and the life they had had. The face of James Jackson always in his mind, his hatred for him all consuming,

He fell asleep. Deep and needed, his physical and mental batteries run down and empty seeking the recharge of rest.

Arthur woke with a start, a sound, what was it? The TV still on, the fire dead, he took a moment to get his bearings. Annette, house, funeral, he looked at the clock, ten past eight, morning or evening? he wondered. He realised that the sound he had heard was the letter box and letters falling onto the mat. He sat, trying to get his mind working. Another day to get through.

He rose from the chair, stretching the stiffness out of his body. The habit of a morning cup of tea sent him to the kitchen, kettle on, tea bags into the pot, the routine returning to his life.

He drank the first cup quickly, needing its warmth and comfort. The second cup he sipped, clearing up the kitchen and tidying the sitting room. He walked to the front door and picked up the small pile of letters and returned to the kitchen where, as he had always done, he opened the mail carefully and precisely slitting each envelope flap with a sharp kitchen knife. Reading each piece before moving to the next. Letters of condolence, difficult to read, difficult to write he thought, and near impossible for him to answer.

Five, six letters all saying the same thing using different words. Letters full of sympathy, offers of help if needed, people trying to understand his grief. Caring people. The seventh letter brought him back to reality, a gas bill. The eighth, an expensive to the touch, plain cream envelope. He opened it carefully. He removed the contents and read them. He dropped the pages, they fluttered gracefully to the floor. He sat still, not daring to think about what the first page had said. He remained stock still trying to sort out his emotions. Minutes passed, several times he bent to pick up the dropped pages but each time drew back. At last, he was ready. He read the first page again and then the other two pages. Finished, he read them again. Taking the letter, he went to the hall and picked up the telephone and sat on the floor. His fingers shaking, misdialled the number twice. Third time he dialled with no errors and listened carefully as the call was answered. As the letter instructed, he asked to speak to Mr Johnstone. He was connected immediately. As the letter instructed, he gave his name and address and the reference number which was on the letter beneath his name on the first page. Mr Johnstone confirmed that the letter was not a hoax or a sick joke. The contents of the letter were factual. Arthur felt weak. Unable to believe what he had read and what he was being told. Despite repeated requests from Mr Johnstone, Arthur was adamant he wanted no publicity.

In the thirty years of marking his ten crosses on the pools coupon every week he had never won. Not a penny. He never expected to win. His father had done the pools and he had followed. It was a ritual, the marking, the listening to the results, calculating the points, hoping for twenty-four but always being disappointed. It was the taking part that connected him to his father and others of his father's generation. Now this letter and Mr Johnstone were telling him that his coupon had been checked and double checked and that he was the winner of six hundred and thirty-eight thousand four hundred and seventy-five pounds and nineteen pence. Mr Johnstone was very particular. Arthur felt no sense of elation, no happiness, no feeling of joy. Mr Johnstone had had the pleasure over the years of confirming to many people that they had won a fortune beyond their wildest dreams and it was usual for the winners to be at least excited and pleased. Today talking to Arthur, it was different. There was no joy, no happiness, no pleasure. It was three days later before Arthur and Mr Johnstone came face to face and by then Mr Johnstone had learned of Arthurs loss, usually it was a happy occasion when the cheque was handed over but this time there was no happiness and Mr Johnstone couldn't find the right words. He left Arthur with the cheque and a copy, as most people wanted to keep a memento of the big win. He also left him a file with a lot of information on banking and financial help and advice on what was available to winners.

Mr Johnstone and Arthur shook hands and Mr Johnstone asked what Arthur intended to do with the money. Arthur answered him and Mr Johnstone was not sure he had heard correctly but didn't repeat his question or ask Arthur to repeat his answer. Surely, he hadn't said 'Get Jackson'. No, he must have misheard.

Another week, more winners, more tears of joy and happiness, Mr Johnstone soon forgot Arthur.

Arthur spent the week in a daze. Unable to comprehend what had happened. He missed her so much. He sat at the kitchen table most evenings looking at her photograph and the cheque. He went to work, visited her grave, cooked his own small meals. No one visited. He checked the newspapers to make sure his wish for no publicity had been honoured.

It was ten days after the meeting with Mr Johnstone when Arthur finally met with his shocked but delighted local bank manager. Arthur had opened his account at this same branch the day he started work, he only visited when he needed cash and, though he knew the manager by sight, had never had occasion to meet with him. There had been no need. He was never overdrawn; his pay had gone in on time every week and his cheques had cleared to pay his bills. Cheque books arrived in the mail as did regular statements. There had been no need to visit other than for cash and that had changed with the introduction of the ATM and a bank card. Arthur's meeting with the bank manager was short. Arthur wanting to ensure his privacy was guaranteed and once he was satisfied, allowed the manager to guide him through the various options open to him to invest and protect his money. Only now was Arthur coming to terms with his newly won wealth.

He left the bank with a faint smile on his face, the muscles aching through lack of recent use.

Yes, he thought, with this amount of money I can keep my promise to Annette.

CHAPTER 8

LEAVING his Mum and Dad standing together on the pavement at the rear of the court building James ran towards the main street, their parting bringing tears to his eyes. He had no idea where he was going or what he was going to do. He felt desperate, not pleased that he had been found not guilty, knowing in his heart that he was. Unable to accept the warmth and love his parents offered him. Ashamed of himself and so sad.

He turned towards the bus station wiping the tears from his eyes with the back of his hand, trying to pull himself together.

The journey by bus to Skegness from Lincoln, where the Crown Court Trial had taken place, was slow and uncomfortable. The upper deck was busy and the cloud of cigarette smoke became thicker as the journey progressed. It gave him some time to think and when the bus reached Skegness, he made his way to his bank and arranged a meeting with his bank manager for later that afternoon.

He arranged for a payment to be made to his solicitor. He told the bank manager, who was fully aware of who his customer was and of the trial, that he had been found not guilty. He expected his motor insurance company to pay his claim in full, as had been agreed prior to the trial, dependent upon the verdict. This amount would be more than enough to pay the balance owed to his solicitor and that balance would depend on his claim for legal aid. He withdrew in cash all the money in his account except for ten pounds which would keep the account open. He told the bank manager he would be in touch as soon as he had a forwarding address. James left the bank with three hundred and twenty-seven pounds in his pocket.

The November evening was cold and damp, the dry sunshine of the day long forgotten. The lights of The Highwayman promised warmth and James made his way to the bar.

'Large vodka please' he said to the barman, the five pound note already in his hand as he watched the barman put the glass to the optic, the clear spirit pouring into it. James looked around the bar. It was busy. Along the bar a couple of drunks were talking drunk speak to each other in aggressive tones. James suddenly realised what he was doing and couldn't understand why.

'No barman, I'm sorry, I don't need, cancel that, I don't want it, forget it' he shouted across to the barman.

'Sorry Sir but I've poured now, you will have to pay for it 'said the barman putting the glass on the counter in front of James.

James threw the fiver down onto the bar, pushing the vodka glass back across the bar where it crashed to the floor at the feet of the barman.   At the sound of the breaking glass all eyes turned in his direction and he heard someone say

'That's the guy on the TV just now who was in court today, killed some kids or something.'

Then the barman shouted

'I know you; you broke that glass on purpose, I'm charging you for it, now get out, you're not welcome here'

It seemed to James that the whole crowded bar was moving towards him. His head was pounding, he was afraid. He moved towards the door but the crowd blocked his way.

'Let me out, let me out' he pleaded as he fought his way towards the door.

A foot tripped him and he sprawled amongst the feet, spilled beer and dog ends on the floor. On his hands and knees, he could only see a forest of legs and, as he looked up, eyes that despised him.

On his knees, he raised his arm above his head to protect himself and shouted

'Jane please forgive me!'

The crowded bar fell silent. The moment of mob rule over. A bottle blonde left the table she was sharing with other bottle blondes and a greasy looking man and made her way to where James was kneeling.

'Come on handsome' she said to him, 'let's get you out of here and cleaned up. Looks to me like you have got things on your mind that need some of my special talents'

James allowed her to help him to his feet and with her arms

supporting him, guide him to the door and out into the cold night and into a taxi. Giving the driver directions she settled James into her ample bosom.

The rest of the evening and the night was a vague memory. He knew he was showered, and he knew the physical warmth and sympathy of the woman. He recollected that he had told her the story, the wedding, the accident, the deaths, the trial. He knew he felt better by telling it to a stranger.

Morning came and he woke not knowing where he was but sharing a bed with a blonde stranger who was gently snoring beside him. He got up, dressed and left without disturbing her.

He found a taxi and asked to be taken to the train station.

'There we go mate, that's a quid' said the driver.

James took his wallet from his jacket pocket. He knew as soon as he opened it that some of his money was gone. There were five twenty pound notes and a slip of paper on which was written – thanks for a nice night -.

'That thieving bitch' he said to the world in general.

'Problem mate?' asked the taxi driver.

'No. Only with my own stupidity' James replied.

He paid the taxi driver and went into the station feeling naive and foolish. On the plus side he figured she could have taken it all.

He found the station café and bought a tea and a Daily Telegraph, a newspaper he liked but had not bought in many months. He scanned it to see if he was mentioned, he wasn't.

Old news already he thought. The paper came with a special supplement - The Oil and Gas Industry.

He read the news of the day and with nothing better to do and no plan he turned to the supplement. As he read, he got more interested. One article caught his eye – it referred to the town of Great Yarmouth in Norfolk being a boom town, because of oil and gas, where wages were high and jobs plentiful for those prepared to work. It referred to Great Yarmouth as the new Klondike with streets paved with gold. He recalled stories his grandfather had told him about his grandfather who had been an original eighty niner who had returned home penniless after failing to find gold in the Klondike. Maybe he would have better luck. That's it then, he thought, his mind made up, Great Yarmouth is as good a place as any to start my new life.

He waited an hour for the train that would take him to it. The journey was tedious with changes at Grantham, Peterborough and Norwich. The train station at Great Yarmouth on a cold November evening was not a welcoming sight. The two-carriage train from Norwich had trundled the twenty or so miles stopping at tiny, out of the way stations to disembark its few passengers. The last part of the journey had been through the flat lands of the Norfolk countryside. He alighted from the train along with a dozen or so other passengers. This was the end of the line for the train; he hoped for him it was the start of something good. An east wind blew cold damp air into the station which was a drab and soulless place. Not what he expected of a boom town, the newspaper article far removed from reality, if the station's ambiance was anything to judge it by. He was very aware that he had a limited amount of funds and he didn't know how long what he did have was going to have to last. He bypassed the one ageing Lada taxi and with suitcase in hand walked the half mile or so towards the Haven Bridge which spans the River Yare and is the connection between East and West Great Yarmouth as well as the route south to Lowestoft and beyond; information gleaned from the newspaper article. He knew that just over the bridge was The Two Bears Hotel, it too had been mentioned, claiming it to be the watering hole of choice for the Americans and locals who were exploiting the country's natural resources.

At first sight the hotel looked drab and cheerless, but he entered and a pleasant receptionist told him they did have a room available, which he took. The room on the first floor wasn't quite as drab and cheerless as the exterior of the hotel, so he unpacked his case, hung up his suit, washed, then changed his clothes before going downstairs to the bar. The Two Bears bar was busy, very busy, very warm and smoky. He was amazed by the different accents he heard as he made his way to the bar. The local sing song Norfolk mixing with the drawl of America. The people too, as different as the accents. The Americans big men with big backsides and big bellies, tall and broad shouldered. He heard some Australian or was it New Zealand, he wasn't sure, then some French. He had never been in or heard such mixed company. James ordered a coke and stayed at the bar taking in the people, listening to the conversations around him. A group of men were talking about dope and joints and James thought he had stumbled upon the local drug dealers. He turned to his left where a tall man in a blue suit was sipping on a pint of beer and watching the television at the back of the bar. James smiled at him, nodded and then asked:

'Excuse me, is there a drug problem in this town?'

'No' said the man smiling, 'the boys get all they need' he chuckled to himself. 'sorry son that's an old joke, no this is not a druggie bar, if that's what you're looking for you are in the wrong place.'

'No, I'm not looking' said James smiling, 'I overheard the men over there talking about joints and dope and frankly I hate to be around anyone who has anything to do with drugs.'

The man laughed out loud, the group who James had overheard looked towards him and one asked

'What's so fuckin funny Jim?'

'This guy, what's your name?' he asked.

'James.'

'I'm Jim, Jim Seager. James here thinks you guys are setting up some big drug deal with your talk of dope and joints.'

They all laughed. James, an ex-comedian, wished he knew why and what was so funny.

'You definitely are not oilfield, are you James? What are you doing in Yarmouth?' asked Jim.

'Looking for a job. I read in the paper that there was work here and I need a job, so I came down from Skegness to find one' James replied, still feeling confused by the laughter his remark had caused.

'Are you a salesman?' Jim asked.

'No. Why do you ask?' responded James.

'I'm looking for a salesman, if you're interested in becoming one come see me tomorrow around noon. You want another drink?' Jim asked.

'Coke please, thank you, are you serious?' asked James, more than a little shocked by the response.

'Of course I'm serious' Jim gave James his business card, 'my office is just down the road, next to the old station building, make it twelve thirty.'

'Okay thanks, thanks for the drink. What did I say that was so funny?' asked James, now totally confused with how the conversation had gone.

'Tell you tomorrow' said Jim smiling, 'be there, okay?' Jim turned and with a 'goodnight' to the crowd in general left the bar.

James sipped his coke. Replaying the last few minutes in his mind. He hadn't asked for a job but now had a meeting about one.

James woke early and was downstairs in the breakfast room at eight. It was empty.

'Good morning.' James addressed the young waitress, 'Bit quiet am I too early?'

She smiled 'bit late you mean, it was very busy earlier' she replied, 'we start at six and most of the guys are away by seven, what can I get you?'

He looked at the menu she offered and realised he hadn't eaten much in the past few days, so he ordered the full

English.

'Tea or coffee?' the waitress asked 'breakfast will be about ten minutes; we cook to order, okay?'

'Tea please, yes that's perfect' answered James, looking forward now to his breakfast.

Breakfast over, he had a couple of hours to spare until his meeting with Jim so James decided to take a look around Yarmouth. The sun was out and the cold wind had died down and the Two Bears didn't seem so drab. James walked back over the Haven Bridge and turned right following the river towards its mouth and the North Sea. Now for the first time he started to see the offices of the companies he had read about in the newspaper, AMOCO, CONOCO, PHILLIPS PETROLEUM, SANTA FE, WILSON SUPPLY. The main road followed the river. He stopped often and watched the boats being loaded and unloaded. Strange looking boats that had flat decks for the cargo and the bridge and funnels taking up the forward third of the vessel. He asked a passerby about them and was told they were the rig supply boats, carrying supplies to the oil and gas rigs in the North Sea. Each of the companies seemed to have their own dock space and the comings and goings of the trucks loaded with containers or pipes and the trundling mobile cranes gave the place a feeling of business and action. Maybe, he thought, he had found the boom.

James made his way back to the hotel to get ready for his meeting with Jim. He was thinking about how best to present himself. It had been a while since he had a proper job and had attended an interview. He went through in his mind the skills and qualifications he had. Firstly, there were seven O Levels, he could speak well, he could type a little with two fingers, do maths and could tell a good joke. His time in the theatre had taught him some management skills, he was good with people, confident and comfortable in company. That's what I've got so that is what is going to have to do, he thought.

He went upstairs, washed and put on his suit and a clean shirt and tie. Checking himself in the mirror he looked good, some colour in his cheeks and a bit more of a healthy glow than he had had in some time.

He found the office easily enough, exactly where Jim had told him it was. The receptionist offered him coffee, which he accepted, and settled him in the reception area.

'Jim phoned to say to expect you, James, but he's running a little late, he is down at Mobil's office and will be here in fifteen minutes or so' she said.

'No problem, thank you' said James, looking around and checking out the reception area and looking into the glass fronted office beyond where several young men sat at desks, all busy on the telephones. Other telephones ringing, waiting to be answered, the atmosphere looked relaxed but professional and the men looked to be enjoying the work. One of them caught his eye and smiled. He saw magazines on the coffee table, all seemed to be related to Oil and Gas. A whole new world he thought and started to get nervous.

A blue painted door to his left opened and a man in a brown warehouse coat came through it allowing James to glimpse a workshop that was beyond. James had no clue as to what this company did, he felt alien.

'Morning. No, sorry, afternoon, James'. Jim had entered the

reception area from the main door and stood smiling, hand outstretched, looking crisp and clean in dark suit and white shirt.

'Had to check a couple of morning reports and a couple of pre spud meetings, sorry I'm a bit late'

The explanation was lost on James who stood up took the offered hand and shook it.

'Afternoon, thanks, no problem' James was flustered. 'Jim, I'm sorry but I didn't understand last night what you were all talking about and now it's, um, I'm even more confused. I don't feel that I should be here, I'm sorry I don't want to waste your time'

'Hey you need a job, I need a salesman, you want to talk about it before you turn it down?' asked Jim, still smiling.

'Yes, okay I guess that's the thing to do' replied James. The whole way of doing business this way surprising him.

'Come on through to the office, let's get started.' Jim led the way.

James followed Jim to a well-appointed office, surprised to see a well-stocked bar in one corner, pictures of drilling rigs, strange looking with even stranger sounding names, lined the walls.

Jim made himself comfortable in a large leather swivel chair behind a huge and beautifully carved mahogany desk. He looked every inch a successful businessman.

'Okay James, welcome to Great Yarmouth and Blue Water Oil Tools. It's all a bit strange isn't it, but don't worry, it's really all pretty simple. I own this company; I make the decisions. Now tell me about yourself.' Jim sat back in the chair still a smile on his face.

James, though surprised, liked Jim's style and for an hour told Jim about his life, his theatre work, every detail of the accident, the court case, the theft of his money, his reason for travelling to Yarmouth. Jim allowed him to talk, never interrupting, ignoring the telephone that rang several times.

'Okay, this is the deal. You start in the warehouse, two months. Learn the equipment, how it goes together, how to service it, learn all you can. Two months in internal sales, get to know how we do business. Then, if you have learnt and really show an interest, I'll put you out on the road as our salesman; company car, expense account, the whole deal. What do you think? Interested?' Jim sat back.

'I don't know, why me? I only met you last night, I don't know if I can do it. I don't know what to do. I want a job but...' James responded excited but nervous.

'James, in this town you have to take what's going when it's going. Oil business is boom or bust, right now its boom; in a couple of months it can still be boom or we may have gone bust. I started this business five years ago supplying paint and brushes and odds and sods, being helped by people I knew who had landed good jobs with the oil and drilling companies, it's called the rope, soap and dope business in the oilfield. I've expanded and now run specialist casing running and hammer services. I'm in debt to the bank and taking chances every day. I love it. You ask, why you? I'll tell you. Before I started this business, I had nothing, I came to Yarmouth from Ipswich, like you, looking for a job. I knew nothing but was prepared to work hard. Someone gave me a chance and I took it. Last night you reminded me of myself five years ago. You want a chance; I'm giving you a chance. If you don't want it someone else will grab it. Pays thirty-eight quid a week to start. Make a good salesman and I'll raise it to sixty quid. You want it?'

James was shocked.

'Yes, I want it, Thank you.'

Jim still smiling said 'Thank me by working hard and making me money, okay? Where are you staying?'

'The Two Bears now but I don't have much money so need to find somewhere I can afford' said James now realising that his funds were limited, and it would be a week or more till payday.

Jim picked up the phone and dialled. 'Charlie come through' he said.

A few moments later the warehouseman who James had seen earlier came into Jim's office.

'Yes boss?'

'Your sister still got the B and B?' asked Jim.

'Yes boss' answered Charlie.

'Is she busy?' asked Jim

'You know if you need anything, she will find space' said Charlie smiling.

'Okay Charlie, this is James Jackson, he's going to be working under you in the warehouse for a couple of months. I want you to work his ass off, teach him all you know. Okay?

Now call that sister of yours and get James settled in with her. Tell her I want it cheap. If it's all good, take James there this afternoon. He will be with you in an hour or so, okay?' Jim didn't stop to have questions answered, he just needed things done.

'Yes boss no problem' said Charlie, already heading out of the office.

'All okay with you, James?' asked Jim.

'Yes, that's fine, I can't believe this is happening, like a fairy tale' said James still shocked by the speed of things.

'Fuck you, you're here to work your ass off, to make me money' Jim smiled while saying it but then his face took on a stern look.

'One other thing, James and its important. Never steal from me, if you do, you're finished in this town, Is that clear?'

'Clear' said James.

'Right, that's it, go move your stuff from the hotel and get back here and go with Charlie' said Jim walking through to the reception area. 'Freda, this is James, he's coming on board with us, have we got fifty quid in the petty cash? Give it to James'.

'Welcome James' said Freda shaking his hand. 'Yes we do' she opened the petty cash box and counted out fifty pounds and gave it to James.

'Freda, Stick an IOU from James in the box, James pay it back when you can okay?' said Jim already on the way back to his own office. 'Freda if it's not paid back in three months let me know'.

James had never met anyone like this.

'Thank you, Jim, I'll not let you down'

'I know. By the way, when you make sales you can call me Jim, in the warehouse you call me boss. Got it?'

'Right boss, thanks' James was delighted.

It took James a couple of weeks to get into the job. One of the first things he found out was that dope referred to the grease that was put on drill pipe connections, and joints referred to the drill pipe or the casing that lined the well after drilling. The work in the workshop was heavy, hard and dirty. Equipment they moved and serviced was designed to withstand rough use and abuse and stripping it and servicing it built up his muscles quickly and he slept well every night at the B&B. Charlies widowed sister Maureen treated him like a member of the family and fed him well.

His IOU paid and his finances back in reasonable shape, James continued to learn all he could about the oil and gas industry and its opportunities and demands. He loved it. The action, the excitement of midnight calls to get equipment to a vessel or helicopter to prevent the rig from having to shut down, not wanting to see "waiting on equipment" on the morning report, the words that could spell the end for a service company.

Blue Water Oil Tools was a small company. An independent, wholly owned by Jim Seager who ran it in a confident and relaxed manner. Very professional and proud of the reputation he had built for great service and reliable equipment. He always knew what was going on, where his service crews were, where his equipment was and what work was going on and coming up. He looked after his employees and treated them well both in and out of the workplace.

A year after James joined the company, he and Jim went to lunch at The Two Bears. James was now the General Manager and second in command of the company. He had worked hard and learnt fast, if he didn't know something, he asked someone who did and he only had to be told once. He had built a good reputation as a dependable man who knew his business. His solicitors had been paid in full, insurance had paid out on the car and so he had moved out of Maureen's and had bought a small flat a mile or so from the office. He was settled into the social and business world of the oil industry and loved going to work. Life was good for James; only occasionally did he dream the dream of the accident and see the horror of death.

'Happy first anniversary, James' said Jim, raising his beer glass in a toast.

'Pleased to have made it Jim. Thank you, I have a lot to thank you for, not least that you kept your word and told no one of my past, which has made it a lot easier for me' replied James raising his coke glass and touching it to Jim's pint pot.

They ordered lunch and discussed some upcoming work and how best they could quote it. James sensed Jim had something important to say but was having difficulty saying it.

'Is there something on your mind Jim?' asked James.

'You know me too well already, yes there is something but it's between us at this stage okay?' said Jim looking very serious.

'Of course,' James assured him.

'I've had a bloody good offer for the company. It will make me a millionaire; I don't know what to do about it' said Jim with a worried look on his face.

'Fuck me' was all James could say, shocked.

'No thanks, I need to get this decision made first' said Jim grinning.

They both laughed. Jim explained the who, why and what of the proposed deal and then asked James for advice.

'It's a good offer Jim, you can retire and enjoy the grand kids, fishing, holidays, all kinds of things, what's stopping you?' asked James, surprised and pleased for Jim.

'I love this company, it's like a baby to me, A baby that I have nurtured and watched grow and mature. Seen it through some bad times but mostly good. It has been good to me and good to all the employees. I would hate for it to be swallowed up by a big corporation and the people treated badly. That's what I have seen happen to many companies in this industry. I know things would have to change, but that's how I feel. That's what stopping me right now.' said Jim, his voice full of concern and emotion. Like a man whose daughter is leaving home for the first time, pleased but worried for her.

'Why not go speak to them and tell them of your concerns, maybe they can reassure you? It's worth a try isn't it?' said James.

'Yes, that's a good idea, no wonder I made you General Manager' Jim said, looking less worried.

'You made me General Manager because no one else wanted

the job' James joked.

They enjoyed the lunch. Jim because he had shared his concerns with a man whose judgement he trusted and James because he felt trusted and respected, a long way from how he had felt when he left the courthouse a year ago.

Ten months later, Jim had asked his questions and received assurances and had sold Blue Water to Knotford Corporation of Houston. All the employees were given new written contracts. Verbal promises and assurances were made regarding long term employment by Knotfords' management and human resources department but it wasn't long before the promises were broken and the assurances were not honoured. The successful company that had been Blue Water was swallowed up, forgotten by a multi-national conglomerate interested only in profit and that didn't give a jot for loyalty. James like many of the other employees sought and found new employment and within six months of the takeover almost all the employees had left and the reputation and expertise that Blue Water had built was lost. For James it was a relatively easy move to find work as the General Manager of the company where he would spend the next twenty years of his working life.

He stayed in touch with Jim who was extremely disappointed with the demise of the company he had built but with several million in the bank he couldn't be too disappointed. James and Jim became firm friends, often spending long weekends together fishing or going to motor sport events.

Jim didn't flash his wealth. He had a lovely home and a good car but his children and grandchildren were looked after but not spoiled or lavished with gifts. His feet were firmly on the ground. One evening just before James moved to Aberdeen, he and Jim had dinner. It had been a lovely evening and they had enjoyed each other's company. Jim, keeping up with the comings and goings of the oilfield and James, still learning from him, as well as passing on his own observations. A coffee and a good cigar, Jim having a brandy, James still not drinking sticking with the coffee.

Jim looked serious 'James, we have been friends for a few years now and I value our friendship. I want you to know that if ever you need my help, financial or otherwise you only have to ask. I know you are stubborn enough to think that you will never have to ask but if you do need anything, don't hesitate. I mean it, whenever, whatever you need from me you got it' he raised his glass.

'Here's to your new life in Aberdeen' he toasted James.

James knew that Jim was serious and that he must answer in a serious manner.

'Thank you, Jim, I appreciate that. I value our friendship and I am going to miss seeing you so regularly, stay in touch, okay? And I thank you very much for your generous offer'. They stood and man hugged, sad that they would not be seeing each other so frequently but both excited for James' future.

They parted good friends knowing that the friendship would endure despite the physical distance between them.

CHAPTER 9

RICHARD Watt was a lean, athletic man. He was not a tall man, at five feet ten inches there were many men who were taller and many who were bigger than his one hundred and fifty pounds. But there were few men who were physically harder. Every inch of him was hard muscle. Muscled and lean from years of action and outdoor activity.

He sat on his haunches; the hunting rifle cradled gently in his arms. The binoculars hung loosely from the well-worn strap around his neck. His khaki shirt and shorts blending in with the scrub and stunted trees. The Land Rover was parked beneath the trees several hundred yards to the rear. Keeping his voice just low enough so the dozen or so people gathered either side of him could hear what he was saying as he explained the plan of action. He looked to the rear and checked that his second in command Mumti Embalasi was covering it; he was, barely visible crouched behind a scrub bush, his rifle at the ready, his body alert. As Richard moved the group forward Mumti kept pace, walking backwards ensuring that there was no danger from the rear. Richard got the group to within thirty yards of their target and in his soft voice, with just a hint of a Scottish accent, he said just loud enough for them all to hear.

'This is as close as we will get without disturbing them, I think the mother is about five years old and the cubs maybe ten or twelve weeks. Let's just watch them play for a few minutes before taking any pictures which may disturb them. Same safety rules as yesterday, if the mother gets anxious or moves towards us, slowly get yourselves flat on the ground. I will take care of her, at worst a tranquilizer dart, don't panic. If you have any questions now is the time to ask them.'

No one spoke.

'Okay, as quiet as possible.'

The group watched the lioness and her three cubs playing in the warm morning sun. One of the cubs had come really close and the group had the opportunity to take some wonderful photographs.

The lioness had not been bothered by the group, she knew they were there but felt no fear, she recognised the lean man in the camouflage clothes and knew he was not frightened of her but posed no danger to her. She allowed the cubs to play and practise hunting, life was good on this game reserve.

The tourist group had a wonderful day. Lots of great photographs and a hint of danger. Now they were back at the field camp with its charismatic huge bellied black chef, who went by the name of Watermelon. His cooking over the open fire would do credit to any five-star hotel anywhere in the world. Waiting on dinner they chatted about their holiday as this was the last night, tomorrow they would be going to Nairobi and then flying off to their respective homes around the world. There were few complaints, maybe the water in the field shower had been a little too hot, the beds a little too soft. Richard ran a good camp.

Richard ate dinner with the group as he normally did, it was part of the job. He enjoyed his work, the outdoors, the bush, the being alert to danger and ready to react. The tourist groups were diverse, in the main Americans, Germans, Italians, British with some Australians and more Japanese this year than last. Whatever the nationality they all wanted to know about him. People always interested in others who they see as having exciting jobs. Big game camp guide was one such job that generated questions. He always lied to them. His story was always the same and well-rehearsed. The questions nearly always came on the last evening of the ten-day safari, a time when they felt they knew him. Everyone was relaxed and they were all friends together, the campfire crackling and after dinner drinks flowing, a time for stories. It happened this evening, the question,

'How did you get into this line of work Richard?'

The answer.

'Well now, that's a long story. My father was a Scot and my mother the daughter of a prominent Boer politician. My father went to South Africa when he left the British army in the fifties, he was a Gordon Highlander and wore the kilt every day of his life even in the heat of Africa. My mother's father, my grandfather, had been a Brigadier in the South African army before entering politics so as the son of a soldier and the grandson of a soldier what else could I do but become a soldier. I joined the South African Army as a boy soldier and received a commission after five years. I was in the special forces for the last ten years of my seventeen-year career. I was injured in a gun battle with the Cubans when we fought them in Angola and retired out on medical grounds. A fellow officer had moved to Kenya some years before and started up a business like this one so when I was injured, I wrote to him looking for a job. Luckily for me he gave me one. Unfortunately, he was killed by a lion a year or so later and his company folded so I joined this company and been here a few years now and love it. It's a wonderful way of life.'

He looked around the group, he knew that his job was pure romance to them, and his story made it more so.

'Sorry if I bored you' he said.

There was general agreement that his story was not at all boring. These bankers, shopkeepers, housewives and salesman, whose trip of a lifetime this was, could only envy the romance of it, the closeness with nature, the obvious pride he had in his work, his field craft, his animal instinct. A man's man, good looking too. A woman's man.

Richard sipped the one beer he allowed himself on every trip. It was always the same on the last evening, excellent dinner, good fire, the guests all believing they had made a friend of you for life. All promising to write.

He sat back and smiled to himself. Half listening to the stories being told around the fire. Christ, he thought if they knew the truth about me these buggers wouldn't be so comfortable.

He thought about how he would tell it.

'Goodnight Mr Smith, Mrs Smith, yes it's been a great day

hasn't it? Yes, you'll see the boys in the morning. Sleep well.'

What would you think Mrs Smith if you knew the truth, he thought to himself. That husband of yours wouldn't have been keen for me to be close to you? How would he start the truth story?

Would he start with his father, the drunken Scot or with his mother, the daughter of a poor Boer farmer? Yes, that would do to start. He daydreamed, yes this is how he would tell it.

My father was a drunken Scot who left Scotland for South Africa because he fought with a cousin and severely injured him. He met my mother the daughter of a poor Boer farmer and got her pregnant. I am the son. He left after twelve years. The only thing he left me was my Scottish accent. My mother died in a house fire when I was nineteen and already in the South African army. She was a wonderful woman who worked hard for us but we were always poor.

'Thanks Mrs Tillotson, glad you enjoyed it, goodnight now. Yes I will see you in the morning, sleep well.'

His daydream briefly interrupted he went back to it. How would you tell your country club friends on your ranch in Texas with your big Mercedes car that a murderer had just wished you good night? He smiled wondering how the story would go on.

I loved the army. I was in the Special Forces trained to fight and kill behind enemy lines, and I was good at it, maybe too good.

Several more of his guests got up and bade him goodnight. He got up himself, going out to check on the three camp guards; as he walked, he continued his mental confession.

When I was twenty three, I married. Life was good, my career was going well, my home life was good. My wife went to college and became a lawyer. I was proud of her. I left a unit exercise one afternoon because I suspected my wife was having an affair. I went to our house, went upstairs and found my wife making love to another man. I killed them both with my bare hands, dumped their bodies in the bush and returned to my unit, no one had noticed my absence. At the end of the exercise, I returned home, reported my wife missing. The bodies were never found. The police suspected me when they found out from my wife's friends that she had been having an affair with a man who had also been reported missing by his family. They had no bodies, no evidence. In the end, with nothing but suspicion, they assumed that they had run off together and set up a new life. I continued my life in the army, no remorse, no guilt.

His checks finished he got back to the fire where just three people remained.

'You want me to put some more logs on the fire or are you ready for bed?' he asked.

'No we're going to bed now' said Beverly Sandersdon turning to her young niece Anita 'aren't we Anita, you ready?'

'Yes, it was a really great day and a wonderful holiday' Anita said.

'Pleasure ladies, good night, see you in the morning' Richard said lighting the way to their tent with his torch.

Yes, how would you feel Beverley if you knew I had raped a girl no older than your niece, you wouldn't be feeling so comfortable and secure I bet, he thought.

He went back to his silent musings. I left the Special Forces regiment when I was caught raping a black girl, we had caught her carrying arms for the terrorists. I had already killed her friend who had threatened me with a knife. Leaving was the easy option and they allowed me to leave with a good conduct record rather than them face the bad publicity of maltreatment of prisoners. I lied my way into the safari business, but I do enjoy it and meeting new people.

He sipped the last of his now warm beer, thinking about his dead wife and the stupid rape of the black girl, the killing of the girl who threatened him. Thinking about his future prospects.

The last guest got up to leave. He walked over to where Richard was sitting.

'I just wanted to say thank you, I've had a really wonderful time, I've got some lovely snaps and you and your people have done us proud' he said.

'Thank you Arthur,' said Richard 'I'm glad you have enjoyed it. We've seen a lot this last ten days, some of the things, especially the baby monkeys being born is most unusual. It's been good, you picked a good time.'

'Yes, I always wanted to come on a trip like this but I could never have done it, it's only now that I have come into money that I can do this kind of thing.' said Arthur.

Richard's senses heightened, many of his guests were

wealthy, it was obvious in the way they dressed and the camera equipment they carried and the way they carried themselves with a confident style. Richard had noticed that Arthur, what was his surname, Summerskill, Arthur Summerskill, was different. A nice man, timid, not at all confident in the group, having a good time oblivious of the others, polite and took instructions easily. A man who was used to doing what he was told.

'Here, sit down Arthur, let's have another beer' said Richard, moving a little so that Arthur could sit next to him at the fire. He threw another log on the fire and it caught into flame almost immediately, throwing light around them.

'Thank you, I don't normally drink much' said Arthur.

'Me neither' laughed Richard 'but it's a warm night the beer is cold and another is not going to hurt us.'

Arthur felt very relaxed and comfortable.

'It sounds as though you have had a wonderful life in the army and now doing this, a job you obviously enjoy, must be great spending your life outdoors doing exciting things' he said.

'Aye, it's been wonderful, and hopefully will go on being wonderful, till I'm too tired and too old to care. Tell me about yourself Arthur' said Richard.

For Arthur it was easy. He did not hold back. The crackling fire and the warm African night air. What a nice man this Richard is, so interested in what I have to say he thought.

Arthur told Richard his life story. Richard's interrogation technique, in which he had once been considered an expert and had taught in army college for a while, kicking in and coaxing Arthur to tell him all about himself. He left nothing out, his work, his wife, the accident, the trial, his hatred of James Jackson, Annette's death, the pools win, his travels; but most of all his desire for revenge on James Jackson, how he didn't know how to get it. How he didn't know how to make the man pay for what he had done to him and his family.

Richard listened carefully to the story. Arthur had seemed such a simple man who would have thought so much anger and hatred lay within him, how much tragedy there had been.

The camp was still. The lamps in the tents long extinguished. The tourists sleeping. The camp fire embers blowing and smouldering on the night breeze. The night calls of the hunted and the hunters occasionally breaking the stillness.

'I could help you get James Jackson, Arthur' said Richard. 'I could do it if you really wanted it to happen badly enough, how badly do you want it?'

Arthur was surprised, shocked, was this man serious, was he himself serious, he sat thinking. How badly do I want this? He was silent for a minute or so, then decided, his voice no more than a whisper, not daring to let anyone else hear.

'I want him more than I can tell you. I want him dead, no, I want more than that, I want him to suffer and feel real pain before he dies, I don't care how he suffers as long as he does. I want him to know the fear of death. I want to destroy him as he destroyed me and my family'

'It will cost you a lot of money, you do know that don't you?' asked Richard, shocked by the intensity in Arthur's hatred.

'I have a lot of money; I will spend every penny to avenge Annette and the twins' Arthur replied.

Richard thought quickly. This had to be settled tonight as the tourist group left first thing in the morning.

'Arthur, I trust you and I think you trust me. I'm going to tell you a different version of my life story, not the tourist version I told earlier. I am going to tell you it so you can know the kind of man I really am.'

Arthur listened as Richard told his true story, left nothing out, every gruesome and gory detail.

Arthur was not shocked, he knew he should have been but he could only see that this was a hard man, the man who could get Jackson. He had now seen two men who had murdered, this man and Jackson.

Arthur looked at Richard.

'That's some story, you seem so, well, normal. It would be quite difficult for anyone to tell by looking at you that you were capable of doing such things. I'm not shocked but I am surprised. If you are serious about helping me how much do you want?' Arthur asked, trusting this man for some reason. He sensed that here was a man of honour, able to do fearsome things, but most of all a man who would do what he said he would do. A man who would keep his word.

Richard thought for a moment before replying. If he got paid to do it, he would do it, that he knew, but it would cost.

After a long silence Richard said.

'You put one hundred thousand dollars into a bank account in my name in Switzerland and send me confirmation that you have, then send me a first class return air ticket to London. I will contact you and we can discuss the final cost and the detail, what do you think?'

'I know I have to trust you not to just take the money, but for some reason I do trust you, I can't explain that but it's how I feel. Yes, I have no other choice, you are the first person I have ever met who I have even discussed this matter with. Yes, I believe you will do it. Where do I send the confirmation?'

The two men, unlikely partners now, shook hands, firmly, knowing it would happen and their lives would be forever linked.

Three weeks later Richard packed his bags, quit his job and with a Swiss Bank deposit slip in his wallet, boarded first class for London. It's first class all the way for me now, he thought as he settled into his seat, the champagne glass in his hand raised in salute.

'Here's to you Arthur' he said.

The air hostess turned around puzzled she could see no one returning his toast.

Two hours later, almost a thousand miles closer to London, she was still puzzled as Richard removed her pants to induct himself into the mile-high club.

CHAPTER 10

TOM McLeod had been a policeman for thirteen years. Born in London he had moved to Edinburgh with his parents when he was seventeen, two years later he joined the police force.

He had always wanted to be a policeman and when he was accepted it was a dream come true for him. At just five foot nine he was amongst the shortest policemen in the force but his broad shoulders and muscular body made him appear much larger than he was. His height, or lack of it, had never been a disadvantage to him in his career. He made sergeant in eight years and spent several years on special royal protection duty where diplomacy and trust were as important as protection of the principals and upholding the law.

The past two years he had been a specialist hostage negotiator. His patience, ability to think under pressure, decision making while staying calm in tense and difficult situations making him an ideal choice for the intensive and thorough training programme. The training took six months, much of it in live situations, with an active negotiator testing his suitability for the work. He passed out with excellent reports.

Tom would never tell anyone that he enjoyed the work, in fact he rarely told anyone what his job was, let alone what it entailed. Mainly it was tedious and tiring with short, adrenalin filled rushes between exceptionally long periods of inactivity. It kept him away from home for long periods sometimes for several months. Few people outside the force knew what his role was but those that did, and who he cared to confide in, knew he enjoyed the job especially when he was successful but never heard about it if the negotiation failed and lives, innocent or otherwise were lost.

Most of the work involved domestic disputes of one sort or another, lovers' tiffs that simply got out of hand often fuelled by drugs or alcohol. Men barricading themselves into buildings with a shotgun and a hostage and threatening to kill themselves or anyone who came near. In these cases, Tom was the one who got near. All too often the only way anyone got hurt in these situations was when the gun went off accidently, tragic but true. The hostage takers in the main being frightened and emotionally disturbed. Not really criminals. Plane hijacks and political or financial hostage taking was thankfully very rare in Britain and he had only ever been involved in one plane hijack while he had been to dozens of domestic shot gun barricades. He had a good record and was considered to be an expert. He studied psychology but did not let what he read override his intuition and common sense. He now helped teach the skills when he was not on active duty.

Tom wasn't married, just had never found the right girl. He enjoyed all sport and still played rugby, prop forward, but now only turning out for the thirds and finding each game harder than the last. It would soon be time to give up and go into coaching.

Molly's kidnap was only his third proper kidnap or abduction. An abduction becoming a kidnap when something was required in exchange. He had been called away from a course in Glasgow to attend the Jacksons home. The course he was on had shocked him. He had been staggered to learn that hundreds of kidnaps took place every year in South America and, while ransoms were routinely being paid, the kidnappers were taking the money and still murdering the hostages. A very worrying trend that he hoped would not be copied in the UK where, thank God, there was still some law and order and a healthy respect for the rule of law by most of the people.

He had now been at James and Karen Jacksons' house for three weeks. The call in the early hours of the third day after Molly's unlawful removal from the house the only contact from the kidnapper. There was no trail to follow, no clues as to who or why, nothing to tie it in with the bombing of James' office. There was nothing, no reports of unusual activity in the area or beyond. No reports of strangers at least none for which there had not been a simple explanation. All they had was the white Toyota pick-up being stolen in Glasgow and no witnesses to that and it being used in Rothienorman and other than Karen or James no witnesses to that.

Tom was undecided as to what to do next. He was keeping up to date with the search for Molly and the continuing investigation into her abduction which was being led by Detective Chief Inspector Sinclair. He met regularly with the Chief Inspector to discuss the case. At their last meeting they had discussed if they should maintain Tom's vigilance at the house, bearing in mind that with modern technology, it was possible to have phone lines routed to anywhere in the country. Tom had argued that once called in on a case it was rare for the trained negotiator to be relieved so, in complete agreement, they had decided to leave things as was for the time being before making a final decision in a month if no further contact had been made.

Tom vetted every call that came to the house, every call was recorded, and the caller checked to ensure it was legitimate. Tom had relieved the tension with Karen and James one day by telling them that double glazing and conservatory salesman would never be calling the house again.

They encouraged their friends to call but kept the calls short, always aware they might miss the second call from the kidnapper.

Tom's relationship with Karen and James was very good from the start but grew as the days passed. They were under a huge stress and he was a good support for them aware that there might be much worse stress to come.

He was fascinated, he hoped not morbidly, by the kidnapper's demand that James Jackson's death would secure Molly's release. In all his training and his study of kidnaps around the world he had never come across this demand. In long conversations with James, he had questioned him about why anyone would want to have him dead and James could not think of anyone and was as confused as Tom was about the twisted mind that demanded this.

It was the forty third day when the phone rang. It was ten fifteen in the morning. The recorder clicked on automatically and they waited the five rings before lifting the receiver.

A short pause then a metallic voice

'An eye for an eye.'

Tom, always alert whenever the phone rang was now fully alert.

'We confirm the password. Is Molly safe?'

The metallic voice, now more distorted than at the last call, spoke again.

'Yes, Is James Jackson dead?'

'No, we must have proof that Molly is alive, we need to talk to her.'

'You know the conditions, I'll call again different password, Dolly Dew Drop'.

'Did you say Dolly Dimple?' asked Tom trying again to delay the caller long enough for the technical experts to trace the call. Again, the call lasted less than thirty seconds. The phone rang again almost immediately, five rings later Tom answered it, once again it was confirmed that the call had been too short to trace.

Tom turned to Karen and James.

'I have just spoken to the kidnapper; he used the right password and is still using the voice distorter. He told me Molly is well and next time he calls will use a new password – Dolly Dew Drop – does that mean anything to you?'

'Yes, it was our pet name for her when she was younger, she must have told him, is that good?'

'Yes, very good, if they are getting on together it is a very good sign. I will be talking to the psychologist later perhaps it would be good if you joined us to hear what it might mean' Tom said, thankful that at least they had had a second call.

He contacted DCI Sinclair and they agreed to meet the following day.

It was no more than thirty minutes later that the phone rang again. Tom had gone to the toilet and James was taking a walk. Karen waited the instructed five rings, the tape recorder automatically clicked on and she picked up the receiver.

'Hello' she said totally unprepared for what she was about to hear.

'Is that Karen?' a metallic voice asked. Much more threatening, Karen thought, heard directly than through the tape recording.

'Yes, I want my baby, please, please let her go, let me talk to her please, I'll do anything, please' Karen pleaded. Her voice breaking.

'Dolly Dew Drop Karen, I am not here to be fucked around. You know the price. Persuade him. Oh, by the way Merry Christmas.'

The line went dead just as Tom entered the room his clothes in a state of disarray as he had cut short his toilet visit.

Karen stood perfectly still. The phone handset still in her hand. The room quiet except for the whirring of the tape deck. Tom watched her as she lowered the phone receiver, her shoulders slumped, and the tears came. He crossed the room and held her gently in his arms, comforting her. She sobbed into his shoulder.

'He wished me a Merry Christmas, he has my baby, how can he be so cruel? Help me Tom, please help me' she pleaded.

James came in and took Karen from Tom who, calmly, showing no emotion replaced the telephone receiver and waited for the call from tracing but already knew it had been such a short call that there was no possibility of a trace.

The phone rang and it was to confirm no trace. Tom thanked them and set up the tape recorder for a replay. He played the tape then rewound and played it again, he did this four more times and then said to Karen and James.

'I am going to play the tape once more I want you to concentrate on any background noise and tell me what you hear.'

He rewound and played the tape again. Karen and James stood silent concentrating on the sounds from the player.

'Hear anything?' Tom asked.

James looked at him with a puzzled look on his face

'Could that be a train I can hear? very faint but sounds like the rumble of a train to me.'

'That's what I thought' said Tom 'there are no trains near us so it must be at his end, we will get this analysed and see if it is.'

Tom thought that at last they had a lead, however slim. He called DCI Sinclair who got his team looking at all train movements within a fifty-mile radius of the house that would correspond to the exact time of the call. If nothing fit, then they would move out in fifty mile increments.

Christmas had not been given any serious thought until the kidnapper had mentioned it. Cards had been coming to the house from friends and relatives and gifts for Molly from well-wishers all over the country. The newspapers and TV had wanted interviews with Karen and James, not just because of the kidnap but also still interested in the explosion three months ago which was very much an ongoing investigation. The police teams working on the explosion and the kidnap had worked closely with the media persuading them to report only what the police wanted reported, not to speculate or run parallel investigations, reminding them that Molly's welfare was the prime concern and that they would be fully involved when investigations resulted in arrests or, better still, Molly's safe release. They were persuaded that this would sell more newspapers and make better headlines.

The press had not been informed of the kidnapper's demand for James' death as the ransom demand to ensure Molly's release. Not least because they feared copycat crime.

Christmas day was not celebrated by Karen, James or Tom, they stayed at the house waiting on any contact from the kidnapper. The thirty or so police who were on duty continuing the search for Molly did not celebrate Christmas Day either.

Unknown to them Molly ate roast turkey with all the trimmings followed by Christmas pudding and cream. She received one gift and one card. The card bore a simple message - Merry Christmas, I don't like holding you, I hope you can go home soon – it wasn't signed. The gift was great, a Sony Walkman with twenty tapes and some spare batteries.

She was really pleased; she had missed listening to music. She had no card to give but her present was a simple kiss on the check and a thank you when he carried her to the bathroom that Christmas evening.

CHAPTER 11

ARTHUR returned from his Kenyan safari holiday feeling more confident and happier than he had felt in many years. At last he had found the man who would take his revenge.

Arthur had been a lonely man prior to the twins deaths and had become even more insular and isolated since Annette had died. The wealth he now had found him no new friends, not that he sought any. After the win he retired from work and spent the time reading, watching the television and three times a year taking a holiday. He had always had an interest in the planet, wild places and wild animals, an interest which he had kept satisfied by reading National Geographic magazine but now with the money he could start to explore and see things for himself. The holidays were always long in the planning and the staff at the small independent travel agent near his home dreaded his visits. They called him Mr Creepy; the owner, though, saw that this client was a valuable source of income and insisted that his staff treat him with respect. Arthur spent a great deal more than the Magaluf lager louts and beach crowd that made up the majority of the agent's business.

Even on his holidays Arthur kept himself to himself, not flouting his money, not getting friendly with the other tourists, always frugal in his habits. His major purchase apart from the holidays had been on a good camera which he enjoyed using.

He had no idea why he had opened up to Richard in Kenya and no idea why Richard had opened up to him but he was glad that they had met and he hadn't had any second thoughts on trusting Richard to keep his word.

A few days after arriving home, Arthur met with his Bank Manager. Despite the Managers' protests and advice for caution, the account with the Swiss Bank was set up and the money transferred just as he and Richard had agreed. Arthur did not like his Bank Manager. Arthur felt that the man always acted as though he thought Arthur's money was his, always trying to tell Arthur how he should invest in this or that company or put money into the various savings and investment accounts the bank operated. Arthur was not pleased when every quarter along with his interest statement he received an account for bank charges. He always queried these charges. He enjoyed watching the manager squirm as he tried to explain how the charges had been calculated. Arthur always managed to get him to reduce the charges a little, not least because Arthur was one of the branches' most affluent customers. Arthur enjoyed watching the man squirm. Arthur's father had never had a bank account; what money he saved was put in a tin and kept under the bed. Anything he bought was paid in cash. If he didn't have the money to pay for it the family went without. He used to tell Arthur – never a lender or a borrower be- and Arthur had not forgotten this.

But he was of a different generation and had opened a bank account the first week he had earned a pay packet, but his fathers' distrust of banks and bankers was deeply rooted in him.

'Right, so that money will be in the swiss bank account tomorrow is that right?' He asked the Bank Manager.

'Yes, Mr Summerskill, it will be. You have paid the extra fee to have that service. You have the account number on that piece of paper, please don't lose it, if you do the money will be lost forever. Perhaps you should rent a safe deposit box with us.'

'No, you will be wanting to charge me for that and I'm paying you enough now' Arthur responded, enjoying the moment.

'And there's another thing,' said Arthur, 'I think I will be starting to spend more of my money in the near future so don't think about giving me your advice, I'm going to do as I please with my money.'

'Of course, Mr Summerskill, we are here to help; of course you must do as you please with your funds.'

'Right then I'm off. It might be a while before I see you again, I'll wish you good day' said Arthur, making for the door, already tired of the man.

'Pleasure as always Mr Summerskill. Thank you for stopping by.' The Bank Manager showed Arthur from his office, passing his secretary's desk he put his fingers in his mouth and silently pretended to vomit causing her to giggle.

Arthur went home.

'Well Annette' he said aloud 'that's the first step, God I hope I can trust this man, but it's only money, and I can afford to lose it but for James Jackson it will be his life'.

The following morning Arthur went to his local travel agent and organised the open first class ticket for Richard, the travel clerks had never done this before so it took a little while. He then went to the post office and sent a telegram advising Richard that the funds had been transferred and that the ticket was organised and paid for and gave a number for the travel agent in Nairobi to call to make the flight arrangements.

Three days later he received the call he had been hoping and praying he would receive. It was Richard.

'Arthur, Arthur, this is Richard, how are you?'

'Hello, Hello can you hear me' answered Arthur, the international phone line crackling and echoing.

'Yes, I can. No need to shout. I will be catching the plane in a couple of hours. I will call you when I get to London, guess it will be about ten tomorrow morning your time okay?' said Richard raising his own voice as the line became noisier.

'Hello! Yes! Hello! Hello!' Arthur shouting into a dead line.

The following twelve-hour wait was agony for Arthur, he wanted the man to be there, set the plan and get it into action.

Arthur spent the early evening at his Doctors. He had been feeling breathless for the past few months and more recently had pains in his chest and sometimes an awful pain in his stomach. He had done his best to ignore these pains but during the safari they had been so bad that he became worried that they might be really serious, so had organised a doctor visit on his return home. He was a man who was rarely ill and he had had enough of hospitals when Annette was there after the accident and for the last few weeks of her life.

'I'm sorry Arthur but that's my diagnosis, I do think we should get a second opinion. I will contact a Specialist; he should be able to see you within a few weeks. In the meantime, I will prescribe some medication to ease the pain' the Doctor told him following a thorough examination.

'I can afford to pay' said Arthur, 'I can go private, you know if it will speed things up, what about all these fancy doctors in Harley Street? Can't they help?' asked Arthur trying to take in what the Doctor had told him.

'Yes, if that's what you want, they won't be able to do anything the National Health can't do but if that's what you want I can arrange it, when could you go to London?' asked the Doctor.

'Tomorrow, if it will do any good' replied Arthur brusquely.

'Well, I don't know if it will do any good but the sooner the better. Let me make a call now' the Doctor said already picking up the telephone before Arthur could respond.

The call lasted about five minutes, the Doctor explaining his diagnosis and arrangements being made. He turned to Arthur,

'Would three thirty tomorrow afternoon be alright for you?'

'Yes I suppose so' said Arthur 'I'll have to go down on the train. I think they are pretty regular, aren't they?'

'Yes, you can leave about midday and make it in good time' said the Doctor who travelled to London frequently with his wife, who enjoyed the theatre.

The Doctor confirmed that Arthur would be at Harley Street at three thirty and ended the call.

Arthur left the Doctors surgery feeling very despondent, he walked to the dispensing chemist and collected his medication and then wishing to be alone in the fresh air he walked the three miles back to his house. The early evening sunshine and the yellow daffodils cheering him up a little.

The house as usual seemed cold and damp. It was spotlessly clean thanks to Mrs Arkwright a woman who came and did for him three times a week, generally cleaning and doing his washing and ironing. She was there when Arthur arrived home but as usual there was nothing more than a civil greeting between them. She needed the money, not the company, she would tell her husband if he asked her about the job and Arthur. Miserable old skinflint he would say, never gives you a penny more than your wages and him what won all that money. The truth was slightly different, she liked the job because it got her away from her miserable skinflint husband and Arthur often used to add extra money to her wages.

Arthur woke early, the pain in his stomach awfully bad. He put off taking the medicine for half an hour, but the pain got worse. He swallowed the tablets and almost immediately the pain lessened. At nine fifteen the phone rang.

'Arthur, its Richard, I am in Heathrow.'

'Morning' said Arthur, 'Look I have to go to London today to see someone, lets meet somewhere down there this evening.'

'Ok, Where?'

Arthur was at a loss for words, he didn't know London at all.

'I don't know, um, let's see' Arthur looked down at the table beside the telephone, searching for inspiration and found it, the Harley Street address of the specialist, 'Right I know' he said reading the address to Richard 'meet me there at six thirty'.

'Right, see you at six thirty' confirmed Richard, wondering what he would find to do all day in London but looking forward to finding out.

Arthur packed an overnight bag; a night in London might be the thing to do he had decided. I've got a big day coming up, he thought to himself.

The card covered scrap book, its yellowing clippings of newsprint, had lain undisturbed in the wooden box at the bottom of the wardrobe. The last things he had stuck in it were Annette's funeral order of service cards and a copy of the death notice from the local paper. He took the file from the box and laid it carefully in his overnight bag. He didn't like opening it, the memories too painful for him.

The train arrived in London on time and he took a taxi to Harley Street. He hadn't known what to expect. The Specialist, Mr Clark had a small and scruffy reception and consulting room. I'm paying a lot of money for this he thought. Arthur, disappointed with the ambiance, was not disappointed with the attitude and thoroughness of the man. Here was a man, Arthur thought, who was an expert. He was with Mr Clark for almost two hours. The examination and taking of blood and urine samples taking only fifteen minutes or so, the rest of the time discussing the various options and alternatives if, as Mr Clark suspected, his diagnosis confirmed that of the Doctor in Nottingham.

Arthur sat in a small café a short walk from Harley Street. He had fifteen minutes to wait for his meeting with Richard. He sipped at his cup of tea thinking about the last couple of hours and what he had been told. He decided the worst part would be the waiting on the test results and the confirmation. Mr Clark had said it would take about five days before they would be available. The café was busy, the hustle and bustle of the street outside which Arthur could see through the plate glass windows of the café alien to him and his lonely existence in Nottingham.

Richard arrived early, checked the address on the piece of paper against the highly polished brass plate on the door of the building. His bags were in his room at the Hilton Hotel, and he had spent most of the day sightseeing and enjoying the city. The street was busy with people and he did not notice Arthur approaching. It was only when Arthur tapped him on the shoulder and said 'hello' that he realised he was there.

'Hello Arthur.' he said 'What a busy place. Good to see you again.'

'Isn't it, how are you, good flight? Listen I don't know what to do, um, shall we go and have a cup of tea and um,' Arthur was confused, he had not thought about how or what they would be doing once they met. He just hadn't thought it through.

Richard felt sorry for him. It seemed to Richard that Arthur had aged in the past few weeks and the tanned face that he had seen on safari was now pale and almost translucent.

Richard took the initiative.

'It might be a good idea if we stayed in London tonight, don't you think? We need to talk and make plans and it might not be a good idea for us to be seen in your hometown. I have a room at the Hilton, let's take a taxi there, have a drink and decide what we are going to do. What do you think?'

'Yes, whatever you think, um, we can do that. I don't know London very well so that's okay, shall we go?'

Richard took Arthur's bag and hailed a taxi.

'A room for how many nights, Sir?' asked the Hilton's receptionist.

'Let's make it two nights, I'm in 701 so you can book me for a second night in there also. Do you have a room close to 701?' asked Richard.

'Let me see.' The receptionist fingered the computer keyboard and waited a few seconds for the screen to change.

'Yes Sir, number 705 is available, will that be okay?'

'That's fine. Okay with you Arthur?' asked Richard checking with Arthur.

'I suppose so, how much does it cost to stay here?' he asked.

The receptionist loved to see the expression on people's faces when they walked in off the street with no booking and were quoted the rack rate. This old man who looked like he would be more used to bed and breakfast is just going to die when I tell him, he thought.

'One hundred and fifty eight pounds, Sir,' he said

'One hundred and fifty eight pounds for two nights, that's outrageous' said Arthur.

'No Sir, that's the rate per room per night, how do you wish to pay?' asked the receptionist, loving the look of surprise on the man's face.

'Put it on my credit card' said Richard smiling as he leant across the counter and put his face inches from that of the receptionist, he whispered 'and don't act like a smart arse, you creepy little bastard.'

The receptionist became flustered and minced around getting the documents and room key organised, determined to keep Arthur and Richard waiting, but Richard knew what was going on.

'When you get organised bring the key to the bar, arrange for Mr Summerskill's bag to be sent up to his room.'

The receptionist could only say 'Yes Sir' to the disappearing backs.

An hour later they sat in Arthurs' room, the file of newspaper cuttings open on the small round table in front of them. Richard sipped a beer from the bottle which he had taken from the mini bar. Arthur was explaining the contents of the file. There were photographs of the crash scene, of Annette and the twins, of Jane and of James. The court case was documented by the cuttings from the many newspapers and there were pictures of Arthur and a story about his outburst in the court room after the verdict had been delivered.

'I want him to suffer, I want him dead Richard. I want it done before I die. I'm begging you not to let me down, no matter what happens to me I want him dead.' Arthur was full of emotion as he spoke the words to Richard, he had not looked through the file for some time and the contents held painful memories that came flooding back to him.

'Arthur, listen to me' said Richard softly. 'We made a deal and you have already paid me my fee. I have done a lot of things in my life that if I had it over again, I would change and you may not think much of me but there is not a man on this earth who will dispute that I am a man of my word. No matter what happens, I will keep my word and James Jackson will be dead.'

Arthur somehow knew he would be. There was something about Richard that Arthur found honest and reassuring.

'Yes, I believe you will' said Arthur smiling, which he hadn't done in a long time.

'Okay Arthur, we have to plan and decide how we are going to trace Jackson and how I am going to make him suffer before he dies. Any ideas?' asked Richard.

'To be honest I haven't given it a lot of thought, I don't have any idea where he is, the last time I saw him was in the court. Can you believe that they were going to charge me with threatening behaviour after letting that bastard walk away' Arthur said angrily.

'Calm down Arthur, we aren't going to get anywhere by getting upset. We need to lay down a plan and then stick to it. Now let's go over what we know and what our options are. Okay?' Richard's army background focusing his mind on a plan of action.

They talked until midnight when Richard suggested they get some sleep and talk again in the morning. Arthur agreed.

Breakfast for two was delivered by room service to Arthurs room at eight thirty and for the rest of the morning they talked and discussed various scenarios, knowing they would have to stay flexible until they had tracked James. He might not even be in the UK Richard told Arthur who had never thought of that possibility. In the early afternoon they walked down Piccadilly grateful to breath in the warm spring air after being cooped up in the hotel with its non-opening windows and air conditioning. They ate lunch at McDonald's, the first time Arthur had ever been into one and the experience was not to his liking; confused by the service and the speed at which the customers devoured the food.

Returning to the hotel Richard scanned the old newspaper clippings before making several calls to directory enquiries and five more calls trying to track down Phillip and Mary Stevenson. The fifth call gave him the information he needed, and he made a note of the telephone number and address.

CHAPTER 12

'MR Stevenson? Mr Phillip Stevenson? Good afternoon Sir, I'm terribly sorry to bother you but are you the Mr Stevenson who has a daughter Jane?'

Richard listened while Mr Stephenson told him that his daughter Jane had been dead for many years.

'Oh, I am terribly sorry to hear that, I can't believe it, I'm so sorry. Listen my name is George Thomas, I was at drama school with Jane and we were good friends, maybe she spoke about me. Anyway, I have been living out of the country since leaving college and I am back for a few weeks so thought I might get in touch with her. I can hardly believe she is dead; she was so full of life. I am so sorry to have bothered you. Look, this may sound silly, but could I come and see you, I'd like to meet you. I have come a long way and I was so hoping to meet up with Jane again. I can't believe it.'

Phillip Stevenson turned to his wife.

'There's a George Thomas on the phone, went to college with our Jane, he didn't know she was dead, wants to come and see us, sounds terribly upset, what do you think?'

'No harm I suppose if he wants to come see us, when is he coming?' Mary Stevenson asked her husband.

'When do you want to come?' asked Phillip 'tomorrow, yes, that will be fine. I get home from work about five thirty, come at seven, is that alright?'

'Yes fine, I tracked you down via an old neighbour of yours in Cornwall, can you confirm the address she gave me, Quarry Cottage, Church Lane, Flax Bourton, near Bristol is that right?'

Phillip confirmed the address and gave Richard directions to enable him to find the cottage easily.

'Right then, thank you, I look forward to meeting you' said Richard.

'Okay Mr Thomas, see you tomorrow then. Goodbye.' Phillip Stevenson put down the phone and walked out into the garden at the back of the cottage. The dust swirling in the wind from the limestone quarry across the hill distorting his view towards the Bristol Channel. Since the quarry had been working round the clock, supplying stone for the motorway extension, clear evenings were few and far between. Never mind, he thought, it's my fault, I manage the damn quarry. Roll on March when I retire from all this dust and aggravation. He thought of Jane, missing her vitality and laughter even after all this time. He so missed her.

Richard and Arthur ate dinner. Room service again. They ate the meal slowly discussing things further and trying to estimate the money that Richard would require to get things moving over the next few weeks. Arthur no longer cared about money; he was happy to let Richard do the calculating.

Arthur went to bed tired but pleased with the days' events but he was in terrible pain and took more tablets. Richard went out for a drink ending up in a cheap strip club where he drank expensive weak beer and watched a slack breasted, skinny woman attempting to titillate a disinterested and sparse audience of middle-aged business men. If this is swinging London, he thought; they can keep it.

The Midland Bank building on the corner of Tottenham Court Road was already busy at ten the next morning as Arthur and Richard entered. They were attended to by a smart young lady at the reception desk who, after making a phone call to Arthurs Bank in Nottingham, showed the two men through to the manager's office.

'Certainly, Sir, we will transfer the amount from your account in Nottingham to a new account for Mr Watt. The cheque book and bank card for Mr Watt's account will be ready to collect in a few days or we could post it to you Mr Watt' said the manager.

'I'll pick it up thanks' said Richard.

'We will also need a couple of thousand in cash if that would be okay' interrupted Arthur at last enjoying spending his money, the result exciting him.

'No problem Mr Summerskill, we can arrange that from your account. I will get one of my staff to have it ready in a few minutes, would twenties be okay?'

'Yes, that will be fine thank you' replied Arthur.

With the cash safely deposited in Richard's pocket and the formalities of the account opening completed the two men returned to the Hilton and checked out. Arthur getting the train back to Nottingham and Richard taking the tube to Heathrow where he hired a car and set out to drive the one hundred or so miles to Bristol.

'Mr Stevenson, good evening. Sorry I'm a bit late there was a lot more traffic than I expected, and I left the motorway at the wrong exit. How are you? I'm George Thomas, we spoke on the phone yesterday' said Richard using the name of George Thomas, his boss in Kenya.

'Good evening Mr Thomas. Come in please.'

Arthur entered the cottage and was introduced by Phillip to his wife, Mary.

'Good evening Mrs Stevenson, pleasure to meet you. Jane used to speak about you both all the time, but that was a long time ago' Richard lied.

They sat in the glass conservatory at the back of the cottage and talked of Jane and what she did after college and of the accident and her untimely death. Richard using the limited amount of information he had gleaned from the newspaper reports in Arthurs files, being vague, and using his practised skills as a liar managed to dupe the couple into believing that he really had been friends with Jane.

'And are you still in touch with her husband. What was his name?' He asked innocently.

'No George, we're not but we have always tried to keep track of him. It is James Jackson. He stopped sending us Christmas cards about twelve years ago. He got married again you know. He was living in Great Yarmouth working in the oil industry. The last we heard, via a friend of ours whose son works in the oil industry, was that he had moved to Aberdeen and was running a company there. We did see him once about fifteen years ago when we were visiting Janes' grave, he was at the graveside, but we didn't want anything to do with him, so we left and went back later by which time he was gone.' Phillip replied.

'Would you like some more tea?'

Richard said he would, and Phillip left the room to put the kettle on. Mary looked at Richard and beckoned him closer, in a whisper she said,

'You will have to forgive my husband, George; he is still very bitter about Jane's death. He blames James Jackson. I don't know what would happen if they met and I wasn't there, when we saw him at the graveside, I had to plead with Phillip to leave. It's been eating at him for years.'

Phillip came back in with the tea and they spent some time talking about where Richard might visit locally for some sight-seeing.

'Wookey Hole is nice and Cheddar Gorge of course, Wells and Glastonbury Cathedrals are wonderful' offered Mary. 'Look it's getting late; would you like to stay here tonight? We have room and it would be nice to have you.'

Richard smiled.

'No thank you Mary, very kind of you but I will get going. I will spend a few days looking around. It's been very nice to see you and I hope we meet again. I am so sorry about Jane and I hope I haven't upset you or Phillip by talking about her this evening.'

'No, it's been very nice, we haven't spoken about her with any of her friends for many years. It's been lovely. Have a nice holiday, come back and see us at any time, isn't that right dear?' said Mary looking at her husband for confirmation.

'Yes, any time' said Phillip 'at least any time before March when I am supposed to retire from this bloody quarry. I'm sure we will move then, away from this dust but the next quarry manager will have my address so contact him if we aren't here'.

Phillip led Richard to the door.

'Good night lad, thanks for coming.'

Richard drove away slowly, the car lights reflecting from the dust covered stunted bushes at the side of the road.

'What a nice young man. Funny though, I can't remember Jane having a friend at college called George, and he would have been several years older than her. What a lot we didn't know about her. It's late I'm ready for bed, how about you?'

'Oh, Mary I do still miss her you know' said Phillip with a deep sigh.

'I know dear, so do I. Come on let's go to bed' said Mary squeezing her husband's hand tightly.

Richard wasn't tired, he waited until he was out of sight of the cottage and then hit the accelerator.

CHAPTER 13

IT was a dark evening, but the sky was clear and the road was dry. He followed the signs for the M5 motorway and at the first services Northbound, stopped, filled up with petrol, bought the best road map they had, stocked up with snacks and chocolate, picked up a coffee and sat working out the most direct route to Aberdeen. He reckoned that if he could stay awake, he would be there by about nine in the morning.

He made excellent progress, the motorway was busy with heavy trucks, but few cars and he had the middle lane to himself most of the time. From the M5 he took the M6 and north of the turn off for The Lakes even the truck traffic was much lighter.

He ate the crisps and chocolate and drank several cans of coke. His eating and drinking driven by boredom to keep him alert. Despite his flight and busy day in London he wasn't tired and he spent the time going over his possible plans. Now with the likelihood that James Jackson lived in or near Aberdeen he was able to take one or two of his ideas a step further. His special forces training was going to come in very handy, he knew.

He arrived at Glasgow just as the morning rush hour traffic was beginning to build, he was tired now and the journey was taking him a bit longer than he had calculated. His tiredness caused him to miss the A90 junction. Not wishing to get caught up in stop-start traffic he found a small café on Glasgow's London Road and ate a large truckers breakfast before settling himself down for a sleep in the car. He woke at eleven refreshed but feeling very grubby.

The traffic much lighter now he quickly retraced his steps the few miles and found the A90 to Aberdeen and he enjoyed his first proper sight of Scotland in daylight.

The Skean Dhu Hotel was a modern building just on the outskirts of Aberdeen in the Altens area. He drove the car into the huge car park and found a space near the main entrance door. The reception was very 'Scottish' with acres of tartan and paintings of castles and hunting scenes.

Richard approached the reception desk.

'Do you have a room' he asked all smiles.

'Yes we do Sir, for how many nights?' asked the pretty red-headed receptionist dressed head to toe in tartan.

'Oh, a couple I think, a couple at least' replied Richard who smiled even more as he realised that for the first time he was hearing a Scots accent in a Scottish setting.

'I feel like I am home at last' he said.

'That's nice' said the girl 'room 241, can I make an impression of your credit card?'

'No, I will be paying cash, if you don't mind.'

'Not at all, a couple of nights in advance; that will be a hundred and seventy pounds please'

The transaction completed Richard went to his room and took a long hot shower, shaved and changed clothes. His café breakfast in Glasgow had been large and appetising and he wasn't hungry. He picked up the telephone book. Jackson, J; there were ten in the book. He looked at the addresses wondering which one, if any, was his man. He went down to reception where he had noticed a wooden rack holding tourist information leaflets, he scanned them, taking the ones he thought might be useful. Sitting in a comfortable tartan covered chair he looked through them trying to get a feel for the city and surrounding area.

At three that afternoon he had reception call him a taxi. Ten minutes later he was in it and asked the driver to give him a tour of the city so that he could familiarise himself with its layout.

'No bother, you a yank?' asked the taxi driver pulling away.

'No, South African, why did you think I was American?'

'We get lots of yanks here, in the oil, you in oil?' he asked.

'No' replied Richard 'but I was, in South Africa, I'm looking to get a job here, you know where I should look?' he asked.

'Well, there are always a lot of riggers and roustabouts in the Star and Garter but the onshore guys, you know the managers and the bosses of the service companies are usually at the Earls Court, that's a hotel on North Anderson Drive. I could drop you off there after showing you around a bit,' offered the driver already knowing he could turn this into a lucrative hour or so of earning.

'That will be great' answered Richard.

The taxi driver who introduced himself as Dod, gave Richard a very thorough guided tour of the city and made the journey interesting by telling him of some of the history. Almost two hours later Richard walked into the Earls Court, the square bar in the middle of the large bar room already crowded.

Richard watched the proceedings for a few minutes while many of those in the bar glanced towards him knowing a stranger was amongst them. He made his way to the bar, gently pushing his way through, he ordered a pint of lager.

He took his drink and looked around for a lone drinker so that he could strike up a conversation. Leaning on the bar across from him was a fat man, early forties, his double chins hiding the neck of his short sleeved white shirt; a pair of gold cross pens clipped to the front pocket, a gold Rolex on his wrist. Richard watched him as he acknowledged several people who were leaving. He watched as the man ordered another drink for himself and calling for the barman by name to set up drinks for a small group who were deep in conversation to his left.

Richard made his way around the bar to stand next to him.

'Excuse me, I can't remember your name, but I know that we have met somewhere before. I just don't recall where, my name is George Thomas by the way' Richard offered his hand.

The man took it and they shook.

'No George, can't say I recognise you, maybe it was when I was pissed, you need a drink? Sandy, a pint here please' said the fat man shouting across the bar to the barman 'you new in town?'

'Yes, it wasn't in Aberdeen we met; I think maybe London. I'm sorry what's your name?' Richard asked him.

'Ian, Ian Lipp. What you doing in Aberdeen, George?' he asked.

'Looking for a job actually' replied Richard 'you know anyone looking to hire?'

'No, George, things are a bit tight at the moment, not a lot of jobs going about, but you will always find something if you look hard enough, this is a good town to find work' said Ian.

'I did have a contact but I don't know the name of his company, James Jackson mean anything to you? asked Richard.

'Oh yea, James, good guy, he runs a company over in Tullos, Cut and Pull Inc, hell he was in here at lunchtime, he never mentioned he was looking for anyone' said Ian.

'Oh, pity I missed him. Thanks a lot for your help. I hope to see you again, can I buy you a drink?' Richard offered.

'No, I need to be getting home to the dragon, thanks anyway. See you again' said Ian already making his way through the crowd.

Richard spent another hour in the bar, the taxi driver had been right, a busy place.

'Cut and Pull Inc' the telephone had been answered very quickly when he dialled the number at eight thirty the following morning.

'Good morning' he said 'is Mr Jackson, Mr James Jackson in the office please' he asked.

'Who's calling please?'

'Tony Smith' said Richard using the first name that came into his head, only trying to find out if James was in or not.

'One moment I'll connect you.'

'James Jackson' the voice sounded pleasant and warm to Richard who immediately replaced the receiver.

Picking up the phone again he called reception and ordered a taxi.

Ten minutes later the taxi dropped him off in front of Cut and Pull's office which was part of a warehouse and office complex just a mile or so closer to town from the hotel.

Richard ran through his story in his head and took the door marked reception.

'Hello, can I help you?' asked the woman behind the desk, a smartly dressed woman who Richard guessed was in her late fifties. 'I'm looking for James Jackson, is he in?'

'Yes, he is, but he is holding a safety meeting right now, he will be about thirty minutes or so, would you like a cup of tea or coffee while you wait? How do you take it?' she asked.

'Thank you very much, tea please, no sugar and a little milk.'

She left the room and Richard glanced at the papers on her desk, invoices and statements, order forms, nothing interesting. He looked at the photographs which almost covered the walls. Drilling rigs and platforms and pictures of men wearing blue coveralls with the Cut and Pull logo on the left breast pocket.

The woman came back in with two mugs of tea, gave him one, sat down behind her desk, took out her packet of cigarettes from the top drawer.

'Smoke?'

'No thanks.' Richard replied 'I gave up. My name is George Thomas by the way.'

'Pleased to meet you George, I'm Marie Coutts' she lit up and disappeared for a moment behind a cloud of smoke.

'I haven't seen you in here before, have I?' she asked.

'No, I just arrived in town yesterday. I am looking for a job. I am in the South African army now but will be leaving in a couple of months so thought I would come over to Scotland where my father was born and see if I can get some work with my explosives background. I was talking to some guys in the Earls Court last night and they told me you guys use explosives so thought Cut and Pull would be my best bet. To be honest I don't know much about the company other than what this guy told me. So, if I'm barking up the wrong tree perhaps you will tell me and point me in another direction' Richard told her, sensing that she had taken a liking to him.

'Well, I've been here since the company started so let me give you a bit of background. We have several offshore guys who are ex-military, marines, SBS and air force. They adjust to offshore life very well I think' Marie said going on to explain to Richard all there was to know about Cut and Pull. Marie loved to talk and she had taken a liking to Richard.

It was forty five minutes after Richard arrived at the Cut and

Pull office before James walked into the reception from what Richard assumed was the warehouse area. Marie was still talking to Richard who was on his second cup of tea but as soon as Richard came in, she made the introductions.

'Who told you about us George?' asked James after shaking hands.

'Sorry, I met quite a few guys last night, I don't remember all the names but he was a well-built guy about forty. Looked like he spent a fair bit of time in the bar' said Richard being as vague as possible.

'Oh, that was probably Ian, Ian Lipp, that name ring a bell?' asked James smiling.

'Yes, that sounds familiar, certainly rings a bell, seemed like a fine guy.'

'Yes, he is, knows everybody around town, been working the oil patch a long time. Now, I have to go to a meeting in an hour, so what can I do for you?' asked James leading the way to his office.

James listened and asked Richard some questions about his background and experience with explosives. Richard had been well trained by the South African army and knew and remembered the technical information that had been drummed into him during training and on operations.

'Look George, I can't make any promises but when you have firm dates for leaving the army then give me a call. I think I may be able to offer you something, but you need to make sure first that you can get residence and be legal to work in the UK. You will also need to get your offshore survival certification; we can give you details on that if we make a deal. That is the best I can do for you George, that okay?' James stood and offered his hand.

Richard took it.

'That's excellent, thanks very much, sorry to have just dropped in on you, nice people in this town, very friendly, thank you very much. You live in town?' The question so innocent, the answer especially important.

'No George, we live about thirty miles out, a place called Rothienorman, small village, very quiet, but that's how we like it' replied James.

'You married?' asked Richard

'Yes, one daughter. You?'

'No, I'm single, married to the army. I'm going to miss it' lied Richard. 'I must let you go, can I have Marie call me a taxi?'

'Sure, where are you going?'

'Just into town, a bit of shopping.'

'I'm going to Holburn Street if that's any use. I can give you a lift if you want' offered James.

'Brilliant thanks, is Holburn Street in town?'

'Yes, I'll point you towards the shops' laughed James.

The journey took less than ten minutes, they small talked.

'Thank you very much, appreciate your time and the lift' smiled Richard as he got out of James' car.

'No problem, call me, okay, George. It's been nice meeting

you.' James smiled and offered his hand through the open door. They shook hands. The lights changed to green, and James was gone. Richard smiled as he watched him drive away.

If only you knew how much I know about you, your ex-parents in law send their regards and Arthur Summerskill still hates you. He chuckled as these thoughts went through his head.

CHAPTER 14

MOLLY sat on the floor beside the mattress. She was bored. The music tapes had kept her amused and occupied and had really cheered her up over Christmas but she soon realised the music did not relieve her boredom. She exercised every day for about thirty minutes she figured. Physically she felt good, strong even, but mentally she was numb. The monotony getting to her.

The physical tie to the room was maybe the worst. She was used to being a free spirit at home able to go into the fields and pretty much where she wanted when she wanted. Here she was being controlled. She found herself looking forward to being carried to the bathroom. It relieved the boredom. She thought sometimes that it wasn't the relief from the boredom she looked forward to but his physical presence. His smell, his body warmth.

Thank goodness he now allowed her to remove the blindfold when she was alone in the room. He had agreed to this at Christmas but on condition that if she didn't have the blindfold on when he entered the room after giving her due warning, then he would have no hesitation in killing her. She believed him. He also allowed her to take off the blindfold when she bathed, that was good as she could now properly wash her hair and brush it.

The routine was okay, the scratch marks she made on the wall now numbered seventy. She knew that it probably didn't match the exact number of days she had been there but she reckoned it was close.

Bored with her diet, her shell suits, her own company and her music tapes she longed for any change in routine, but change was rare. Once he had been gone for two nights leaving her food neatly wrapped and packaged in tinfoil, a bowl of water, soap and a towel along with toilet paper and a bucket. Eating and drinking as little as possible she had avoided having to use the bucket for any more than a pee. She had been so happy when he returned.

Several times he was away overnight, and he was gone almost every day. She knew this because she could hear the engine sound of what she guessed was a diesel Land Rover. The same noise that the Land Rover belonging to Robert a farmer neighbour in Rothienorman made.

He always used the box on his throat to distort his voice, she thought it made him sound like a character in an arcade game and it no longer frightened her. Molly wondered what his real voice sounded like, she fantasised that it would sound like Mel Gibson or Patrick Swayze. Just once he had started to speak with the box switched off but only one or two words before she realised and at the same instant he realised his mistake and switched it on. She hated it as she felt the distortion put a distance between them that she knew wasn't there when they touched.

He didn't smoke, she knew that as he never smelt of cigarette smoke. He always smelt fresh and outdoorsy. Fresh air and damp earth. He didn't drink much as only a couple of times had she smelt whisky on his breath and once beer.

He had taken her picture twice, getting her to hold up a newspaper. He had worn a mask each time and had removed her bandage and he had allowed her to brush her hair. On each occasion he had told her how pretty she looked. Twice she had to speak into a microphone attached to a small tape recorder. The first time just to say the word "mother". The second time he had written a message that she had to read out and had left the machine with her so she could practise and get it right. After several attempts she eventually got it right and then wound the tape on and left a message of her own. He collected the tape recorder and was gone about half an hour when he returned in a terrible rage, threatening her and taking away her Walkman and tapes as punishment for trying to deceive him. He returned them a week or so after but warned her they would be gone for good if she tried anything like that again.

Molly cried a lot, mostly at night. It wasn't through fear, although she was frightened, she was never fearful. She cried because she missed her Mum and James and Kettles, school, and her friends. Thinking about how long it would take her to catch up on school work and how she might explain to her registration teacher why her homework had been late and where she had been for the past weeks. Had anyone told the school? What did they think? She wondered if her mother had written a letter and thought about how it would be worded. Dear Mr Smart, Molly will not be at school today as she has been kidnapped and we don't know when she will return home. Best regards, Mrs Jackson. Just thinking about that made Molly smile. Gosh she thought if no-one's told the school I will be in detention for ever, for being absent without permission, when I get back.

Mostly she wondered why she had been taken. Her parents were not rich, they didn't own expensive things, there was no reason she could think of. She asked him several times. Why? But he never answered.

'Please God this is so boring. If you can arrange for him to let me go, I promise I will never sit doing nothing again, ever. Please.' Molly said to the four walls.

Sitting on the mattress she hugged her knees and listened to her tapes.

CHAPTER 15

RICHARD spent the three weeks following his meeting with James at Cut and Pull driving around in a rented car with maps and binoculars at hand. He kept his room at the Skean Dhu, after arranging a rate reduction for a longer stay, but spent several nights away at hotels and bed and breakfasts and meticulously covered an area in the North East and the Moray Coast and as far as Inverness.

He bought a phone card and called Arthur from a phone box on Aberdeen's Union Street. He smiled to himself as he read the cheap stick-on advertisements for sexual pleasures that local entrepreneurs plastered on phone boxes everywhere. One in particular at this phone box caught his eye. Printed on a tartan background it read simply, Cabers Tossed, and of course a name and a phone number. He thought it was nice that Sandra whose card it was, had a real sense of national identity.

'Hello Arthur, it's me, how are you?'

'I'm fine. Where are you?'

'Arthur, I've found him. I've spoken to him. I know where he works. I know where he lives. How about that? I'm in Aberdeen, Scotland. Look I have done a lot of thinking and checked a lot of detail up here and I have built on our plan. I will write it down and send it to you by courier. You should have it in a couple of days. Arthur, it is going to cost a lot of money to set up, but it will work I'm sure of it. When you get it, read it, do what I ask you to do, then destroy it. If you want to back out when you've read it that's okay. I will call you in a week or so. You understand?'

'You've spoken to him!?' Arthur was stunned 'how can that be? What did he say? Why didn't you kill him?'

'Hey Arthur, I said I would kill him but I don't intend to get caught doing it.' Richard answered him sharply knowing that Arthur was shocked. 'You'll get my letter. I'll call you in a week or so we will talk then. I'm hanging up now. Goodbye Arthur.'

Richard hung up the phone removed the phone card and bypassing the winos and druggies loitering at the rank of phone boxes hailed a cab back to the hotel.

He took a miniature whisky from the mini bar, poured it and added water then sat at the small table writing and thinking for nearly four hours trying to get the detail right and explain it in a way that Arthur would understand and agree to.

He completed his writing and put it in an envelope. The next morning having slept on it and deciding that no changes were necessary he delivered it to the local TNT office and sent it on its way to Nottingham.

He spent the next three days taking his plans a stage further, taking the chance that Arthur would go for it.

Arthur was resting in his chair. The knock at the front door disturbed him. He had been feeling very sick for the past couple of days, the painkillers failing to dull the ever-worsening pain. The doctor had telephoned that morning just before breakfast and asked him why he hadn't come to the surgery, as he had promised to do several times, to discuss the Specialist test results. Arthur had told him that he wasn't feeling well and hadn't been going out. The doctor told him he would call on him after his morning surgery. When Arthur went to the door it was the doctor he expected to see and not a man in uniform with a large envelope in his hand.

'Sign here please Sir.'

'What for?' asked Arthur never having received a courier package before.

'Package for you Sir; it's from TNT.'

Arthur then recalled that Richard had said he would send a package.

'Oh yes, very good' said Arthur 'Do I need to pay?'

'No Sir, all taken care of, you just need to sign here.'

Arthur signed the proffered slip and took the package.

The Doctor arrived as Arthur was still at the door watching the courier van pull away.

'I'm feeling a good bit better now Doctor, the painkillers seem to be working but taking a bit more time. Thank you for coming.'

'Arthur, you have missed several appointments with me, and I called the specialist this morning and he tells me he has called you several times but you always make some excuse about not having time to talk to him. He has the test results, Arthur, and you really do need to talk to him. Please do not put it off any longer. If the test results confirm my first diagnosis, then any options we have for treatment need to be decided on as early as possible. You are not doing yourself any favours by delaying. Please promise me you will call him.'

'Yes, okay I will call him. Thank you for coming' said Arthur curtly, then realising the Doctor was only showing real concern for him 'sorry Doctor, you're right I will call him, thank you.'

Arthur bid the doctor good day and closed the door.

Arthur was more interested in the package he had just received than knowing his test results. He knew they would not be good news. First the package then the specialist he decided.

He settled himself into his chair at the kitchen table. His pools winners' chair. He opened the package.

Fancy paper with some foreign sounding name at the heading. Skean Dhu, what the dickens is that he thought.

The letter was handwritten, small precise writing, neat and legible. It took him several minutes to read the three pages, then he got up made himself a pot of tea and re-read the letter three times. The last page of the letter was a calculation of the expense involved, itemised with notations and a total figure at the bottom.

Arthur went through to the lounge; the curtains were closed

and the room cold and smelling slightly damp and musty. He hadn't lit the fire in here for several weeks. The four photographs on the mantlepiece were beautifully mounted into silver frames, polished and bright. The twins, the twins with Annette, Annette alone, the four of them taken days before the holiday so he knew the unborn baby was in the picture. He picked up the photograph of Annette and the twins and lovingly held it to his heart, his eyes moist, his shoulders slumped, the grief and hurt he felt today as bad as it had been every day since the accident. Caressing the picture, he spoke to Annette.

'My Darling, you will know how ill I am. I will be joining you all soon but I am going to hold on long enough to avenge you and the babies. I love you all so much, I miss you all so much.'

He put the picture back in its place on the mantlepiece, neat and in line.

He went back to the kitchen, sat at the table again and put the three pages back into the package and put it to one side. He picked up the telephone, checked the number from the card in his wallet and dialled.

'Mr Clark please' he said when it was answered, 'this is Arthur Summerskill.'

The phone played music to him for a minute or so, then,

'Mr Summerskill, Mr Clark here, thank you for calling. You know I have been needing to talk to you for several weeks. We need to make an appointment, as soon as possible, can you come to London tomorrow?'

'It's bad news isn't it?' said Arthur, knowing that it was and that the illness was going to end his life. He just needed to know how long he had.

'Yes, I'm afraid it is' said Mr Clark, not a man to avoid the truth.

'How long?' asked Arthur, his voice showing no emotion.

'That will depend on treatment and how positive an attitude you have, we need to discuss that, can you make it tomorrow?' responded Mr Clark, much preferring to discuss the options face to face.

'Do I have six months?'

'Possibly, possibly longer, we need to talk, let's say three tomorrow, my office.'

'Yes, yes, I suppose so' Arthur responded.

'Very good then, see you tomorrow' said Mr Clark, wondering how many times he had given the bad news to people.

The phone went dead. Arthur stood, the phone hanging in his fingers. He looked to heaven and in a whisper said

'Please God, let me see him dead, please give me the time.'

CHAPTER 16

RICHARD was genuinely shocked and upset when Arthur told him of his visit to the specialist and the confirmation that his cancer was inoperable and terminal.

The phone conversation was warm and there was a genuine friendship and respect between these two polar opposite men. Arthur telling Richard several times how much he trusted him and how he felt Richard was a man of honour and Richard telling Arthur that no matter what happened he would complete the contract.

Richard summed up the plan for Arthur.

'I am going to make him suffer by kidnapping his stepdaughter and the price of her release will be him taking his own life. I am not going to kill him he is going to kill himself. If he doesn't, I will kill his stepdaughter and he will die of shame, that's getting revenge Arthur.'

They spent some time going over the plan and Richard went into a little more detail on some points but deliberately kept most of it vague. He explained that if the police trail ever got to Arthur as it might it was best that Arthur did not know every detail.

Richard gave Arthur the bank account number and name for the account he had opened in Inverness and Arthur agreed to transfer the required sum into it. They agreed to communicate if they needed to via two post office boxes that Richard had set up, one in Inverurie and one in Huntly, two small towns north west of Aberdeen.

Arthur said goodbye to Richard and, as they had just agreed, he took the TNT package to the fireplace in the living room and set fire to it; watching it all burn away until there was nothing but grey ash.

Richard packed his bag at the Skean Dhu, settled his account in cash. He waited at the hotel for a representative of the car hire company to pick up the car that he had rented at Heathrow and take it off hire. He had been expecting some excess charges for mileage but there weren't any and the representative and car were gone in a few minutes.

This is the point, he thought to himself, where Richard Watt becomes George Thomas. During his three weeks in Aberdeen Richard had discovered the darker side to the city and in exchange for a reasonable sum of money he now had a beautifully forged driving licence and passport in the name of George Thomas as well as an electricity bill for a fictitious address in Huntly also in the name of George Thomas. He had already used them to set up the Inverness bank account and now with the added benefit of a George Thomas cheque book and credit card he was set to go.

He went back into the hotel reception and settled into the tartan warmth waiting on a sales rep from the local Land

Rover dealer whose business was situated just along the road from Cut and Pulls office.

'Good morning Sir, good to see you again, the Discovery is outside' the young man who Richard had met a couple of days before was dressed 'country set' in tweed jacket over check shirt and light brown needlecord trousers with brown highly polished brogue shoes.

'Morning' said Richard smiling, shaking the offered hand 'I'm ready, let's go.'

Tossing the keys to Richard the young man said

'Well, it's going to be yours for a while so you had better drive.'

'Fine' said Richard, catching the keys the young man tossed his way, he followed him out to the Discovery and put his bag into the back.

Richard drove to the dealers office, pleased with the vehicle and the pleasant power of the diesel engine.

'Right Sir, we need your driving licence and some personal details. As agreed, we will rent you the vehicle for twelve months, the price includes ten thousand miles of driving. If you exceed the miles you will pay an extra twenty pence per mile, servicing must be done here or at our branch in Elgin or Inverness. Service is included in the price as is the fully comprehensive insurance and damage collision waiver you requested. So, we need a cheque from you for two thousand pounds as a deposit and this direct debit form completed for the monthly payments. Is that all okay with you Mr Thomas?'

'Yes, that's perfect' said Richard taking out his cheque book and writing the cheque. 'I told my bank that you might call to verify the cheque was good so if you want to do that then go ahead.'

'No need for that Sir. Thank you' said country sets' boss who was dressed like a country squire.

The formalities completed, country set salesman familiarised Richard with the various knobs and levers of the vehicle. An hour after leaving the hotel Richard was driving the Discovery to London.

His first visit was to the Midland Bank in Tottenham Court Road, the branch he and Arthur had visited several weeks before; where he picked up the cheque book and cheque card in his own name and withdrew some cash.

His next visit was to Harrods' book department where he bought some books on wildlife photography and several specifically on big cats, pumas and panthers. The visit to Harrods photography department took longer than he had expected several hours longer in fact, discussing his requirements with a knowledgeable assistant before writing a cheque for almost eight thousand pounds then arranging for delivery to be made to the Hilton Hotel in three or four days, once they were satisfied his cheque was cleared. A further two thousand pounds was spent in the gentlemen's and outdoors departments where he bought clothes and equipment for all weathers to look the part for the role he was about to play. Wildlife writer and photographer.

Late that afternoon he checked into the Hilton, being greeted once again by the smart-ass receptionist.

'Welcome back Sir, staying with us again?'

'Hello there, how are you? Nice to see you again. I'll be staying three or four nights if you have a room for me?' Richard didn't need any issues.

'Certainly, Sir, no problem, you will get our special client rate, we have your details from your last visit so room three twenty. Have a pleasant stay.' The receptionist giving Richard his key remembered Richard's last visit and had told his flat mate, Malcolm, that the look in Richard's eyes had been really cold and cruel and he had been upset at the way Richard had spoken to him. He did not want a repeat performance. The job was difficult enough anyway and he tried to keep everyone happy.

Richard spent that evening and the next in the East End of London. Quietly and discreetly asking questions and handing out twenty pound notes. It was late on the second evening before he made the right contact. He dialled the number he had been give.

'Who did you say gave you my name?' asked the woman who answered.

'I didn't but it was a man in a pub who said you could supply' said Richard.

'What's your name then?' she asked.

'Doesn't matter. I don't need your name you don't need mine. All I need to know is am I talking to the right person. Am I?'

'Okay, let's talk. Meet me at Littlewoods cafeteria on Oxford Street ten thirty tomorrow morning. What do you look like?' She asked.

Richard smiled.

'I'll be reading The Telegraph and will have a photography magazine on the table in front of me. See you in the morning.' said Richard breaking the connection.

That evening he sat on the bed at the Hilton unwrapping packages that had been delivered by Harrods earlier than he had expected. The bed was cluttered with two cameras and lenses of varying length and size. It had been some years since Richard's surveillance course with the special forces had taught him about photography but as he handled the equipment it came back to him and he was pleased with himself.

He scoured the wildlife magazines for any mention of the panther-like creature that had been the subject of a special report in the local north east Scotland newspaper, The Press and Journal. He couldn't find anything but there was a story about a similar creature seen on Bodmin Moor, The Beast of Bodmin, they called it and there were many sightings reported and several photographs. He was surprised that there were no reports of the North East of Scotland animal as it was big news in and around Aberdeen. No matter he thought that animal is going to be my cover.

He was a couple of minutes late for his meeting at the cafeteria, he had forgotten to pick up the photography magazine and had to return to his room for it. The café was warm, Richard bought a coffee and sat down at a table with his back to a solid wall and a good view of the rest of the room. He opened the magazine at an advert for a Nikon camera and opened The Daily Telegraph. He sipped his coffee and read the paper. Alert to what was going on around him.

'Could I look at your magazine please?' the short fat West Indian, who was sitting at a table some ten feet away, asked.

'Sure' said Richard handing it to the man as he moved to the next table to Richard.

Richard nursed his coffee, going cold now. The magazine borrower had made no move and appeared engrossed in the magazine. No one else had approached Richard and the café was clearing, getting ready for the lunchtime rush.

Richard got up.

'I'm leaving now, have you finished with my magazine?' he asked the fat West Indian.

'Yes, brother thank you, I'm leaving myself.' He handed it back and they walked together not speaking, to the exit onto Oxford Street.

A grey-haired woman, sixtyish, with a hard face and thinning hair, brushed his shoulder as he stepped onto the street.

'You called me. Walk with me.'

'Did I?' said Richard, looking at here and keeping an eye out for the West Indian and anyone else who might be with her.

'What do you need?' she asked.

'Sniper rifle, scope, AWSM preferred and 200 rounds ammunition plus throat voice changer' he said not looking at her.

There was no hesitation 'No problem, three grand cash, take delivery tomorrow morning at nine at the Burger King just up the road. Bring cash.' She turned and was gone, disappearing into the crowd. He saw the West Indian across the street watching him. Richard gave him a mock salute then walked away himself.

Richard withdrew the cash from the Midland Bank and spent the rest of the day with his camera equipment and the tourist spots of London.

The Burger King was busy, breakfasts, coffees and orange juices being ordered and dispensed from ten cash points. He ordered a juice and a coffee and carried his tray upstairs to the seating area. The West Indian was already there eating a cheeseburger and large fries. He looked up saw Richard and indicated to him that he should take the adjoining table. Richard took it.

'What you ordered is in the bag' looking down at a grubby holdall on the floor at his feet.

Richard looked around to see if they were being watched before leaning over and pulling back the zipper on the bag. He put his hand in the bag but couldn't check it properly. He straightened up.

'I need to check it.'

'Take it to the toilet, you got three minutes' the West Indian told him while indicating to a thin faced man across the room.

Richard looked across at the thin faced man who was already standing up and moving to a table closer to the toilet door.

Richard picked up the bag and took it through to the toilet. He locked himself into a cubicle and carefully took the contents from the bag. Taking his time he assembled the rifle which he was pleased to see was in excellent condition, checked the bolt action, ensured the ammunition fitted, then disassembled it and put it back in the bag. The scope was brand new still in its original box. He took out the voice changer, which was also still in its box, there were no batteries with it so he couldn't check it, but it looked new and in good condition.

He unlocked the cubicle to see the thin faced man and the West Indian both standing at the urinal.

'You satisfied?' asked thin face.

'Yes.'

'Payment time then, three thousand five hundred' said thin face.

'No' said Richard, moving so that his back was against the wall and laying the bag on the floor at his feet. waiting for the rip off. It never came.

'Okay' said the West Indian smiling 'three grand as agreed.'

'My associate is waiting outside with the money' said Richard still cautious.

'Leave the bag and go get it' thin face snarled, nervous now as things weren't going as they had planned.

'No son, we all leave together, you take the bag, I'll hand over the money, you give me the bag. Okay?'

S'pose so' thin face said indicating to the West Indian to pick up the bag.

Richard led the way out of the toilet and down the stairs, the West Indian behind him carrying the bag and thin face right behind him. Richard pulled open the big glass swing door and waited just a split second before moving on, by which time the West Indian was no longer behind him but parallel to him with the thin faced man tight behind him. Richard half turned and had the West Indian by the throat in a vice like grip with his right hand while his left hand thrust a fat envelope into thin man's face.

'You go count it son while I talk to your friend' snarled Richard.

He was back in less than a minute.

'Okay it's all there, let him have the bag.'

Richard snatched it from the West Indian's hand, released his grip on his throat and turned and walked away listening to the coughing and wheezing behind him that he was responsible for.

A taxi got him back to the Hilton in five minutes.

The following morning, he checked out of the hotel at six, loaded the Discovery in the hotel car park and started on the long drive to Inverness. He fuelled up at Perth and set off up the A9 on the last part of the journey. He enjoyed the drive through the unspoilt landscape and was surprised to find The House of Bruar representing all things Scottish, he pulled in and enjoyed a late lunch. He arrived in Inverness early evening and made for the Kingsmills Hotel where check in formalities were completed in a few minutes and his room was large and comfortable. He telephoned an estate agent he had met and briefed a few weeks before and arranged to meet him at nine the following morning. He ate a late dinner of Cullen Skink followed by a delicious grilled salmon steak with petit pois and new potatoes. He went to bed and slept soundly.

Peter Hepburn liked renting out property, especially when his customers were writers, artists, or fishermen. As a group they all seemed desperate to find get away from it all property that they were happy to pay above market price for.

Black Burn Cottage would suit Richard very well thought Peter. In fact, it met his brief exactly. It would need a bit of tidying up, but he had owned it for twenty years and no one had lived in it for the past two, but, for a one-year rental at four hundred a month, he was prepared to spend a little on it to secure the deal.

Peter picked up Richard at nine fifteen and drove him to view the cottage. On the journey Richard told him about his plans to track and photograph the big cat that was supposedly somewhere in the North East of Scotland. Peter was sceptical about it but had seen the newspaper reports himself so did not completely poo hoo it. Richard knew as soon as he saw the cottage that it would be perfect. Sixty miles from Inverness, midway between Keith and Huntly and two miles off the main road. An unclassified road led through some forestry and then a T junction to two tracks with one track marked 'Danger Flooded Quarry' the other, unmarked, several hundred yards long, unmetalled but in good order with grass growing tall up the centre section, led to the cottage. The fields either side rough with grasses and sedges, the barbed wire fences and fence posts sagging and broken. The cottage was surrounded by a beech hedge which was so overgrown that the cottage was almost completely hidden. The granite walls and slate roof blending into the dark copse beyond. Surprisingly for a cottage so remote it had mains electric but the poles carrying the power did not follow the line of the track instead they came in from the side of the building. Richard asked why this was and Peter explained that the power supply was installed as an extension of the quarry supply when the quarry was working some twenty years previously.

The cottage was basic. Its name taken from the narrow but deep burn that ran by it on the south side and which still provided the water pumped up by an electric pump. A small kitchen, a bathroom and two other rooms one with a fireplace, the lounge, Peter called it, with a back boiler for heating the water. The internal electrics had been upgraded three years ago and a new hot water tank with electric immersion fitted. The floors were solid with carpet in the living space and linoleum in the kitchen and bathroom. The walls in the lounge were pine panelled, the pine darkened by years of smoke from the fire. The other room, the bedroom, was plain painted plaster walls with carpet on the floor. The cottage was dry with no sign of any roof leaks or damp.

'That's about it' said Peter, 'not much more I can tell you. It is very quiet here, there are no neighbours, the track ends at the door here and there is no one at the quarry. It really is very secluded.' If anyone comes down the track, they are either lost or coming to see you'.

'Its fine' said Richard 'I am going to have to put a board up at the window in the bedroom so I can make a proper dark room for developing my photographs, is that a problem?'.

'No, not at all, anything else you would like' asked Peter, feeling a little guilty about the amount he was charging for such an out of the way run down cottage.

'Well, I would like a washing machine, dryer, cooker and microwave, and a fridge and freezer, tell you what, you want four hundred a month, you put in what I need, and it doesn't have to be new, just serviceable, and I will pay you five fifty and you pay the electric bill. Does that suit, do we have a deal? It would really suit me as I don't want any bills in my name, you know how the tax man can track you down and I don't want any hassle. I will pay you in cash in advance of course. Say three months, what do you think?'

Peter did some fast mental arithmetic, reckoned he could buy all that Richard needed for a couple of hundred second hand, and the electric bill would easily be covered. He stuck out his hand.

'That's a deal, as long as its cash, that way we can both benefit from the tax man not knowing.'

'Sure, that's good' said Richard, 'we can scratch each other's back, one last thing, I like to live a quiet life and would appreciate it if you didn't advertise my living here. I don't want a lot of nutters at my door. If I am going to get this panther, I have to do it with little fuss, I'm sure you understand.'

Peter thought this was great, he was already thinking about buying the second-hand stuff for the kitchen. They drove back to Inverness and Peter's office where they both agreed that a formal contract was not necessary, and Richard paid over the sixteen fifty to cover the first three months. They agreed that Peter would have the electrical goods delivered and installed within the next five days and once that was done Richard would move in.

As agreed, five days later Peter called Richard at the Kingsmills and told him that all the goods were delivered, installed, and tested, and the key was ready to collect from his office. With key collected Richard visited the large DIY centre in Inverness and bought nails, sheeting, power drill and hand tools and arranged to rent their trailer the following day to move the stuff to the cottage. Over the following two days Richard had completely boarded up the cottage. Every window and the front door. From the outside it looked as though the cottage had been boarded up to protect it from vandals which was exactly the impression Richard wanted to create. He checked at night to see if any light was visible, and where it was, he covered in duct tape. The back door he rigged so that it looked like it was boarded up but could in fact be used.

He spent hours watching the unclassified road, checking on who used it and when. He watched the track for signs of use, he checked the track to the quarry for signs of use. There was none. At night there was no road noise, no car headlights, no one came anywhere near the lane. He walked the line of the power poles that came from the quarry and found that they followed the route of an old now overgrown track. He made this track which ran from the side of the cottage to just below the quarry his main access, not using the direct track from the junction to the cottage. Just down from the junction and on the main track he made a barrier with some large stones and some old railway sleepers he found near the quarry. Vehicles could not get through now, it looked like the track was not in use.

In the darkest hours of the night, he practised driving from the unclassified road to the cottage at high speed with no lights. He became expert.

The rifle was thoroughly checked and cleaned. He spent an afternoon at a deserted glen south of Tomintoul setting up the sights and ensuring the silencer was effective. He test fired twenty rounds. Satisfied he stripped the rifle, oiled it and wrapped it in sacking that was lightly greased. He collected up the used cartridge cases and dug a deep hole and buried them. He returned to the cottage, dug another hole and buried the rifle.

Richard was a very thorough man; he had thought through all the steps of his plan and how best he could avoid detection. He knew the best way would be to be in plain sight, this would blend him in with his surroundings, his camouflage would be his own actions.

Over the next month the checkout operators at the supermarkets in Huntly and Keith began to recognise their new customer. The, mostly part time, cashiers had little to stimulate their dreary lives and the presence twice a week of a good looking tanned man was better than a Christmas bonus. They didn't know who he was or what he did. They guessed he was single by the contents of his shopping basket. Nothing about him or his actions gave them any reason to be anything other than curious. They would have been more curious if they had known that he bought almost identical shopping at both supermarkets. Twice he had also travelled to shop a little further to the market town of Inverurie just 12 miles or so from James Jacksons. All his household rubbish was bagged and dropped off at the local council tip or in rubbish bins at laybys on the main road. Nothing was left at the cottage.

He didn't shave and grew a full dark beard, he let his hair grow and it reverted to the curls of his teenage years. He bought a pair of round glasses and wore them. He began to look every inch the stereotype naturalist. He also wanted to ensure that anyone else he had met during his time in Aberdeen including James Jackson would not instantly recognise him. They might recognise the name George Thomas, but he had changed his appearance so much that only a very observant person would put the two Georges as the same person.

He had been in residence at Black Burn cottage for six weeks when he decided the time was right. He contacted the newspaper reporter through an advert he had seen in a shop window which had read "NEWSHOUND requires STORIES of LOCAL interest". He had dialled the number and told his story or at least the story he wanted to tell. The local town papers gave the story to The Press and Journal. His picture and the headline – Wildlife Writer and Photographer Hunts North East Panther - was there for all to see. He was interviewed by Grampian Television. A one minute spot on the local news gave him everything he needed. In six weeks, he went from being a stranger to becoming a five minute celebrity and better still a well known face, no longer a stranger in the area, people now believed they knew him but he had given no more information than he had control over. He never told anyone where he lived. In the months ahead when the police were searching for strangers, he would not be a stranger.

Richard threw himself into the role of panther hunter. He

followed up reported sightings and talked to people who claimed to have seen it. As he drove around the area stopping at pubs, cafes and restaurants to eat, people recognised him and would talk about the panther in their area and tell him of people who they knew who had seen it. Starting out pretending to be an authority on the subject he quickly became one, and he realised that beyond any reasonable doubt there was indeed such a creature. In fact, his findings led him to believe there were maybe as many as twenty creatures living in family groups of four or five. He had seen tracks, examined the bones and carcasses of dead deer and sheep and was convinced. He stopped at remote farms and talked to farmers who in nearly all cases had lost sheep or lambs, finding them dead and part eaten by what they assumed to be hunting animals, the damage done to the animals quite different than that caused by dogs or foxes. He kept a meticulous journal documenting all his meetings and observations. He enjoyed using the camera and its various lenses and his skills improved. He had even been approached by a policeman in Huntly who wanted to give him details of a sighting on the main road while driving his patrol car a couple of nights previously. His efforts at capturing a panther on camera did not go unrewarded and over time he had some amazing shots.

Richard was certain that with the exception of the estate agent no one else knew where he was living. He would not turn into the lane if he saw any vehicles on the unclassified road, simply driving until all was clear when he would double back. There was no rush and no pressure on him.

His shopping trips continued. The checkout girls now

knowing who he was and what he was doing, still unaware that he duplicated his weekly shopping. Everything he bought he paid cash. Diesel, film, shopping, meals all paid for in cash.

At night in his camouflage clothing and blackened face he would move on foot and explore the surrounding area, he was fit and often travelled more than twenty miles in a night. The long daylight hours of late summer making travel easy but staying hidden more difficult. His night navigation and avoidance skills so hard earned in the military on the plains of Africa made life easier for him and were put to good use in the forests and hills of the North East of Scotland.

At least four times in the first month Richard travelled overland on foot to James Jackson's house. It was eighteen miles from the cottage but there was only one main road to cross and a few minor ones and the area was very sparsely populated. He would observe the house and any movement around it, he guessed he knew the area better than Richard did. Once he had been observing from behind a small wall close to the house. He had watched James' wife building this wall earlier in the evening, placing the stones without using any mortar to hold them together. He had noticed that most of the field walls in the area were built this way. The back door had opened, and the little Yorkshire terrier had been put out. The little dog had sensed him and came right up and nuzzled into him, not at all frightened or cautious. It licked his hand and scampered off when James' stepdaughter had called her.

It was a beautiful September day and he had decided to travel the eighteen miles to James' house to observe the house in daylight. He arrived on the hill to the north east of the house in the late afternoon and could not believe what he saw in the track leading to the house. It was crowded with people, cars, and large vans. Edging closer he saw that the large vans were marked with various logos of radio and TV stations. He had no idea what was happening. With so many people and the light still good it took him an hour to get into a position closer to the house where he could maybe find out what was going on. He waited in his new position and watched as the group of reporters and camera crews got ever larger. It was shortly after ten when James Jackson came out of the house and began talking to the assembled crowd which he now saw included some uniformed policemen. Richard could only hear a few words of what James was saying but the words, dead colleagues, courage, bereaved, told him that something serious had happened.

Richard headed back to the cottage, travelling fast over the fields and woodland. It was nearly three before he got back to the cottage, the night sky and full moon making his journey a very pleasant experience. He sat in the Discovery and turned on the radio tuning it to North East Community Radio which was one of the only stations he could pick up in the remote location. The news came on and it was almost completely taken up by a report of an explosion with deaths and many casualties at the offices of Cut and Pull in Aberdeen. One of them wasn't James Jackson he knew that much. He was shocked. What the hell was going on, had Arthur tried to get rid of James by another method using another killer. He slept fitfully, waking early and headed to ASDA in Elgin where he bought several newspapers. The explosion was front page in them all and pictures of James Jackson, now known as Mr

Lucky; featured in all of them.

Richard found a phone box, he needed to talk to Arthur. As they had agreed he had had no contact with Arthur except to pass him a PO Box number for the Post Office in Inverurie, today was an emergency.

'Arthur its Richard. How are you?'

'Just terrible Richard, very weak and in a lot of pain. I don't think I have long to go. How are you?' his voice was weak and trembling 'Have you done it yet?'

'Sorry to hear you are not well. I'm okay. Look we have a problem. I need to ask you something and I need an honest answer. Have you hired anyone else to get rid of James?'

'What? No! What are you talking about I don't know anyone else. What's going on?' asked Richard confused.

'Have you seen the papers today?' Richard asked.

'No, no interest in papers, why?'

'We have a problem, it's going to mean a delay, totally out of my control. Read the papers today. There has been an explosion in Aberdeen at the company that James works for. You might see him on the TV. I'm going to delay our plan until the fuss dies down' Richard said, trusting that Arthur had no idea about it and had not hired anyone else.

'What? Good God, what are you talking about, just get it done' Arthur said now totally confused and in pain.

'Don't worry about it' said Richard realising Arthur wasn't taking it in.

'Okay, now listen. I don't know how long I have; I'm trying

to hold on to see him dead. I was reading about the Rio Carnival in National Geographic, so I decided to go, it's in February so it will give me a target to aim for. Give me hopefully another three months. You're on your own now, you have all you asked for and you have access to my money so I am trusting you to get the job done. Don't let me down' said Arthur regaining some strength and passion in his voice.

'Arthur, you have a good time. Trust me to do the job. You hold on, you will get your wish, Good luck Arthur.'

'Thank you, God bless. It was nice meeting you. Goodbye' Arthur put the phone down the tears welling in his eyes.

The line was dead, the two men alone hundreds of miles apart. One knowing he was going to die the other knowing he was going to make someone else die and then enjoy the fruits of his labour. Or at least that was what he hoped would happen.

CHAPTER 17

STEALING the pick-up truck in Glasgow had been easy.

Richard had caught the train from Keith Station and via Aberdeen travelled onward to Glasgow. He hadn't been particular about the vehicle he intended to steal but had seen several Toyota Hilux pick-ups in the area and if there happened to be a stealable one in Glasgow that's the one he would go for.

The train from Aberdeen arrived at Glasgow Queen Street Station and a short walk to Buchanan Street Bus Station gave him easy access to the airport shuttle bus. The well-appointed restaurant buffet at the airport gave him an excellent view of the parking area situated at the front of the airport terminal building. He ate a fine lunch and watched and waited.

He chewed a piece of his steak slowly as he watched a white Toyota pick-up drive into the parking area. The driver took a ticket from the barrier machine and put it on the dashboard. He found a space and reversed neatly into it. The driver got out and picked up a holdall from the bed of the pick-up. A woman of similar age got out from the passenger side and together they walked the short distance to the terminal.

Richard did not rush his lunch. Ten minutes later he went downstairs to the check in desk area and saw the couple checking in for a flight to Atlanta. Now he was interested. He watched as they went through to passport control. He bought a paper and a coffee and went to the arrivals waiting area and stayed there until ten minutes after the scheduled departure time for the Atlanta flight. He checked the departure board and it confirmed that the flight had departed on time.

The theft was easy. Getting into the truck and hot wiring the ignition, skills learned in special forces. The parking ticket had been left on the dashboard, so he drove to the barrier, paid the few pounds that the parking time cost and drove out of the airport and headed to the cottage. He figured a four-hour easy drive. The Toyota had an almost full tank of diesel so that was a bonus, but he refuelled as he entered Aberdeen taking the Perth to Dundee route instead of the A9 Perth to Inverness. It was early evening when he arrived at the cottage, a wet evening, the rain not looking as though it was ever going to stop. He spent a very wet hour hiding the Toyota in a dense part of the woodland near the quarry. The coffee tasted good, he was getting excited, the months of planning, the playing the part of the panther hunter taking its strain on him. The delay caused by the explosion at James Jackson's was an inconvenience but the news coverage had subsided so there was no need for further delay.

In a couple of days, he would start to make James Jackson suffer.

The following morning, after his return from Glasgow he unearthed the rifle from the ground at the back of the cottage.

Cleaned it and checked it. He checked that the bedroom was ready for her, the mattress and bedding, the clothes he had already bought, the food, towels, and toilet paper, he knew the detail was important. From his military days it had been drummed into him that planning without action was futile, acting without planning was fatal.

He slept late, knowing that for the next couple of days he would be living on adrenalin and nerves.

From the hilltop overlooking the farmhouse he watched, his powerful binoculars letting him see movement in the house through the windows. He had chosen the day carefully. He knew that Molly had a day off school, the school janitor had told him it was a school in service training day. It didn't matter if Karen and James were at home, he could deal with them; it was Molly who was important, her abduction the way to make James suffer.

The rain and mist obliterated his view of the house and it was several minutes before it cleared. He saw James walking away from the house, the little dog at his heels. Molly was in the doorway watching her stepfather who turned and waved to her.

His chance had come, the opportunity not to be missed. Richard got up and sprinted to the Toyota which he had parked behind bushes hidden from the narrow road. He took off his wet jacket, put on the balaclava pulling it down so only his eyes and mouth were showing. He picked up the rifle and rested it through the open window of the passenger door. He drove slowly up the lane, watching James and the dog three hundred yards away from him up the hill from where he had been observing. As he watched, driving slowly, he saw James stop and turn. He stopped, picked up the rifle and aimed at James' feet. He squeezed the trigger and watched through the scope as James heard the CRACK! of the silenced rifle and the realisation on his face that he was being shot at. He watched as James picked up the dog and ran zig zagging to his right, away from the pick-up. He fired two more shots, aimed just in front of the running figure. He gunned the pick-up; within a few seconds he was at the house and slewed around the large gravel area so he faced the way he had come. He burst into the house the rifle in his hand, Molly was standing in the kitchen a look of amazement on her face. He grabbed her, she screamed, Karen came into the kitchen, her mouth open, ready to ask her daughter what was happening, he hit Karen, the blow catching her on the side of the head, she went down, still conscious. He dragged Molly out of the kitchen to the back door. He saw James running down the field towards the house several hundred yards away. He pushed Molly to the ground and aimed and fired the rifle again, a warning shot only to slow James' run but he thought he had hit the dog which tumbled through the air. He picked up Molly but her mother was now hanging onto her daughter's legs, he hit Karen in the head, once, twice, she let go and lay still. He bundled Molly into the passenger side of the pick-up pushing her onto the floor. He ran to the drivers' side got in and accelerated away. The track from the house took a sharp left and fifty yards later a sharp right turn and then another fifty yards to a sharp left before a hundred yards to the metalled road. He looked for James who he saw was heading for the second left bend, it was going to be close as to who got there first. He gunned the truck, slewed it around the left band and in his mirror saw James' fingers clawing at the tail gate but failing to get a grip. He left James sprawled in the dirt looking at his tail lights heading towards the metalled road. At the bottom of the track he stopped, checked the rear view mirror to see if James was still chasing him, he wasn't. He grabbed Molly by the hair, pulling her head up he put the sack over it. He secured her hands and feet with the tie wraps and pushed her back down into the footwell. He threatened her with death if she moved. She didn't. He checked the rear view again. No sign of James, so he put the gun in the holdall and put that under the seat. He removed his balaclava, tidied his hair, took a deep breath, and drove as normally as possible to the cottage.

The drive to the cottage was uneventful, Molly had squirmed and wriggled several times but mostly she lay still and silent.

Arriving at the cottage he put on his balaclava and carried her into the bedroom. He removed her clothes and dressed her in a shell suit, securing her and bandaging her eyes. He laid her on the mattress and using his voice changer told her to be quiet and still.

He left her, getting back into the pick-up he took the clothes he had removed from her and stuffed them into a plastic sack and stuffed it under the front passenger seat. The gun he stripped and put it back into the holdall and stuffed that behind the driver's seat. He turned onto the track that led to the waterfilled quarry. It was dark now, but he needed no lights. He had driven without lights on this track many times. He parked the truck with its handbrake on and got out and double checked its position in relation to the quarry edge. Satisfied he opened the driver's door, leant across and wound down the passenger side window, ensured it was out of gear, wound down the driver's side window and released the handbrake. He stepped back slamming the door. The truck did not move. It should have moved; the ground sloped towards the quarry edge. He walked to the front of the truck and with one index finger pushed. The truck rolled slowly backwards. He stepped forward and gave it a mighty shove. The truck picked up speed disappearing over the quarry edge and falling the fifty or so feet before hitting the water, tailgate first, and continuing down the underwater quarry face sinking slowly to the bottom. It lay sitting on its tailgate with headlights up some two feet below the greeny black water of the quarry.

He watched as trapped air bubbled up effervescent in the moonlight. For twenty minutes air bubbled and popped, then there was silence, the forest noises reclaiming their rightful place.

He slept fitfully that first night with her in the cottage. He went over the day's events, wondering if he had made any mistakes. Was Molly okay, he didn't want her dying. He checked on her several times. Was his cover going to be good? Would the police check on this cottage? A hundred questions, many without answers, coming into his head.

He woke early, a difficult day ahead. He went cross country to Keith and got in his Discovery just as the northbound train was leaving. He drove to Huntly and ate a late lunch at the Huntly Arms hotel pointedly telling the waitress he was just back from Glasgow. He told her it was a bloody awful place full of drunks and thieves and that he had missed the last train and had great difficulty finding a hotel.

'Aye, that's the big city for you' she had said 'aren't you the man that's hunting our panther?'

'Yes I am. Have you seen it?' he asked her expecting the usual negative reply followed by, 'but a friend of mine knows someone who has', but this time it was different.

'I feel so silly, I mean I don't believe it exists, but I think I have seen it. In fact there were three of them, my husband was with me. We were walking just down from the castle and there were three of them just playing by the side of the river. I thought they were dogs at first, you know, black labs, but as we watched them it was obvious they were cats. The shape of the heads and sleek coats, long tails, they were big, heavy looking. We watched them for maybe four or five minutes before they stopped and looked over to where we were standing. I think they saw us, and they ran off, really fast, you know like the tiger on the petrol advert. We weren't frightened but my husband said not to say anything 'cause people would think we were stupid. But yes, I've seen them.'

Richard was fascinated, this was as good a report as he had had and one first hand was rare. He went out to the Discovery for his notebook. A policeman was standing next to it making a note of the registration number. Richard didn't know what to do.

'Problem?' he asked.

'Is this your vehicle Sir?'

'It's on hire to me, yes' Richard replied asking again 'What's the problem?'

'You're not showing a tax disc Sir, on your windscreen. Do you have one for the vehicle?' asked the policeman tapping the bottom right hand corner of the windscreen.

Yes, yes, of course I do' Richard replied 'the plastic holder came unstuck the other day so I put it in the glove box for safe keeping. Here let me show you' Richard said, unlocking the passenger door and the glove box and taking out the tax disc in its holder and handing it to the policeman.

'That's fine Sir, thank you. It is an offence not to display it so please get it fixed, will you?' said the policeman more as an instruction than a question.

'I'm sorry, yes of course. I'll do it right away, thank you.'

'No bother Sir, don't want you locked up before you find our panther do we?' the policeman walked away laughing.

Richard leant against the passenger door of the discovery. His heart pounding. Sweating.

'Well,' he thought 'I've learnt two important things in the last few minutes, number one, it's the small details that catch you out, number two, I'm a panther hunter not a kidnapper.' He tapped his knuckles to his head. 'Stay alert to the little things you stupid panther hunter.'

He went to the small hardware shop just off the square and bought some tape, he then fixed his tax disc.

He walked back into the bar, notebook in hand.

'Now dear, can you give me some of the details again, firstly what's your name?'

It was about three in the afternoon when he made a phone call from the box in Huntly square. The call lasted just a few seconds.

'Arthur, I have her, good luck.'

'Good luck to you' replied Arthur, smiling, the pain leaving his body.

CHAPTER 18

A few days into his first visit to Aberdeen and after he had tracked down James Jackson and while putting his plan together Richard realised that he might need to really get James Jackson's attention. His plan to abduct Molly and use her to force James to kill himself might require real pressure being put on Jackson. The practise in the South African Special Forces if they took over a town peacefully or after battle was always to take control of the local radio and TV stations. Having control enabled them to transmit any message to the local community or to the bad guys who might be in the area. It was a fast and effective way to communicate and get attention. Thinking about this he decided to investigate if this might be a suitable way of communicating with James if the time came and it was necessary.

NECR was a small independent commercial radio station that transmitted as its name suggested to the North East of Scotland. He had listened to them several times on his car radio and they were always playing adverts for companies in the Huntly, Keith and Inverurie area; exactly where he would be operating. After an easy investigation he found that they operated from an office and studios located in the Old Town House of Kintore. The Town House was six hundred years old, built when Kintore was an important Royal Burgh and not just a small commuter town some ten miles from Aberdeen.

Wearing a new suit, pinstripe blue which he had bought from Marks and Spencer's in Aberdeen, with new black shoes, hair neatly combed, he looked every inch the successful businessman. He entered the NECR door at the Old Town House and took an inner door marked Reception. The reception was tiny, two glass windows on one side of an internal wall gave a view of two studios, through one window he could see a scruffy, middle aged thin man sweating over a couple of turn tables, a cassette deck and a CD player. A telephone and a mixing desk completed the equipment he was surrounded by with a stack of records and tapes and CDs on the shelves behind him. A large clock was on the wall and an illuminated sign that read in red ON AIR. He assumed the same scene was behind the second window, but it was in darkness.

He asked to see someone in charge of advertising. The receptionist, Mandy, her name badge read, pressed two buttons on her phone.

'Doris, there a loon here needing to know about advertising' said Mandy her local accent so strong it was almost not understandable.

Richard already knew that a loon was the local slang for a man, but he was smiling to himself as an elegant, thirty something, attractive, generous sized woman came into the office. She looked at him, smiled. She liked what she saw.

'Hello, my name is Doris Clutterbuck, I'm the Sales Director, how can I help you?' she asked, offering her hand and smiling into his eyes.

Richard looked at her, he liked what he saw, she was his type of woman. Her white blouse was straining, assisting her one size too small bra in keeping her ample bosom contained. He felt himself looking at her breasts and forced his head up and his hand out to introduce himself.

'Hello, Doris, pleased to meet you. I'm George Thomas. I was passing through Aberdeen and heard your station on the radio and thought you might be able to help. Let me explain. I am a partner in a large hotel group and we are currently looking at purchasing two hotels in the area, I'm afraid I can't give you more detail than that. If we conclude the deal, we will be doing an extensive advertising campaign for them both so I will need your rates, any creative ideas you might have and importantly what a campaign might cost us. How does that sound? Listen I'm starving could we maybe talk about this over lunch. My treat.' Richard hadn't stopped smiling.

Doris was in love. As soon as she had seen Richard she knew. God, he was handsome.

'Um, yes, let me just pop up to my office and check my diary, won't be a second.'

She bounded upstairs. She didn't check her diary, she checked her underarms for body odour, squirted perfume and almost fell down the stairs in her haste to get back to him.

'Yes, I'm free for an hour or so.' She purred, trying to sound sexy but in control.

'Oh brilliant, anywhere local you fancy? No wait, I drove through here the other day, isn't there a hotel, Thainstone House, or something like that, do they do lunch?' he asked.

'Yes, yes, I believe they do' Doris said, knowing full well that they did and that it was expensive and very nice. The last time she had eaten there was three years before when she went out to celebrate her divorce.

Lunch at Thainstone House hotel was wonderful. They talked, flirted, talked some more, got the business details out of the way. Then he had booked a room and they didn't leave it till seven that evening. He now knew everything there was to know about her, her body, her preferred sexual positions, but more importantly how the radio station ran, its security, how it made its money, the people who worked there. He couldn't have learnt anymore if he had been writing the play lists and allocating the airtime.

He drove her home; he had enjoyed her body. She wanted him to come in for coffee and more sex but he told her he had to go to Edinburgh and was already running late.

'Can I see you again in a month or so?' he asked her. Knowing that the answer would be yes, which it was.

He kissed her again, got back in the car and headed for Aberdeen.

CHAPTER 19

RICHARD played out his role every day as panther hunter, writer and photographer. He left the cottage every morning early and travelled the roads and tracks of the area talking to farmers and other locals. He was ever more convinced the panther or panthers were real. He had heard too many stories to think it was a hoax or imaginations run wild. For several weeks after he had abducted Molly, she was the talk of the area; newspapers and radio news always had some item about the ongoing search or this or that lead being investigated but now several months later it was as though it had never happened. He had noticed the same thing happen after the explosion at James' office, big news for a few weeks then not news at all. Other stories filled the airwaves and the newsprint. The only news he wanted to see was the report of James Jackson's death.

Richard wasn't concerned about Molly; she was in good health and he was feeding her well and looking after her as best he could, considering she was his prisoner. He was in fact becoming fond of her, she seemed like a nice girl, polite and sensible. From the start she had done what she was told and hadn't complained or caused him trouble. He wanted it over and was sure she did. It was time to force the matter and put maximum pressure on Jackson.

On his last visit to the NECR studios he had been the smart businessman in a pinstripe suit; this time there was no suit. Dressed in his camouflage and balaclava he waited in the shadows of a small front cottage garden across from the studios. He had a clear view of the studio door. It was a cold and wet evening and a dark night. It was midnight. He had watched as Andy Knight (Knight Time on the Radio) had entered the building to do his midnight to six graveyard disc spinning stint. Richard moved from the garden to the shadows just by the door. He waited for Ned Edge (the Voice of the North East) to leave the building; he hoped the routine that he had observed over the previous three nights was not going to change. It would only be bad luck and not bad planning if there were changes to the programme format or presenters. He heard the door locks being drawn back. The door opened, and Ned was silhouetted in the open doorway. Ned turned to close the door but before he could he was being propelled back into the building with a knife at his throat and a vice like hand gripping his cheeks and covering his mouth. The metallic whisper in his ear was threatening.

'Keep quiet or I will kill you.'

Ned was petrified, he could only think of wee Jock, his partner, who would be waiting up for him with his cocoa and quiche. He nodded his understanding. Shielded by a partition wall from the tiny studio, Richard pushed the door closed and the security locks clicked into place. He hit Ned a blow across the temple. It was a hard blow, not designed to kill but it might; it was a blow that would lay a man low for several days. Richard lowered Ned gently to the floor. He stopped. Listened. Knight Time on the Radio was into his show. He was reading requests. Richard waited until he heard music. Crazy by Willie Nelson started.

The knife was at Andy's throat before he saw the balaclava or the black leather gloves.

He sat perfectly still. The mixing desk, turntables and piles of records and CDs preventing him from moving far even if he had wanted to.

'Keep your hands in your lap, do not move until I tell you to' Richard ordered him. 'Leave your mic off, now cue up another record and play it immediately this one ends. Do you understand?'

Andy nodded. Richard watched carefully as the record was cued up. Andy sat still until Willie finished then pressed the start button on the second turntable and Kris Kristofferson started.

'Okay Mr Knight, this is what is going to happen.' Richard's explanation that followed was short but clear.

Andy was frightened, he had no intention of doing anything to antagonise this man who had crashed in on his life.

As instructed, he took a CD from the pile and readied it to be played. Next, he inserted the C60 tape Richard gave him into the tape player and cued it up ready to play. Kris finished and as instructed Andy started the CD – Mark Germino track one playing. The phone rang and went unanswered by Andy. Mark Germino track one finished and as instructed the tape play button was pressed.

The two thousand seven hundred and nineteen people listening to NECR at this time heard a strange metallic voice.

'This is a special request for James Jackson of Rothienorman. We have her, James, and no matter how hard you look you won't find her. Do you recognise my voice James, I wonder? I wonder if you would recognise me? But that is of no importance James. What is important is that we have Molly and to gain her freedom you must die. We don't want money, we don't need to negotiate. You know exactly what it takes. We don't joke, we don't make idle threats. We are serious, you must realise that. Do what you know you must do.'

Andy on instruction stopped the tape, ejected it and handed it to Richard, then pressed play on the CD, pressed repeat, and Mark Germino was playing track two and would be until someone pressed stop. That someone would not be Andy Knight who now lay unconscious next to Ned. The phone in the studio rang. Richard took his knife and cut the phone line. The phone stopped ringing.

Richard left the building. The CD on repeat, The two disc jockeys unconscious on the floor. He pulled the door shut as he left making sure the locks set and without keys no one could enter the building.

Richard was back in the cottage before the police broke down the NECR door to find two unconscious men on the floor and Mark Germino singing Back Street Mozart for maybe the thirtieth time. Billy Jean the station Managing Director was a few minutes behind them. He had arrived home at two to his phone ringing and messages on his answering machine. He had been to a Ritz Records party celebrating the new Johnny Stronach, bothie rap record, that was the hit sensation of the North East. It had been a good party and he was full of whisky and haggis and he didn't feel like answering the phone, but he did.

'What do you mean he's played the same record over and over again?' he asked.

The person on the phone wasn't making any sense.

'What message? What tape? Threats? James who?'

'Oh, did you call the police?'

'Okay I'll take care of it, thank you.'

He put the phone down then played his messages. They were all saying much the same thing. One was from Bucksburn Police.

'Bucksburn police here. Please call us back if there is any problem at the radio station. We have visited but can't gain access. The same song is being played over and over and we have reports of a strange message being broadcast. If you haven't called us by two thirty, we are going to force entry'.

He arrived at the station just as the two policemen forced open the door.

Twenty minutes later the ambulance was leaving, blue lights flashing and a crime scene had been established.

'What do you want me to do?' Billy asked the police sergeant.

'Leave everything please sir.'

'We are still broadcasting can I turn off this CD and go over to Classic Gold?'

'How do you do that?' asked the sergeant.

'I press that button to stop the CD and that switch to go to Classic Gold.'

'Okay do that.'

The three men looked around the studio.

'Apparently there was some message broadcast' said the sergeant.

'Well, we video everything that goes on in here so if there is anything, we will have it on video' Billy said, hoping that the tapes had been changed the previous evening as per instructions.

'In that case I think we will wait until the Inspector arrives' said the sergeant not wishing to mess anything up that might spoil his upcoming retirement.

It was in fact DCI Sinclair who arrived twenty minutes later. The sergeant briefed him, and they took the video tape and put it in the player. They rewound the tape then fast forwarded until there appeared to be some unusual action.

The tape showed the threatening figure in a balaclava with the knife at Andy's throat. The tape didn't pick up external sounds only that which was broadcast so they had a clear recording of the tape message meant for James Jackson.

That message was sinister enough.

CHAPTER 20

DCI Sinclair was despondent, frustrated, and disappointed. His team had been working for three months investigating Molly's abduction. His colleagues working on the explosion at James' office were, he knew, equally despondent and for them it was four months of frustration.

He called Tom who was still manning the phone at the Jackson's and asked him to come into the office for a meeting with the whole team.

They met in the major incident room at Bucksburn Police Station. A representative from the explosion investigation team also attending. In all there were thirty police officers. Most of them had been on the case since the abduction and thousands of hours of investigation had given them almost nothing.

The number 92 was written in large red chalk on the board indicating the number of days the abduction investigation had been ongoing. Next to it was a picture of Molly and below it, James and Karen. A large map showing the area south to Dundee, west to Fort William and north to Inverness was taped to the board with circles marked on it indicating the miles radius distance from Rothienorman. These were marked at 5 miles, 10 miles and every 20 miles on.

The DCI called for order and opened up the meeting by reviewing the incident and the actions that had been taken so far.

'What haven't we done, Tom?' he asked, 'there must be something we have overlooked.' He looked around the room but no one volunteered anything. He continued 'until last night and this message broadcast at the radio station we hadn't heard anything for almost fifty days. Our telephone tapping operation has been unsuccessful; the only thing we have is the faint sound of a train from the call on the forty third day. From that we convinced ourselves that the kidnapper or kidnappers is in a one-hundred-mile radius of us. We have a stolen Toyota pick-up that we can't find and can only assume has been dumped somewhere. I want us to redouble our efforts on looking at every isolated cottage, farm, outbuilding, anywhere that Molly could be hidden.' He stopped talking as there was a rumble of dissent from the gathered officers.

'I know, I know, you guys have done it, but we are going to do it again, maybe we missed something. Next, I want everyone with that radio station interviewed, and I mean everyone: cleaners, part time helpers, no excuses, everyone. Matey had information on how that station worked, the routine, who gave it to him? It's all we have got new right now. Let's do a good job on it. Next have we fully investigated James and Karen's background? Who handled that in the beginning? It would have been done after the explosion.'

Tom looked up from his note book. Looking across to the explosive incident representative for confirmation, he said

'Detective Sergeant Ewens did that Sir,' Tom received a confirming nod from across the room.

'Let's get him in here, Tom, let's make sure he handled every angle. James spends a lot of time overseas, have we checked that angle? Let's make sure it was done.'

'That is what DS Ewens was told to do Sir, he is a professional officer, I'm sure he did it' said Tom defending DS Ewens who he had known for some time and had worked with in the past.

'Let's check with him Tom, today.' ordered DCI Sinclair. He tapped his pencil against the black board 'this has been going on too long, double our efforts, double checking is the name of the game. Thank you everyone, you have all been working hard and long but we need to get this girl back to her Mother and Stepfather. Molly is innocent in all this and it is our duty to do all we can to make it happen.' He dismissed them and stood looking at the blackboard for some minutes before leaving for his own office.

Tom McLeod was in the DCI's office forty-five minutes later.

'Boss, I'm afraid we have a weak link. I've just spent fifteen minutes on the telephone with Sergeant Ewens. He is at home on sick leave now. When I was asking him about his investigation into James' background he broke down, just wept and all he could say was, I'm sorry. I called personnel they told me Sergeant Ewens is off with stress, his wife has left him and left the kids with him, he isn't coping, he is drinking and has money worries. The worst news is that it was last August when his wife left. I called him back and asked him some direct questions. The upshot is that he did not do what he was ordered to do. He can only remember that he checked convictions going back five years. Nothing else so we have no background checks. He reported that he had done everything asked of him and put in a report to that effect but in fact he hadn't done it.'

'That's a bastard Tom!' said DCI Sinclair his face red with anger. 'are we running the checks again?'

'Yes Sir, doing it now' Tom said reassuringly.

Four hours later a police constable delivered a package to DCI Sinclair. An hour after that DCI Sinclair and Tom McLeod were driving to Rothienorman.

James made them coffee and they sat in the lounge.

'Where's Karen?' asked Tom.

'She's at the Doctor, touch of flu, we thought it best she go as we don't want her to be run down, she is worrying about enough already. Expecting her back in half an hour or so. Any news about the NECR message?' James asked.

'No James, we had a big review meeting today and as a result we are doing a lot of double checking, new searches plus going over old ground. Looking at things in case we missed anything. Looking again at any connection there might be between you, the explosion, the abduction, to see if they are interconnected. There has to be something we have missed and today we did find something that concerns you.'

'Me!?' exclaimed James visibly shocked.

The DCI looked across at Tom and nodded to him.

'Why didn't you tell us about your previous marriage, the accident and the court case?' asked Tom, his voice quiet and the wording precise.

'Oh God, that can't have anything to do with this. It was all more than twenty years ago. You're not serious, it can't have any connection, it doesn't make any sense.' James was distraught, up and pacing the room, wringing his hands, his head bowed, and his shoulders slumped.

DCI Sinclair was angry.

'Make sense or not James, I wish you had told us. Maybe there is no connection but at least we would have checked it out. In fact, we did issue orders immediately following the explosion but regrettably the officer assigned the job didn't do it well enough and will face a disciplinary hearing over his incompetence, but James you had the information, surely you thought about it?'

More gently he repeated the question.

'Did you think about it James?'

James was silent for a few moments, gathering his thoughts.

'You're right, I'm sorry, I did think about it. I didn't see it was relevant. If I had I would have told you. I thought anyway that you would have checked on me and had dismissed it as irrelevant.'

'James, we have the official records here in this envelope' said Tom putting a large brown envelope down on the coffee table. 'We want you to tell us in your own words and then let us decide if there is any relevance.'

Again, James was silent for a few moments, then he dropped a real bombshell;

'Ok' he said sitting down 'but Karen had better be here as she knows nothing about that part of my life, nothing about my first wife, Jane. Nothing.' His voice trembling.

Tom couldn't help himself.

'Jesus Christ, James, you can't be serious? She has enough to be worrying about now without this' he snapped.

James looked up at Tom, a look of resignation on his face.

'You're right Tom, of course you're right but it never seemed like it was part of my life. I just put it away and don't care to think about it. Time heals and only occasionally does something trigger a memory and it comes into my mind. Frankly Tom, I am so ashamed of that part of my life, the accident, what I did, the pain and grief I caused to so many people. I like to think that now I am a different person. I have been that different person for a long time so it's going to be as painful for me telling Karen as it is for her to hear it.'

Unheard by the three men Karen had returned from the Doctor's and had heard James speaking. She stood in the open doorway.

'What's going to be painful for me?' she asked her voice fearing bad news about Molly.

Tom was calm.

'Hello Karen. We have no further news on Molly. Come and

sit down, James has something to tell us.'

Karen took off her coat and sat next to Tom on the settee, directly facing James across the coffee table. James looked at his feet, cleared his throat and fixed his eyes on his coffee cup empty on the table, too nervous to look into Karen's eyes.

'Some of the things I am about to tell you I am ashamed of. I can only ask that you consider how long ago this happened and how immature I was back then.'

He looked up into Karen's eyes and saw the worry in them.

'Karen, forgive me please for not sharing this with you, there never seemed to be the right time. You have made me so happy; I couldn't risk losing you. I tried to bury these things and I have lived with the shame.'

'James, what are you talking about!?' exclaimed Karen, her voice trembling.

Tom McLeod took her hand and held it gently, stroking his thumb along the back of her hand trying to give her comfort and support. He knew what she was about to hear.

'You should have known this years ago Karen.' James took a deep breath, getting his thoughts in order, he continued 'I was working in Skegness as a comedian, compere at a summer show. I met a girl. She was a dancer; her name was Jane. I fell in love with her. I married her. I killed her and others.'

'What?' Karen shrieked 'you what?'

Tom squeezed her hand gently.

'Go on James, take your time' he said.

James focused again on the coffee cup unable to look at the

hurt in Karen's face. He breathed deeply, the long-buried emotions coming to the surface. He felt the tears forming in his eyes.

'There was a car crash you see, I was responsible.'

For thirty minutes James told the whole story. Jane, the marriage, the accident, the deaths, the court case, the disgrace he felt he had brought on his parents whom he had sworn to secrecy shortly after he met Karen. He even told them about the blond whore who stole his money and the train ride to Great Yarmouth.

They had all listened intently, DCI Sinclair making a few notes as James spoke.

Karen sat motionless but full of emotion. She had listened and taken in what he had been saying but couldn't believe it. How could this man that she loved so much, this man who she trusted without question have kept this from her. Her heart told her it could not be true, but she had sat facing him while he told the story, so her head told her it must be.

She looked at him, sensing his torment.

'Oh James. Why now? Why haven't you told me this before? A wife, deaths, surely you loved me enough to tell me before. Didn't you trust me? I love you. You should have told me.' She stopped, feeling herself getting angry.

Tom put his arm around her.

'Karen calm down, our prime concern is Molly. We want to know if any of James' past is linked to Molly or to the explosion for that matter. Let's make Molly our priority. Okay?'

Karen nodded. DCI Sinclair looked at the few notes he had made and said.

'James, that was fine, well done, but I want you to go over it again, from the beginning, we may have to do this several times. I want you to recall the detail, every little item, I don't care whether or not you think it's important or relevant, I want to hear it all. Let me be the judge. Karen do you want to hear it again?'

Karen thought for a moment.

'Yes. I think I do, maybe the next time I hear it I can make some sense of it.'

James told the story again, and then again, each time recalling a little more detail.

'Right,' said DCI Sinclair 'this time when you tell it I'm going to interrupt and ask you questions. Karen you may want some time alone. You have had a shock I know. How about going and making us all some tea?'

'Yes, okay, God I can't believe it, Oh James you must help me understand why' she cried, her head buried in Tom's broad shoulder.

He let her cry for a few minutes and beckoned to James who stood and went to his wife, taking her from Tom and enfolding her in his arms, whispering to her, telling her how much he loved her and how sorry he was. They were in each other's arms for several minutes, the DCI and Tom trying to be patient but anxious to start the questioning. It was the DCI who ended the embrace by saying to them,

'Come on, it's Molly we must be thinking about Karen, some

tea please. James let's get back to it.'

Reluctantly Karen left the room and the three men talked for more than an hour. Karen plied them with tea and as the time passed, sandwiches. The DCI reviewed his notes, he didn't think there was anything else that James could tell them. The room was warm and the daylight fading.

'I've never seen such hate in a man's eyes' said James quietly, his voice little more than a hoarse whisper.

Tom jerked alert.

'Whose eyes James?'

'Arthur, Arthur Summerskill' said James 'the driver of the other car the man whose children I killed.'

'When did you see the hate, James?' asked DCI Sinclair.

'He was in court every day of the trial, he never took his eyes off of me, so full of hatred; good reason of course' said James the memory clear now.

'Have you seen him since?' asked Tom.

'No' replied James 'the police told me to let them know if I had any problem with him, but they also said they would have a word with him.'

Tom asked 'A word about what?'

'Oh, for his outburst in court, haven't I mentioned that?' James asked but before anyone answered, 'I will remember his look of hatred and his words for ever.'

'What words? What did he say?' asked Tom.

'You're a dead man - bastard' responded James 'but I have

never seen him again, never heard from him. I don't know where he lives or even if he and his wife are still alive. He would be about seventy now I suppose.'

'This is what we have been looking for James. Now, is there anything else?' asked DCI Sinclair, turning to Tom and addressing them both. 'Let's get on it, Tom. James, you need to spend some time with Karen, thanks for being honest with us, I appreciate that wasn't easy, better late than never, anything else?'

'No,' said James 'I'm sorry, I should have told you before. It really didn't seem to be anything that Karen or Molly should know about me, not after the time that had passed when I kept it to myself, only one other person knows the whole story and that's my friend and old boss in Great Yarmouth, Jim Seager.'

'Oh, that name's familiar' interrupted Tom, 'he's called you nearly every week, a good friend isn't he?' Tom knew who he was from listening to the regular taped phone messages between the two men.

'Yes, he really is' said James.

'We will contact him' said Tom, 'there may be something you told him that sticks in his memory, something that maybe you've forgotten.'

The two policemen got up to leave, thanking Karen for the food and drinks. Tom gave her a warm embrace.

'Don't be too hard on him Karen, he will be feeling very guilty, let's hope what we heard today puts us closer to Molly.'

'Thanks Tom. I won't, I love him for who he is, he's still the same man I fell in love with.'

'See you soon, will be in touch soonest' said Tom, following his boss through the back door.

Karen stood at the door and waved as the two men drove away. She turned, locking the door and going through to the lounge where James was staring out of the window into the dark. She moved to his side.

'Well, you are a mystery man' she said gently.

He turned and held her face in his hands, tilting her head up and looking into her eyes.

'Karen,' he said 'I never told you for what I think, or at least thought, were all the right reasons. My pain before we met is not your pain. Maybe I should have told you about Jane. No, I should have told you, but our marriage was so short and the end so tragic that I just wanted it all behind me. I hope in time you will understand but if you don't then I have to say that I don't know if I would have done it any other way. I'm so sorry if this has hurt you or God forbid has hurt Molly, I'm so sorry Karen.'

Karen listened intently, not taking her eyes from his. Feeling his hands on her face she felt his gentleness and tenderness. She knew that no matter what he had done her love for this man was complete and all forgiving.

'I think I do understand James, it will take some time to get used to it but you're still you and I love you, so we can work it out but there is a big but, if this harms Molly in any way I will never be able to forgive you, no matter how much I love you. You need to understand that.'

'I know' he replied.

They sat together taking comfort from each other. At ten they turned on the TV expecting to see the kidnapper's message, which had been broadcast on NECR, as the main story. It wasn't the main story; it wasn't even a minor story; it didn't feature at all. The media still cooperating with the police in Molly's interest.

CHAPTER 21

ARTHUR Summerskill's house was being guarded by a constable. He watched as the curtains of the terraced houses on the street twitched. The occupants seeing but unseen.

A young mother, her child in a pushchair, stopped at the gate.

'Has something happened to the old man?' she asked the constable.

'No madam, not to my knowledge. Do you know him?'

'No not really' she answered 'I live just down the road, I haven't seen him in a while. I sometimes saw him at the door taking his milk in when I took my eldest to school but not in a while. My husband is away working in Germany. I'm at number thirty one if you need anything,' she smiled at the young constable 'anything' she repeated 'I'll be in all weekend.'

'Thank you, madam, I'll bear that in mind' he blushed as she walked away.

He thought that he might have been interested if he didn't

have tickets for Manchester United on Saturday.

Two detectives were inside the house. Entry gained by breaking the glass in the back door. Their governor had said it was important to pick up Arthur and get him in for questioning. If he wasn't home, gain entry and report anything suspicious. It was a favour for an old mate now a DCI up in Scotland so best to get it right he had told them. When there had been no answer at the door, they radioed in for confirmation that they should break in. They got the go ahead plus the constable to keep inquisitive neighbours at bay. Thirty minutes after gaining entry the senior detective, a detective sergeant, called their inspector.

'We got some interesting stuff here guv, a copy of a Littlewoods cheque from a few years ago, big money, some six hundred and thirty odd thousand in Mr Summerskill's name. Pictures of children and family group but looks to me like the home of a single man. Its clean, neat and tidy but not homely if you know what I mean. Nothing suspicious though. The other thing we have is a load of travel brochures, all stamped with the name of that travel company in the High Street. You want us to go there see if they know him?' He waited for an answer 'right guv we'll call you from there.'

They left through the front door.

'Constable you stay here, make sure no one goes in.'

The travel agent owner was not in but the staff were quick to give the detectives the details.

'Yeah, we call him Mr Creepy. He won all that money and still quibbles about which class to fly and which hotel to stay in. If I won all that money it would be first class all the way for me' said the young man who introduced himself as the travel manager.

'Now, let's see, yes, here it is, booked to Rio, that's Brazil you know, left here mid-December. We booked him into the Rio Palace Hotel for five nights but we don't know if he is still there or not. He has an open ticket. Is he complaining about us or something?' asked the young man pulling the file from the cabinet.

'No, we are looking for him. Could he still be there?' asked the DS.

'No reason why not, we have always booked him on tours before, safari tours mostly, and they all had fixed return dates. This is the first time we didn't know when he was returning, but a lot of people have open return tickets, you know, people that can afford to travel.'

'Okay son, thanks, we need that file.'

'No, that's private and confidential company property' said the young man trying to be important.

The DS looked at him, shook his head and shrugged.

'Okay son, pick it up and you and it will accompany me to the station.'

'No, that won't be necessary, it's not a problem' said the young man thrusting the file into the detective's hand.

The two detectives returned to the station and put the file down in front of their DI. He picked up the phone and dialled.

'Detective Chief Inspector Sinclair please' he said, a short pause.

'Sir, this is Chris, we gained entry but he is not there, looks like your man Arthur has gone travelling, maybe in Rio de Janeiro, that's the destination on his ticket bought back in December and he has an open return. We have a hotel name but that was for five nights only, we have the travel agent's file. We also found a copy of a pools winner's cheque at the house, over six hundred thousand a couple of years ago.' He listened as DCI Sinclair responded. 'Okay we will go back to the house and give it a very thorough search, anything we come up with we will let you know.' He listened again, 'yeah, we will copy and fax the file to you, yeah, very urgent, we're on our way.

This time they searched the house methodically and thoroughly. The clippings file they found in a wardrobe, the bill from the Harley Street specialist in the kitchen drawer, along with bank statements for the past twelve months.

They went through the unopened mail that was in a pile behind the front door, two more bank statements, twenty pieces of junk mail, an electricity bill, no personal letters.

It was late when they finished, all the documents loaded into a car and sent to the station. The constable waited until the glazier had replaced the window and with the house secured, he left. At least a day off tomorrow for him and the football to watch while the detectives would still be working. Another weekend when they wouldn't be taking their wives out.

'Ok, good job, let's fax up the important bits and the rest we will courier up, they should get it all by Monday. It will be up to them to get the banks to release detailed information, good luck to them. I'll call DCI Sinclair and confirm that with him.' said the Inspector. 'Good work boys, see you tomorrow, goodnight.'

The call made, the faxes sent, the courier despatched, the inspector went home. Neither he nor his detectives would know what a vital role they had played in Molly's release.

Tom McLeod spoke with DCI Sinclair late that Friday night and agreed that Tom should visit James and Karen the following morning.

'Hello Tom, nice to see you' said Karen, 'how are you? any progress?'

'You're a remarkable woman, Karen' he said. 'How are you managing to stay so bright and upbeat?'

'You, Tom' she replied.

'Me, why me?' he asked surprised.

'Well, when you first came here you told us that it would be alright, that we would get her back, we believed you and still do, you have never stopped working for us and with us Tom. You haven't faltered or changed your opinion.' She paused, 'Or have you?' she asked.

'No, I haven't. In fact, I've come with some news that convinces me we are making headway, where's James? I'll tell you together.'

'He's upstairs I'll call him' she said excitedly. 'James, Tom's here' she shouted up the stairs 'are you coming down?'

'Yes,' he shouted back 'be there in two minutes, just getting changed.'

'Hello Tom' said James coming into the room. 'What's new?'

'Good news, Karen, James, we have located Arthur Summerskill's house. We think, well in fact we are pretty sure he is in Rio de Janiero, been there since mid-December, we have a hotel name where he was booked and he hasn't been seen at home since then, so our guess is he is still there. The lounge at his house is like a shrine to his wife and children, unfortunately his wife is also dead now, a couple of years ago strangely about the same time that he won a lot of money on the football pools, more than half a million, so if he has set anything up he can afford it. But we don't know if it is him who has organised the abduction of Molly, we need to continue our investigation but my gut feel is that it is, but don't quote me on that.' He paused as they both wanted to ask questions but he put his hand up palm out to stop them. 'Let me finish' he said. 'We will be checking his bank accounts as soon as we can get a court order or the banks agree to our requests, but their agreement is doubtful no matter the reason for the request. So that may take a little while, but we have to observe the law, that's how it is.'

'What pressure can we put on the banks Tom? asked James 'they have to know how important it is.'

'None, James, the courts will have to make the decision. We will explain all to the banks but' he shrugged. 'but that's not all were doing, Interpol is working with us, but these things take time.'

The room went quiet, James and Karen taking in the information, excited, frustrated, anxious.

'Oh, one other thing' said Tom 'it looks like Arthur is ill, physically ill, we are checking with a specialist in Harley Street, it might be Monday before we can get to him and again, he may not agree to tell us anything. Arthur's local Doctor is away on holiday but again if we find him, he may not give us any information; patient confidentiality.'

'Jesus Christ Tom, you are telling me that bureaucracy and professional standards are stopping us from getting Molly. We need to do something!' shouted James, angry now.

'Calm down James, we haven't stopped working' said Tom gently 'things take time, we live with it every day. I know it's difficult but please don't let it get to you. We need to be methodical and thorough. Okay?'

James took a deep breath. Then another.

'Yeah, I know Tom, just frustrated' said James much calmer now.

They stood quietly each of them thinking things through. James was the first to speak.

'So, Tom, am I right in thinking that you believe Arthur has paid someone to take Molly and to claim my life as ransom?' asked James looking for confirmation of his thoughts.

'Yes, it seems that way' answered Tom, not wishing to expand on it.

'So even if you find Arthur you don't necessarily find Molly. Right?' he asked.

'That's right' said Tom' we can only take it a step at a time. We can only get Molly back by looking at every detail, checking every piece of information until eventually we get a result. Sometimes of course its luck that brings the result but most times, in my experience, it's tedious and painstaking investigation and hard slog, that's how it is, that's how it works. That's why and how we are going to get Molly back and I am sure we are going to get her back safely.' Tom was as emotionally involved as Karen and James, he had lived with them for several months and had got to know them well. He liked them both as people. He had been in daily contact since moving out of the house and he considered himself to be not just a policeman on the case but a good friend to them both. He believed what he was telling them.

'There is an alternative Tom, you know that' said James his voice tense and hard.

'No! No!' shouted Karen, shoulders slumped and knees weak; she sat down.

'No James, that isn't a viable alternative. Your life does not guarantee Molly's safety or her release. How can you consider giving your life for a man you don't know' said Tom, desperate to steer the conversation away from this ultimate sacrifice.

James was calm. 'It wouldn't be for him; it would be for Molly. If I could see this man; he would tell me, I would make him tell me. If he thought I was ready to die for her he would tell me.' said James, now seriously considering the choice of his life for hers.

'Please James, take these thoughts out of your head. It would be a total waste and would achieve nothing. Karen, don't let him think this way, don't let him consider it as an option' pleaded Tom.

Karen spoke, her voice clear and strong.

'We have been talking about it, Tom. I think we both know that it would be futile but all we want is our Molly back. Nothing else is important to us. We don't care if the kidnapper is punished, we don't care if he is caught, if it means freedom for Molly, we would help him go free. That's how we differ Tom. We only have one thought you have more to think about.'

Tom had not seen Karen so focused. Her voice had a cold edge to it. He was impressed with her spirit and her single mindedness.

James put his arm around her, trying to give her some of his strength but instead felt her strength feeding him.

Tom thought this was a good time to leave. Together they walked to the back door. Tom hugged them both. They said goodbye.

James and Karen sat in the lounge. They had talked many times about James doing what the kidnapper wanted; James taking his own life. James had told Karen that he would gladly do it if it would guarantee that Molly would be released. They both knew there was no guarantee. Now with the police suspecting that Arthur Summerskill had something to do with it, here was his chance to find out about the man who had Molly. Their big worry was the lack of contact from the kidnapper. The radio broadcast had ended that. It really did seem that Molly was still alive and the conditions for her release set by the kidnapper remained the same.

James thought about the options and alternatives. They were limited. There had never been any opportunity to negotiate. The terms had been laid down at the first contact and now months later they were unchanged. He and he alone had witnessed the hatred in Arthur Summerskill's eyes all those years ago in the court room and that look was as clear today as it was then. He had filed that look away to the deep recesses of his mind on his marriage to Karen but now it was back, as clear as if it was yesterday rather than twenty odd years ago. He knew now that it was Arthur who was behind this and James knew more than anyone why he had a reason to be doing it.

James spoke.

'Karen, I have decided on what I am going to do. I am going to Rio and going to find Arthur Summerskill before the police do. I know I can. I'm going to call Jim Seager, he has been doing some consultancy work with a company in Rio, he may be able to help me. I know he won't tell anyone what I am planning and will keep it a secret. If I can find Arthur, maybe I can reason with him to let Molly go. Maybe I can help him and whoever is helping him get away with it, maybe even negotiate with the police not to take any action. Karen, I have to do something, anything, this is the first real lead we have had, I can't just sit around waiting for something to happen.' He sat still, hoping that she would not argue with him.

Karen too had been thinking, thinking and praying. More than anything she wanted Molly back. She wanted her back even more than spending her life with James. Why does life have to be so complicated, she wondered? She was so happy with James, he had brought her love and happiness; more than she would have thought possible after the awful years married to Molly's father with his drinking, awful temper and his violence. My darling, selfless man ready to give his life for a girl who is not his blood daughter. Please God don't let it happen.

She had listened to James, knowing that, whatever argument she put forward, he would do as he thought best. In fact, she realised that she wanted him to go, not to kill himself, not to sacrifice himself but to be doing something, anything, to get Molly back.

She put her arms around him, moving her body as close to him as possible.

'Oh darling, I love you so much, you know that, I'm not going to agree with you. You love Molly so much, in fact, sometimes I think you love her more than I do. I know,' she put her hand up to stop him interrupting 'I know it's a different kind of love, you love her and she loves you. You love her more than her own father does. I'm not going to argue with you, we both know it won't do any good. Just promise me you won't do anything unless you are certain, absolutely positive, that it will free Molly. Please promise me that.' She was crying now, fearful for her man.

'I promise' he whispered holding her tightly to him.

'James.'

'Yes.'

'Take me upstairs and make love to me' her voice trembled.

He pulled her gently from the settee, they undressed each other as they went up the stairs. The wanting and love so complete.

Their love making was slow and tender. It was three thirty when James got up, dressed into his jeans and jumper. Karen stirred.

'Where are you going?' she asked quietly.

'I'm going to the phone box in the village to call Jim.'

'Why, why not use the phone here?' she asked.

'Because I don't want the police to hear what I have to say to Jim' James replied.

'How would the police know?' she asked inquisitively.

'It's not just incoming calls that get monitored, it's outgoing as well; I thought you knew that.'

'Yes, I did know, I guess I just forgot it's been so long' she paused and laughed.

It was the first time in a long time that James had heard her laugh.

'What's so funny?'

'Oh, nothing really, it's just I phoned Elizabeth the other day and we got talking about the Ann Summers party she had been to. Our chat got a bit rude. I didn't think about the police listening in. I bet they found it very amusing. Oh Christ, I hope it didn't get reported to Tom, I would be so embarrassed' she said.

'Don't worry, Tom and the rest of them will have heard it all before, they won't have given it a second thought' he reassured her, not really believing what he was saying but not wanting to worry her.

'I'll be back in thirty minutes' said James picking up his change from the dressing table.

The night was black, the telephone box a haven of light in the deserted village.

He dialled Jim's number. It rang for a while and a sleepy voice answered.

'Hello.'

'Jim, wake up mate, it's James.'

'Shit, what time is it?' asked Jim rubbing the sleep from his eyes, his wife stirring beside him.

'Who is it?' she asked.

'It's James, what time is it?' he asked her.

'Almost four' said James before Jim's wife had time to answer.

'Four, sorry James I was in a real deep sleep, where are you? What's happened? Have you got Molly? Not bad news is it? asked Jim excitedly, the string of questions all coming into his head as the reason for the call.

'No Jim, we don't have Molly. Listen Jim, can you remember when we first met, I told you about my first wife Jane, the accident and Arthur and his children who were killed, well it's all raised its head.'

'What do you mean raised its head?' asked Jim, now very much awake but confused by James' answer.

'The police think that Arthur Summerskill, he was the other driver, it was his kids who were killed, financed Molly's kidnap to get to me. They think, well they are pretty sure, that he has paid someone, or a group of people, to kidnap her, basically to get revenge on me.'

'Jesus Christ!' exclaimed Jim 'after all these years he still hates you that much!'

'Appears so. Jim, listen, you once told me that if ever I needed your help just to ask for it. Well, I need it now Jim. I need it really badly. I'm really sorry Jim to have to...'

Jim interrupted him.

'You don't have to be sorry mate. I'm proud to be your friend, just tell me what you need from me, anything, don't be afraid that I might say no because I won't. What I have is yours. What do you need?'

'Jim, thank you, you always had the knack of making things easy. Okay the police are ninety-nine per cent certain that Arthur is in Brazil, I need to go there and find him. I want to leave today. Can you fix me a flight? I don't want to do it from here in case the police cotton on. Next, you mentioned to me that you are doing some consultancy work for a company in Brazil, can you give me a contact and see if they can help me find Arthur. Third, and this is the hardest thing that I've ever asked any man, Jim. If I don't come back will you please keep an eye on Karen, and God please, Molly. Will you promise me that Jim?' James' voice was pleading.

'Hey James, nothing's going to happen to you. If you are thinking about what the kidnapper wants then don't do it. It won't work things out for Molly. Let the police work this out, they know what they are doing.'

'Jim if you don't want to help me just say so, I'll understand. But know that my mind is made up. I'm going, with your help or not, I am going.' James was angry but knew that his friend had his best interests at heart.

'Hold on James, hold on' pleaded Jim 'of course I'm going to help you. I just don't want you doing anything stupid' he paused; 'you still there?'

'Yeah, I'm sorry Jim, I'm still here.'

'Okay. Good.' Jim smiled down the phone trying to send the warmth of his friendship to James 'you want to leave today; I'll get my travel agent to get you an open ticket, Aberdeen to London, waiting on you at the airport and he can reserve a seat for you on all flights from the red eye on. Can't see you making the red eye though its already four fifteen, so, you would have to be at the airport in an hour and a half. Call me from London and I'll tell you what Rio flight you are on and where to pick up the ticket. You may have to go to Amsterdam or Lisbon so you will be travelling a long time today. I'll have the travel agent book you into the Rio Sheraton, I was there just after Christmas, very nice. You will be met at the airport. So that's it. You need to hurry now if you are going to make the airport. Good luck mate. Call me from London. Keep me updated. If there is anything else, you know where to find me. Tell Karen to call anytime, but hell you know that. Good luck.'

'Jim, you may be twenty years older than when we first met but you can still think on your feet faster than any man I know. That all sounds brilliant. Thank you.'

'Hell yeah, I know' laughed Jim 'you haven't heard about the contract, have you? Listen, the company I consult for have a retired police general on the board. I had dinner with him when I was there. He did say to me that if ever I needed anything I only had to ask. Well, that's exactly what I'm going to be doing in an hour or so. We will see if it was an empty offer or not. If he meant it, he will certainly have the contacts to help you. Do you know where Arthur is?'

'That all sounds fantastic Jim. The police told me that he was booked into the Rio Palace Hotel; that was back in December so he could still be there but who knows, anywhere'.

'That's fine it gives us somewhere to start. Does Karen know you're going James?'

'Yes, she does. We discussed it and she knows I must do it. She isn't happy about it, but well, anyway, that's how it is' James replied.

'Okay. Well give her our love. She needs anything she calls, you got that?' said Jim, desperate now to do whatever he could for them.

'Yes, I'll tell her. I can't thank you enough, you know that don't you?

'It's nothing, if anything happens, I'll look after them, don't worry about that. I'll look after them as if they were my own, I promise you' said Jim, his voice and intonation leaving no doubt in James' mind that he meant it and would be true to his word.

'One other thing, if anything should happen to me for whatever reason then let Sergeant Tom McLeod know, he will decide how to handle things.'

'Right no problem I have spoken to him before'.

James didn't know what else to say. He had nothing to add and any words of thanks or gratitude would be inadequate, so he simply said.

'I'll call you later, bye.'

Before Jim could respond the telephone purred in his ear, the line dead.

James stood in the telephone box, headlights illuminating the box, silhouetting James in the blackness of the night. A vehicle slowed and stopped. The driver got out; James watched as the man went through his pockets looking for change. The man moved towards the box.

'You okay mate, you finished? He mouthed through the glass.

James opened the door.

'What! Oh sorry, yes, yes, I'm finished, sorry' said James stumbling out of the box into the darkness.

Yes, thought James, maybe I am finished. He breathed in deeply, the cold morning air filling his lungs. He looked around at the darkened buildings in the village, the bank, the pub, the garage, the shop. Places he had known for a long time, places he had visited, shopped in, chatted in had fun in. He smiled to himself and shook his head.

He ran to his car and drove it fast the two miles to the house.

He burst in.

'Come on Karen, get my bag packed, let's see if I can make the red eye.'

CHAPTER 22

KAREN was forty, they had celebrated her birthday in August. Just a month before the explosion.

She had been working as an administrative assistant in the purchasing department of BP when she first met James. Her department had organised a seminar for suppliers and she had gone along to take care of any photocopying or typing that might be required on the day.

They sat opposite each other at the lunch where a couple of hundred of Aberdeen's shakers and movers of the supply and service side of the oil industry discussed the benefits and problems of a diverse range of oil related initiatives.

She liked him immediately. He was interested in her and what she did and she was pleased he had paid attention to her, not allowing her to be excluded from the lunchtime chatter that was taking place around the table.

'Does your husband work in the oil industry' James asked.

'When we were married, he did' she had replied. 'We divorced some years ago, I think he is working in Saudi

Arabia now, he's a drilling engineer, but we never hear from him. He sometimes remembers to send our daughter a Christmas or birthday card.' She hated talking about him so stopped abruptly.

'Does your wife work?' she asked.

'No, I don't have a wife' he had replied.

Karen lay in their bed, James calling his friend Jim from the village to avoid the call being taped by the police.

What a long time ago, she thought, when we first spoke; she remembered it as if it were yesterday. He had found her at the end of the seminar and asked her if she fancied going out one evening, pictures and dinner or whatever she fancied doing. She had wanted to say 'yes please' but instead told him that she would think about it, giving him her phone number asking him to call her in a week or so. It would be a long week waiting for his call and she hoped she hadn't made a mistake by not saying yes to his invitation immediately. Sally, her friend, who had been babysitting a three-year-old Molly on the day of the seminar, had told her, if he is interested, he will call.

Karen cried then, alone in the bed, she thought of Molly, her beautiful daughter, where she might be, who had her. Karen wondered if Molly might be crying as well.

James hadn't waited a week to make that first call to her. He had called her the day after the seminar and when he asked her again if she wanted to go out. She had said yes, she would love to.

Their courtship was passionate and short. Her friends and

her parents all agreed that James was a lovely man and would make a wonderful husband and father to Molly, but six months was not long enough to really know him. Karen ignored them and knew she had found her soul mate. She had been right. The past twelve years of marriage had been wonderful. There was not one day she regretted. James was a loving father to Molly and a kind and a considerate, loving, hardworking, partner to her. Quite different from the hard drinking, chauvinist, narcissist pig who had been her first husband and Molly's father. She so wished that James was Molly's dad and that they had met and married and he had been her first and only husband.

The explosion at his office and the insecurity and guilt he had suffered since had only increased and deepened their love and thank God, she thought, they had each other now that Molly was in danger.

She wondered why she hadn't been angrier with him for hiding his first marriage and its tragic ending. No, she hadn't been angry, more hurt that he hadn't confided in her, but no, not angry. She understood the reasons behind his decision not to tell her, it was typical of him that he had told no one about it except his friend Jim. What a good friend Jim had been to them both. Jim shared and enjoyed sharing with them, his family, his home, his wealth, no finer friend in the world.

Karen looked at the clock on her dressing table, almost four fifteen, she wondered how the phone conversation was going, how much longer he would be and what he had decided with Jim. She knew in her heart what he would do, it would not be what she wanted, it would be what he decided. He would always stand by any decision he made. This time if it was wrong, he would not be able to defend it. Karen knew what she wanted, and it was the best of all worlds, one which any woman with a loving partner and child would choose. Her man and her child safe and a good future before them.

For some reason, her thoughts turned to Tom McLeod. This policeman, she thought, a good policeman, had been a real friend, a broad shouldered friend whom she and James had relied on heavily during the past months. His solid dependability and assured confidence that Molly was safe and would be home had never wavered. There had times when they had been down and despondent but Tom had always been there, reassuring, always ready to have his shoulder cried on. Oh, she thought, he is going to be very unhappy if James does decide to go to Brazil to find Arthur. She hated to think of Tom unhappy, this bear like man who had so gently caressed her hand a few days ago, who had taken her in his arms and enfolded her when the pain of Molly's ordeal was too great. Oh yes, she thought, he is going to be unhappy, disappointed too that we didn't discuss it with him. No, James had been right; Tom and the rest of the police team on the case had a dual responsibility, the release of Molly but as importantly the apprehension of the person or persons who had taken her. For her and James there was only one responsibility and that was to Molly. She hoped that Tom would understand.

Karen looked around the bedroom, the pictures, and knickknacks, the perfume bottles from around the world, gifts from James, the photographs. Everything she looked at had a memory of Molly or James or both. The rest of the house was the same, every ornament, every picture holding its own secret of them together. No matter what, she thought, I will have the most wonderful memories.

Kettles barked as James came in the back door.

'Karen, Karen,' he called bounding up the stairs the dog jumping and yapping at his feet. 'Come on Karen, get my bag packed, let's see if I can make the red eye.'

Karen was suddenly wide awake.

'You have decided then, you are going, what did Jim think?'

'Yes Karen, I have to go, you know that don't you? Jim's fine, worried of course, sends his love. He is putting some things together for me, flights, hotel and meet and greet at Rio, that will help. Come on, let's get me packed.' He gently pulled her from the bed, her body still smelling of their love making.

He held her close 'I love you Karen, please tell Molly I love her when you see her. I'll do my best for her Karen. I don't intend just to give into them, you know that but if the worst happens, and we won't mention this again, Jim will look after you both. I have his word on that, and you know Jim, he is a man of his word. You'll be fine Karen.' He kissed her then, a kiss of passion, of compassion, a kiss that had all the I'm sorrys and all the I love yous rolled into it. A kiss that makes two people one.

They threw his clothes into one soft suitcase and his suit and jacket into a suit carrier. He took his passport from the dresser drawer, checked his wallet for his credit cards and cash and dressed in jeans, shirt and sweater he was ready.

'Will you drive me to the airport?'

'Yes of course, I was going to whether you asked me or not'

she answered using her hand to pat his hair into place and then caressing his face.

'I'm ready' he said 'can we please go before I get emotional?'

She drove steadily and carefully the flashing yellow lights of the gritting lorry they passed warning them that the roads were icy.

The journey took an hour. An hour of silence. His hand resting on her thigh, feeling her warmth.

The welcome lights of the airport car park and single storey terminal building heralded their arrival.

'Don't come in Karen' he said 'it will only make it worse, go home and wait for news of Molly. I will call you when I can, when I find him, okay. Don't worry it will be alright.'

'Oh James' she cried 'please come back to me, I love you so much, please come back.'

He got out of the car, tilting his seat to pull out the two bags from the back seat. He put them on the pavement, he sat on his haunches looking at her across the passenger seat.

'I love you' he said.

Karen closed her eyes, squeezing the lids together trying to clear the mist of tears that was fogging her vision. When she opened them the door was closed; James was gone.

Karen had no idea how she drove home. She could remember nothing of the journey. The house was cold and empty.

The phone rang as she was taking off her coat. She looked at her watch, six forty five, he would just be boarding. She would have a chance to say I love you.

She picked up the phone. An electronic voice said.

'Did you hear me on the radio?'

'You fucking bastard!' she shouted into the phone before slamming it down.

CHAPTER 23

ARTHUR sat by the pool. Rows of sun loungers neat and geometrically aligned four or five deep around the pool. The South Atlantic surf pounding the hotel's private beach thirty metres away.

He looked north across the swell towards the beach at Ipanema. Arthur felt well, the sun warm on his body. The pool was busy, it was mid-morning and, in an hour, or so would be too hot for him. and he would go inside to the reception area, tranquil, and with efficient air conditioning. He felt fit, his pain bearable.

Today as he had done every day since arriving in Rio in December, he read the English newspapers, he had them delivered to his room early morning. It was old news when he got them, often two days late, at worst, four, but that was no matter. He had never been an avid reader of newspapers but now he had the time he enjoyed reading them and, for the first time, being up to date with politics and news from around the world. Every day, and today was no exception, he looked for any story that would mention Molly and her kidnap, her release, or a report of James Jackson's death.

There was no such story.

He put the papers down and sat watching the children playing in the water, fathers and mothers playing with their children, having a good time, shrieking, and laughing. Memories came to him, the holidays in Skegness, the joy of being with his beautiful children. His eyes filled with tears, he sobbed aloud. People close by looking at him, embarrassed for him and looking away so as not to intrude on him.

The matronly Brazilian lady on a sun bed just two away from Arthur's looked at him and then to her husband with a questioning look. Turning back to Arthur she spoke to him in Portuguese. Arthur did not understand and he mumbled.

'Okay, I'm okay. I'm sorry. Okay, sorry.'

Realising he was attracting attention and making a fool of himself Arthur sniffed hard, wiped the tears with the back of his hand and looked across at the woman thinking to himself: ;

'If you had any idea what I have done you wouldn't believe it.' He laughed aloud, tidied up his newspapers, put them under his arm, put on his panama hat and walked into the hotel.

'Crazy English' said the Brazilian lady to her husband.

'Yes, they all are;' he replied with conviction 'he does seem a little odd, I think I might check him out.'

'Oh, come on' said his wife 'you are supposed to be on holiday, you can't be the Chief of Detectives in Rio as well as Sao Paulo.'

'I know but I do worry about people like that, they are

simply different and people like that nearly always have secrets' he said smiling. 'I'll not do it myself though I'll talk to Emilio and let him handle it.'

Emilio Gustav took the call from his old partner Julio Garcia and went straight round to the Sheraton Hotel to see him. The met in the bar next to the reception area and Julio pointed Arthur out to Emilio. Arthur was dozing in a deep leather armchair.

Emilio went to the manager's office, showed his police identity card and obtained details of Arthur's passport and the length of his stay, his home address and his credit card details.

'That's quite a long time for a guest to stay with you isn't it? More than a couple of months now, that must be costing him a lot of money'.

'Yes, it is, it is an extended stay, most unusual, but he is an excellent guest, very polite and courteous, he pays by his credit card at the end of every week, no quibbles' said the manager not at all phased by the questioning, visits from the police being a fairly regular occurrence.

'Please check his bill, I need to know if he has made or received any phone calls' asked Emilio.

'No need to check, I know he has not made a single call to anyone except his local doctor. I don't know about incoming calls as they don't register on our system' responded the manager smugly priding himself on knowing his guests. 'As a matter of fact, I have spoken with Mr Summerskill several times, he is a sick man recovering from cancer and the doctor calls on him at least twice a week and has done since shortly after his arrival.'

Oh, I see, excellent, may I have the pass key to his room please?' asked Emilio.

'That is most irregular Senor' said the manager a worried look on his face.

'Yes, it is but it is necessary, of course if it's a problem for you then I can go through all the correct formalities, all the proper time consuming routine, all the paperwork, I hope you don't want to inconvenience me by having to do that?'

The manager put up his hand to stop Emilio.

'No, no. I want no problem. The hotel is always ready to assist the police as you know. I will give you the key but Senor, please, do not make a mess of his room and create a problem for me' pleaded the manager only too aware of the difficulties an upset senior police officer could cause him.

'No problem amigo, oh by the way we could have a look in his safety deposit box on the way, eh?' said Emilio smiling.

The safety deposit box contained Arthur's passport, a letter and a business card from a Harley Street medical specialist, fifty thousand dollars in one thousand dollar American Express Travellers Cheques and a thick roll of one hundred dollar bills.

Emilio made notes and checked the currency to see if it was counterfeit. It wasn't. He closed the box and left the manager to lock it away while he went back to Julio who was keeping an eye on the still dozing Arthur.

'I am going to check his room, number 719, call me there if he makes a move. Okay?'

'Sure, no problem' said Julio ready for another whisky while his wife was still at the pool.

719 was tidy, nothing other than the room of an old single man. On the message pad next to the phone was a telephone number and name, Doctor Carlos Santos.

Emilio returned to the bar and reported to Julio. Julio shrugged, thanked Emilio and returned to his wife poolside.

'Sorry darling for being so long, but that's done, Emilio took care of it.'

Emilio watched Arthur who was now awake and himself watching the comings and goings of the busy hotel. Emilio walked across and sat in the chair next to Arthur.

'Good morning, Senor, another lovely day' he said in Portuguese.

'I'm sorry' said Arthur 'I speak English.'

'No problem, Senor' said Emilio in his perfect English 'I was merely saying good morning, another lovely day'.

'Yes it is' said Arthur 'good morning to you, you speak excellent English are you Brazilian?'

'Yes I am. In business one must speak English, you understand. I am Emilio. Are you enjoying Rio? Are you staying here in the hotel?' asked Emilio trying to start a conversation.

'Emilio, I am Arthur. Yes I am staying here, it's very nice, I haven't seen much of the city'.

'Oh, but you must visit the sights, the Statue of Christ, Sugarloaf, the rain forest, it is beautiful. How long are you staying?'

'Well to be honest with you I have been very ill, I am convalescing, I don't have a lot of strength, I get tired.'

'Oh Senor, I am so sorry to hear this. Nothing too serious I hope.'

'Well actually I have cancer but it's responding well to the drugs.' Arthur continued to tell Emilio that he was a widower, his children's death, his wife's death, how he had wanted to see Rio before he died. They talked for some twenty minutes. Emilio felt sorry for the wealthy old man.

'That is a very sad story Arthur, you must be very lonely.'

'Yes I am' said Arthur 'but enough about me. What do you do? What do you do for a living?'

'A living, oh I see, you mean what do I work at. I am in import and export' lied Emilio.

'Oh very nice' said Arthur not really sure what work in export and import was.

'Arthur, said Emilio 'I must leave now, I have an appointment, it was nice talking to you and thank you for allowing me to practise my English.'

'No, thank you, nice to meet you' said Arthur standing to shake Emilio's proffered hand.

Emilio pushed through the glass revolving doors, no problem there he thought, just a sick lonely old man. He decided to go back to the office and plough through the paperwork that was building up on his desk. Another few hours and then my weekend, he thought.

Arthur went to his room, that was a pleasant change he thought, what a nice man, very polite.

Emilio woke early on Saturday morning his wife Maria sleeping peacefully beside him. He pottered around the apartment for a while tidying the kitchen and some magazines that were lying around. The phone rang, he grabbed it quickly so it would not disturb his wife.

'Hello' the reply brought a big smile to his face 'General, it's been a long time, how are you? how is civilian life and big business?'

The General answered Emilio's questions asking him about Maria, the job, asking about the escalation in crime in Rio and the violence.

'Yes, General it is very bad now, you must be pleased you retired, but you surely didn't track me down and call me to discuss my crime figures, what can I do for you?'

'Well Emilio, my old friend' said the General 'there is something that maybe you could help me with, it is not for me you understand but for a business friend of mine, an Englishman who my company is working with. It is a simple thing. Do you mind if I ask you to help?' asked the General; keeping to the recognised informal procedures for the pay back of previous favours.

'General, it would be an honour for me to be able to assist your associate' replied Emilio equally formally, secretly hoping that the General's request would be simple and not connected to drugs or worse. Emilio was well aware that retired police officers, especially very senior ones, often lived well above their pension and sometimes got involved in shady business dealings as a means of maintaining a good lifestyle in retirement.

'Ah good Emilio, your continued loyalty will be remembered' said the General 'as I said I think this will be very simple. My associate is looking for a man, an Englishman who is supposed to be in Brazil, he thinks in Rio, the name is Arthur Summerskill, he is an older man, quite a wealthy man.'

Emilio cut him short.

'General you won't believe this but I was talking to this man only yesterday. Why does your associate need him?'

'That is of no concern to me Emilio. Where did you speak to him?'

'At the Sheraton, General, he is staying there, Room 719. He is a sick man General; cancer.

'Ah, that is not good. I will pass the information on to my associate. Thank you, Emilio, most helpful. What good luck for us both. We can now enjoy our weekend, eh?'

'No problem General, anything you need you only have to ask, you know that. Maybe in a few years you will have room for me in the company. I will need to do something to keep me occupied.'

'We can talk later about that. Have a good weekend' the General ended the call.

'Who was that?' asked Maria from the bedroom doorway.

'General Constantino.'

'Oh Christ, he's not blackmailing you about the drugs, is he?

She asked, looking very worried.

'No, he needed some information, simple stuff, he will only blackmail me when it's not simple. Come on, we live to fight another day. Let's go enjoy ourselves.'

CHAPTER 24

JAMES watched from the shadows as Karen drove away. The tail lights of the car disappearing into the darkness of the early morning. He sighed a deep sigh. Hoisting his bags, he entered the cold terminal building, it was already bustling with hundreds of offshore oil rig workers taking fixed wing flights to Shetlands or Unst from where they would continue by helicopter to the rigs and platforms starting a two or three week, twelve hours on twelve hours off shift.

He nodded to some of the men he recognised. Turning left he went to the British Airways counter.

'Morning, you should have a ticket for me, James Jackson.'

The bright eyed corporate suited clerk checked the tickets in front of her, not finding one with his name.

'One moment Mr Jackson' she said turning to her computer terminal. She typed in his name.

'No, we don't have a ticket for you, but we do have a message, it says 'change of plan, ticket at Air UK, call me from Schiphol' that's it' she said, then added 'it's from Jim.'

'Ok,' said James, smiling his thanks and already turning towards the Air UK desk.

With ticket in hand, he checked his bags and passed through security and passport control to wait with his fellow passengers for the flight to Amsterdam.

Schiphol, his least favourite airport was antiseptic and chrome in the winter sunshine. James wondered what to do, should he call Jim now or go through passport control and reclaim his bags. Decided, he reclaimed his bags and called Jim from the rank of public phones next to the information desk.

'Jim, its James. I'm in Schiphol, what's happening?'

'You made good time to catch the early flight,' said Jim 'I've got you booked on a KLM flight to Rio it leaves at twenty-three thirty tonight. Best I could do, sorry, I know how you dislike Schiphol.'

'No problem, that's fine Jim, thanks. Do I pick up my ticket from KLM?'

'Yes mate, the desk on the departure floor' said Jim who like James knew Schiphol's layout very well 'one other thing, my General is supposed to meet you. he is a big swarthy man with a large dark moustache, a big authoritative looking man, I've given him your description so don't worry he will find you.'

'That's great Jim, thanks' said James impressed with Jim's efforts over the past couple of hours. 'Don't suppose there is any news on Arthur?' he asked.

'No, not yet, the General is looking, putting out his feelers, he is okay, he will help I'm sure of it. When I called him it was just as if I had asked him for a read of his paper, he never questioned why I needed to know' replied Jim.

'That's good, I can't thank you enough, you know that?' a lump coming to James' throat.

'No problem, that's what I'm here for, call me if you need anything, let me know what's happening if you can okay; safe journey' said Jim trying to sound strong.

'Jim, you're like a brother I never had. I love you.'

'Get out of here' said Jim wiping his eyes with his hand. 'Good luck brother, be careful.'

'Bye Jim' said James not hearing the reply as he put down the phone.

James took the airport bus to Amsterdam after putting his bags in left luggage and picking up his ticket. He wandered the Amsterdam streets, a lone tourist. He walked from the bus drop off point at Central Station down to Dam Square, he ate lunch before visiting the Rijksmuseum and looking at one of his favourite paintings, Rembrandt's The Night Watch, for maybe the last time he thought sadly.

The day went quickly. The evening did not. He arrived back at Schiphol at eight and was able to check in for his flight immediately, killing the next three hours was a real chore. He ate again, drank several coffees, he toured the shops, visited the new airport Casino where he lost twenty-five dollars in as many seconds. Still only ten he wondered if he should call Karen but decided against it as he did not want the police to know where he was. That's stupid he thought, they will have checked the airport if they wanted to find me. Reconsidering he still decided against calling her.

The flight was called and he was lucky, the seat next to him was unoccupied. He ate, again, and slept fitfully. The cabin warm and quiet, the aircraft smoothly cruising the sky heading south west.

At seven on a bright sunny morning the plane touched down in Rio. A bus took them from the plane to the airport terminal and already he felt the heat, from the cold of winter to the heat of summer in a night's flight. Very accustomed to international travel and arriving at strange airports he did what he always did, went with the flow.

The queue at the immigration desk was already long when James joined it. The snake of poles and tape directing the hundred or so people to a sign which read in English and Portuguese 'Wait behind the line until an officer signals to you'. There were five officers on duty each behind glass in a small booth. They moved the queue quickly and efficiently. Soon it was his turn. He pushed his passport, immigration form and currency held form through a small slot in the bottom of the glass panel.

'Where you stay?' asked the officer gruffly.

'I don't know' answered James 'I am being met.'

'Okay. Have a good stay' the passport was stamped and pushed back to him.

James just had time to pick it up and say thank you when he was tapped on the shoulder by a tall, lean man in a crisp, short sleeved, white shirt with four gold crowns on the epaulets.

'Mr Jackson' come with me please.

James' heart raced, surely the UK police hadn't put a stop on him already. He was shown to a small office, a square table and chair on each side the only furniture.

'Wait here please' said the man leaving and closing the door behind him.

James felt uncomfortable, unsure and insecure. The wait lasted five minutes. Five long minutes of tension for James.

The door burst open, a big man with an equally big moustache filling the door frame.

'James, amigo, I am General Constantino, my friend Jim has spoken to you about me, no? Did you have a good flight? Yes? I have good news. You would like coffee? No. Tea? Yes. Have you booked hotel? How long you stay? It is good to meet you.' The General anxious to please and practise his English.

James smiled.

'Good morning General, it is good to meet you' James offered his hand which was taken in a firm grip by the General and shaken hard. 'No, I don't need anything to drink, thank you. What good news do you have?'

'Your friend Arthur Summerskill he is in Rio, at the Sheraton Hotel Room 719' the General beamed a mouthful of gleaming white teeth.

'That's fantastic, so quick, thank you' said James smiling, the General's beaming smile infectious.

Good, very good, shall we go see him?' asked the General.

'No, no. It's a surprise, you haven't told him I'm coming have you?' asked James aghast.

'No, tell me James why do you want to surprise him? This man owes you money, no?' asked the General 'I have friends, we can make him pay. Yes. You know' the General taped his nose conspiratorially.

'No General, I just need to talk to him, family business.'

'Okay, I understand amigo, anything you need you call me, eh?' he handed James a business card.

'Thank you General that's very kind. Now about a hotel, the Sheraton would be as good as anywhere, how do I get there?'

'With me amigo. I will take you. Yes. It is no problem, my pleasure. It's on my way to my home anyway.'

The General, followed by James who now felt like a page boy to the king, strode from the office to the baggage reclaim area where James' bag and suit carrier were being guarded by a young man in uniform. On seeing the General, the young man picked up the bag and carrier and followed behind James as the General returned salutes from the customs officers; and with no further checks James and his bags were in the General's large American car on route to the Sheraton.

The General gave James a running commentary on the sights as they passed them.

'There, you see there' he said pointing ahead 'see the cable car going up to Sugarloaf Mountain, beautiful, eh? Oh, and see there the beach Copacabana eh, beautiful.'

James looked around him, it was not yet nine and the broad esplanade in front of the beach was crowded with people walking, walking with a purpose, exercising, a busy place he thought. The car passed through a residential area and then the General was off again.

'See the beach, Ipanema, beautiful, eh? You know, where the girl came from?' he laughed 'lovely eh? There you see the white building on the point, that is the Sheraton' the General pointing to it.

James found himself whistling, the words in his head.

'Young and lovely, warm and tender the girl from Ipanema goes walking.'

'You know it. Yes, the girl from Ipanema, beautiful.' The General laughed again. Ignoring a no entry sign he drove into the hotel car park and parked directly in front of the "No Parking" signs at the main door. The bell hops came running out, saluting the General and shaking his hand.

'How many nights will you stay sir?' asked the receptionist.

'I am not sure' said James 'let's say seven'

The manager now joined the receptionist and greeted the General and James.

'Seven nights Sir, certainly. As a friend of the General you get our incredibly special rate and special room. Anything you need just call reception if they can't help, you ask for me' the receptionist looked at the General who smiled and nodded.

'Thank you' said James 'What room number?'

'812 Sir.'

'Okay, thanks.' James picked up the key card and turning to the General 'Would you like some breakfast with me General, it's the least I can do?'

'Thank you. but no. I will go to my home. Call me if you need me, you have my card, anything' the General again smiled and tapped his nose with his forefinger.

'Thank you General. Thank you very much.'

CHAPTER 25

MOLLY couldn't believe her ears.

'What did you say?' she asked.

The electronic voice replied.

'I said, take off your blindfold.'

Molly didn't do anything. The voice said again.

'Take off your blindfold.'

It's a trick, isn't it?' she said. 'You are trying to trick me into seeing you, so you can kill me.'

'No Molly, I'm not. I thought you might like to go for a walk. It's a lovely evening, it's been snowing for a couple of days but today the sun was shining, the sky is clear and starlit and a lovely bright full moon. Come on some fresh air will be nice for you.'

Still Molly didn't move. She was thinking, her brain almost overpowered. Tempted to tell him to go to hell. She didn't need any favours from him. He had kept her locked up for long enough. Eighty seven marks on her wall. Why did she need to go out now? Because he had decided, he decides everything She would tell him no.

'I'll go out when I am released and not before. I don't know why you are holding me, I don't know anything. I eat when you say, I sleep when you say, I pee when you say, I hate you, leave me alone.' She was angry and her voice showed it.

He was calm, the electronic voice even sounding gentle.

'Come on Molly, it will be nice. The fresh air will be nice. You will enjoy it. Please take off your blindfold, I am not going to force you to, it's up to you but I think you will enjoy going out so please take it off.'

Molly, didn't move, wanting him to know that any decision was going to be hers and not his. Slowly she removed the tape and the bandage, she turned her head to where she thought he was standing, seeing only his eyes through the holes in the camouflage balaclava he wore.

She put her hands out to him and he gently pulled her to her feet.

He bent and cut the tie wraps from her feet. Pointing to a pile of clothes by the mattress he said 'get dressed, there are warm clothes.'

Molly dressed herself in a pair of thick trousers that were too big for her but had a tie waist band, a thick jumper, a thick padded coat, a pair of woollen socks and a pair of cheap green wellingtons.

She looked at him, hating the control he had over her but now she had made her mind up to take off the blindfold she was determined to enjoy the going out.

Smiling, she did a twirl,

'How do I look?'

'You look like you will be warm' the voice replied, then 'okay Molly, I am going to tie this rope around your ankle, I don't want you thinking you can run away, you can't; you know the rules. Is that clear?'

He tied a thin rope around her ankle over the top of the wellington, the rope was about fifteen feet long and the other end was in his hand.

'First you hold me in this place,' she said her arm indicating the room and now you tie me up like a dog on a leash. Leave me here, I don't want to go anywhere with you, I hate you, leave me, go and enjoy the snow on your own, I'm not interested.'

'Come on, too late to change your mind, we're going.' He pulled the rope, it pulled her leg and she thought about just sitting down and refusing to move but really, she wanted out of this prison even for a moment so she moved towards him.

'Okay' she said resignedly.

'Okay let's go. Listen if you try to run off, I will stop you, if we see anyone and you cry out, I will kill you. I am trusting you to be a good girl. Be sensible.'

Molly made no reply and followed him through the door.

He had told her the truth. It had been snowing and it was a beautiful night. Very cold with the ice crystals sparkling and the sky a solid black but full of twinkling stars and the biggest brightest moon she had ever seen. Before she had taken a step out of the door, he had picked her up and carried her for a hundred yards so as to leave just one trail of footprints. On the track that he had been driving, along the line of the power poles the snow was just a few inches deep, the trees lining it stopping the snow from accumulating. It was easy walking, but her legs quickly became tired through lack of activity during her confinement. The snow was deep and pristine in the clearings between the trees nearer to the quarry and the walking was very tiring and difficult and she quickly became fatigued.

'I need to rest,' she said to him 'my legs are very tired, I don't want to go back, just to rest a bit, it is lovely.'

He looked at her and gave a thumbs up indicating a fallen tree some thirty yards ahead. They sat together, she rested against him, catching her breath, and resting her legs. He was alert, listening and looking for anything unusual. He pointed out the lip of the quarry to her.

'The pick-up is in the quarry, under the water.'

She made no comment. She sensed him become very alert, his body tensed. He put his hand up to his lips, she knew he wanted her to be quiet. He pointed to a spot about thirty yards away, a gap between two large trees; her eyes, accustomed to the dark, saw the two deer grazing on some grass in a snow free patch. What graceful creatures they are Molly thought. Richard whispered to her his voice box no longer on, only the second time she had heard his voice, the first being the day he had taken her.

'Two young hinds; pretty, aren't they?'

Molly nodded. Not wishing to disturb them, she sat as still as she could and watched them grazing. They seemed totally unaware of Molly and the kidnapper. Every twenty seconds or so they would raise their heads to sniff the air, but they went back to eating after a few seconds, calm and confident. They watched the deer for several minutes enjoying the scene then he squeezed her arm and whispered excitedly,

'Look beyond them just below the tree on the right, do you see two yellow eyes?'

Molly strained to see but it was a few seconds before she thought she saw the eyes and she whispered back.

'I think so. What is it?'

'Not sure, fox maybe, stay still.'

They sat as still as possible, her nose started to run from the cold but she didn't wipe it, frightened to move and scare the deer.

The yellow eyes were still watching, unmoving and as far as she could tell unblinking. Then in an instant the yellow eyes moved, followed by a dark body that was moving at high speed, towards the deer who, equally as fast, were gone. The dark body stopped not twenty feet from Molly and the kidnapper. A long black tail swished and twitched. The animal sat on its haunches and yawned; she could see the hot air from its breath in the cold air of the night. Then it sensed them and turned and was gone. The forest, startled for a moment by the deer running, returned to silence.

'What was that?' she whispered excitedly.

'What did you see?' he asked.

'I don't know' she replied, 'no idea.'

'No, really, what did you see, describe it to me' he whispered, she sensed he was very serious.

'Okay, it was black, its coat was shiny, I think. It had small ears, a long tail and long legs. It was like a black Labrador but it wasn't one, it wasn't a dog, a big cat I think but I've never seen anything like it. Scary. What did you see?'

The electronic voice was back now

'Same as you. It was amazing, have you ever seen a picture of a panther? Could it have been one?'

'Yes, yes, very much like a great big black cat, but it wasn't like a house cat, a pet cat, it was much bigger.'

'Wow, close to my cottage, amazing' the electronic voice said. 'Let's go you're getting cold'

They walked first to the spot where the animal had sat down, the snow compacted and disturbed but no real sign that anything had been there. The walk back to the cottage passed in silence but as they neared the cottage, she asked him,

'When will I be freed?'

'Soon, let's get back.'

He carried her the last hundred yards and got her settled back in her makeshift prison, taking away the outdoor clothing and securing the tie wrap on her ankles. She put on the bandage and tape over her eyes.

'Thank you' she said 'thank you for taking me out, it was lovely and exciting. Can we go again?'

'Maybe Molly, maybe. I'm sorry about this I'm just doing a

job.' Molly sensed he was smiling.

'Goodnight, sleep well' the electronic voice said.

'Mmm' Molly removed her blindfold when he left the room and was asleep in minutes.

CHAPTER 26

ARTHUR lay in the hotel bed. His body was wracked with pain. Yesterday he had felt so well, the pain totally under control as it had been for some weeks. He had woken this morning with a pain worse than he had known. He felt awful, weak and his body shaking. He rang the Doctor.

'Canziana' he said to the Doctor's assistant who was also acting as his interpreter 'please bring the Doctor to see me urgently, the pain is terrible, so much pain this morning' he paused, listening. 'Yes, yes, I have taken the tablets but there is no release from the pain. It is worse than ever before.'

'Yes, Mr Arthur' Canziana replied 'let me explain that to the Doctor' her English as ever, perfect.

Arthur waited, holding the phone to his ear and rubbing his stomach with the other hand in an effort to get some relief from the pain, Canziana came back to the phone.

'We will be there in an hour, the Doctor says to take two more of the painkiller pills, the pink ones.'

'Ok thank you. Please be quick.'

He took the tablets and waited for the pain dulling effect but this time there was none. He lay in the bed soaked in his own sweat.

The Doctor and Canziana arrived forty minutes later, let into the room by the hotel manager. The Doctor fully examined Arthur, tutting and clucking, sighing, and grunting while he did so. There was much head shaking and sucking of lower lip.

With Canziana translating the Doctor gave Arthur the news that he had been putting off for some time but could put off no longer.

'Well, my friend, I'm afraid the end is close. The cancer is very advanced now and very aggressive, your kidneys and liver are both diseased as we know and now, I believe your stomach is also affected. These organs are finding it exceedingly difficult to continue to do their job for your body. They are shutting down. I can only provide stronger painkillers for you, stronger drugs. As I have told you before, if we can admit you into hospital, we can make the end much easier for you. Here at the hotel it will be difficult but I will do my best. That's it I'm afraid I cannot put a sweet coating on it, it is very serious and somewhere you have found some inner strength and I hope that you continue to find it. Please consider the hospital, it is my recommendation. I am deeply sorry.'

Canziana began to cry. Arthur finding the strength from somewhere pulled himself up in the bed.

'No Doctor, no hospital, I want to die here, not in hospital. Please help me.'

Canziana through her tears continued to translate.

'Arthur, I cannot do much to help you, stronger pain medicine, you have maybe one week, possibly two, not much longer. I can have a nurse stay with you; I will talk to the hotel to see if we can get the adjoining room. But it will be expensive. Do you have enough money?'

'Yes, plenty of money, I can afford to pay. Haven't I always paid your bills on time. Tell him, Canziana, you know I have paid him'.

The Doctor smiled and acknowledged that Arthur always paid on time.

Arthur continued.

'Look Doctor, I have some unfinished business I want to be around for as long as you can keep me going. I am not afraid to die, you understand. It's just that I want my business completed. Then I can die happy.'

The Doctor listened as Canziana translated, her voice breaking as she continued to cry.

'Arthur what possible business can you have that is so important?'

'Old unfinished family business Doctor, old unfinished family business.'

Arthur's head slumped forward, his eyes closed as the sedative and pain killers took effect.

The Doctor and Canziana made him comfortable and left him sleeping while they organised his future care.

CHAPTER 27

JAMES made himself comfortable in room 812, a sea view room on the eighth floor of the hotel. The room was spacious with a king size bed, large TV, a small fridge, and ample storage which he used to hang up his clothes. The bathroom had both a walk-in shower and a large bath. There was a sliding glass door to a sizeable balcony with a white plastic table and four matching chairs. The balcony looked out over the swimming pool and the sea beyond. James left the room to explore the layout of the hotel. The hotel was built on a steeply sloping site. The west side entrance to reception was the high side and the pool area was three floors lower on east side. The floor indicator buttons in the lift were confusing at first with the fourth floor marked as reception and the first floor, swimming pool/ beach, he figured he would get used to it. There were several places to eat including a tenth floor gastronomic panoramic, at least that's how it was advertised, and a first-floor pool side bar and snack bar, the main hotel restaurant and bar being on the fourth floor. He returned to his room, called reception, and asked for the room number of Arthur Summerskill, they gave it to him without question, 719 dial 2 first for room to room. He wrote it down, 2719.

He dialled 2719.

In 719 Canziana and the Doctor were telling Arthur about the arrangements they had made regarding the nurse who would commence her duties in a couple of days. Arthur was feeling a lot more comfortable, though still very weak and still in bed. The phone rang Canziana answered it.

James was shocked to hear a woman's voice, for some reason he had expected to hear a man's voice answer the phone in English.

'Is this the room of Arthur Summerskill?' he asked.

'Yes, who is calling please?' Canziana asked.

'It's a friend.' James put the phone down, talking to a woman was not what he had expected.

In 719 Arthur was looking quizzically at Canziana.

'Who was that?' he asked.

'You have a friend asking if this is your room' she said.

'No one but you know I am here' said Arthur 'can't understand that; apart from you two, the only people I speak to are the hotel staff or a man yesterday in the lobby, a nice man, maybe it was him.' Arthur shrugged, too tired to care.

James had made his way to the floor below his and found room 719, it was almost directly below his own room on the same side of the hotel. There was a fire exit stairway a short distance away from the door to the room and he waited there, thinking about what to do next. He saw the door open and two people come out, a man and a younger woman. They went to the lift, waited for it, entered, and left. James waited. He heard the rattle of glasses and saw a room service waiter pushing a trolley coming down the hallway towards him. James walked towards door 719 tapping his pockets as if looking for his key card. James stopped, the room service guy stopped, James made gestures indicating his key was in the room and at the same time asking the waiter in English if he had his pass key. The waiter understood, took his key card, and slid it into the opening in the door lock. The green light came on.

'Thank you' said James smiling as he gently opened the door a fraction.

The waiter smiled and walked on pushing his trolley. James quietly opened the door and eased himself into the room, assuming that the room would be the same design as his. It was. A short corridor leading to the bed area with a bathroom door on the right and built-in wardrobes to the left. He stopped, listened. He could hear soft snoring. He composed himself and took two paces that put him into the bedroom, at the bottom right-hand corner of the bed. He watched Arthur laying on the bed, just a white sheet covering him from his lower chest down. Arthur's eyes were closed, sleeping. James recognised him, all those years had not changed Arthur's features, less hair but still the face of hate from all those years ago.

James thought about Molly and became angry.

'Good morning Arthur Summerskill' he said harshly.

Arthur's eyes opened, blinking he looked around trying to focus on the voice or the face of the speaker.

'Who are you, what are you doing in my room?' he asked, his voice shaking, a little frightened and unsure.

'Don't you know me?' asked James 'Have I changed that much? Maybe it's the beard and the grey hair.'

Arthur looked, staring hard at James' face and a look of recognition came to his face

'It can't be.' stuttered Arthur. 'Is it, is it you James Jackson?'

'The very same.'

'What are you doing here? Arthur asked.

'A few questions for you first, Arthur. Question one. Do you know who is holding Molly?'

'Yes' said Arthur, smiling now.

'Question two. Do you trust him?'

'That's a funny question' said Arthur looking puzzled.

'Funny! Funny! None of this is funny! Answer me. Do you trust him?'

'Yes' answered Arthur.

'Question three. Do you know what is required for Molly to be released?'

'Yes I do.' Arthur smiled cruelly now. 'You have to die' he said pointing at James.

'How could you be so evil, she has done nothing to you, if you wanted me so badly you could have just come after me, what you have done is hurt other people, I ask again how could you be so evil?'

Arthur pulled himself into a sitting position in the bed, he stared at James and then with all the bitterness and hatred stored over the years, his face sneering and twisted he venomously whispered,

'Because I hate you, I hate you with all my heart, with all my being. I have hated you for years, you destroyed my family, my happiness. You deserve to die so I had to be sure you would die but more than that I wanted you to know what it feels like to suffer, to lose someone you love, I wanted you to suffer like I have suffered, I hate you with all my being. If you don't die, then, she dies, then you will slowly die with shame and remorse. Your life will not be worth living. That's not a choice I think you will make. Crawl away and die and we will release her.'

James was calm, his mind clear, the actions he would take playing in slow motion in his mind.

'I ask you once again. Do you trust the man who is holding her, if I die will he release her? asked James

Arthur, still sat up in the bed, nodded. 'Yes. He will release her'.

James walked across to the sliding doors leading to the balcony. He opened them wide. The wind blowing off the sea gentle and warm.

Turning back into the room he took a letter and placed it on the coffee table and put a glass on it to keep it in place. The letter began: 'I James Jackson being of sound mind and body.........'

'It's time to go Arthur' he said.

'Go where?' asked Arthur confused.

'We are going over the balcony, we are going to die together, you can live the last few seconds of your life in terror' said James calmly and clearly.

He walked to the bed and easily picked Arthur up. He was too weak and sedated to struggle much, he did struggle, but to no avail. He barely managed a shocked shout as James ran, with Arthur in his arms, towards and over the balcony railing and together the two bodies fell, crashing through the thatched roof of the poolside bar before hitting the tiled floor seven floors below. Their screams as they fell filling the natural amphitheatre of the swimming pool and its surrounds. James and Arthur's screams cut off as they hit the floor only to be taken up shocked moments later by the adults and children at the pool. People were running in all directions unsure of what had happened; others were looking up wondering if anything else would be falling down. The screaming was followed by a shocked silence with mothers gathering up children to get them away, while the curious gathered around the two intertwined bodies whose blood and bodily fluids were slowly seeping across the floor of the poolside bar. Several were sick, others more used to accidents and incidents took control and held people back, calling for help and seeing if there was anything, they could do to help the two men lying on the floor. There was nothing. The damage to the bodies was obvious and severe.

Within an hour the bodies were gone, the police had taken reports and were searching rooms 719 and 812. The hotel management had provided information. The hotel maintenance team had repaired the thatch, power washed the tiles, replaced a few broken chairs and a table. The bar staff were taking orders, holidays continued; children played.

At the police station a full investigation was in progress. Emilio Gustav had been shocked to see Arthur's and James' name on a police report relating to deaths at the Sheraton Hotel and immediately called Julio and then Emilio called General Constantino. They were all involved and now the British Consul was on the telephone demanding to know what had happened. In addition, they had also had a request from the British police wanting to know the whereabouts of Arthur Summerskill. The Interior Minister became involved, as the reputation of Rio de Janiero as a safe vacation destination could be damaged. The only thing linking the two dead men together in Brazil was the note that James Jackson had left in Arthur Summerskill's room. While it was a note that contained an accusation, there was no threat of retribution in the note. The Interior Minister had the final say. He advised the police to destroy the note, advise the British Embassy that there had been a tragic accident that had left two British nationals dead at the Sheraton Hotel, no foul play was suspected and cause of death would be recorded as accidental. The Rio police were instructed to advise their counterparts in the UK.

The following morning The Rio Times, the main newspaper in Rio de Janiero, carried a report on its third page about the accidental death of two British tourists in a poolside incident.

Jim Seager had been contacted by General Constantino and was the first in the UK to learn of the death of his friend and of Arthur. He had called Tom McLeod. Tom told Jim that before they told Karen they should wait for official confirmation from the UK Embassy in Brazil. The twenty-four hour wait on the confirmation was tough on both of them. The British Consulate General in Rio received the official notification of the deaths of James Jackson and Arthur Summerskill within twenty-four hours of the deaths occurring. The Consulate General notified the Ambassador in Brasilia and from there the Foreign Office in London was advised. Within a couple of hours DCI Sinclair had been notified. He contacted Tom McLeod and together they went to Rothienorman to deliver the awful news to Karen both knowing they had been aware of the deaths for more than twenty-four hours.

With sirens blaring the ambulance took Karen from the farmhouse to the hospital in Aberdeen, the strain of the past months and now the death of her husband proving all too much for her. The intensive care unit, trained to manage all kinds of accidents and emergencies, sprang into action. The staff visibly moved when they heard the cause of Karen's physical and mental breakdown.

DCI Sinclair and Sergeant McLeod were distressed. These intelligent, compassionate, yet tough policemen had never been involved in such a demoralising case. A man forced to kill himself to save another human life, it was a plan from an evil mind. The accidental death story coming out of Brazil just too clearly a cover up for political reasons. They knew it wasn't the truth but there was little they could do about it.

DCI Sinclair had considered requesting a news blackout on the deaths in Brazil but knew that international news affecting UK citizens always somehow got back to the UK, so he didn't request it. He also thought that there was at least a chance that the kidnapper would see or hear the news and release Molly and for that reason he decided to put a news request out for the deaths to be reported.

The Sun and The Daily Record carried the news on inside pages two days later.

With Karen in intensive care Tom McLeod stayed by the phone at the farmhouse, in the hope that the kidnapper would see the newspaper reports or hear the story on BBC or local radio. A week after the deaths there had been no call.

Tom was getting ready to settle down for another night on the settee next to the phone. The phone rang, Tom waited, the tape clicked on. A metallic voice said

'Let me speak to James Jackson.'

'Not possible' answered Tom his voice level and calm.

'Who is this?'

'Sergeant Tom McLeod, we have informed Mrs Jackson that her husband, James Jackson, is dead.'

'Proof.'

Tom forgetting his training got angry.

'Proof, you want proof. Two men are lying dead in Brazil and it's all over the newspapers there and here and you want proof. Call your boss, call Arthur, see if you can speak to him. You won't be able to because he is lying dead as well, and you want proof.'

'I need proof' said the metallic voice.

'Listen you bastard, the man killed himself, he did what you wanted, now release…'

The metallic voice interrupted him

'I'm sorry, I need proof.'

'What more proof can we give you?' asked Tom exasperated and upset with himself for getting angry.

'The body needs to be in the UK, and I need to see the funeral take place. I am sure you can arrange it. I will call in two days.

The phone link was cut.

Tom sat with the phone in his hand, the dial tone telling him the call had been terminated. He sat there for several minutes before setting the phone down; it immediately rang, his tracers telling him once again the call had been too short to trace. He rang DCI Sinclair and through his superiors, requests were made to the UK Foreign and Commonwealth Office to urge the Brazilian Government to cut short the red tape and allow the two bodies to be released from the Rio City morgue to get the bodies back to the UK.

The wheels of diplomacy and foreign affairs ran surprisingly smoothly. The Duty Officer at the British Embassy in Brasilia took the call from the Duty Officer at the Foreign Office in London. In turn calls went to the Consulate General in Rio, the Ministry of Interior Affairs in Sao Paulo and within a few hours, approval had been given for the bodies of Arthur Summerskill and James Jackson to be released and allowed to leave the country. The Duty Officer at the British Embassy called his contact at KLM and alerted them that they required two dead bodies to be flown to the UK; one body to Aberdeen and one to Manchester. Both bodies would be shipped via Schiphol where KLM have their own mortuary. Richard and Arthur would just be another statistic to add to the fifty thousand dead bodies that are flown every year. When the British Embassy Duty Officer in Brasilia was completing his documentation and reports at the end of his shift, he paused as he wrote James' name, he thought it was familiar and he was sure that it was a James Jackson from Rothienorman who had been involved in some explosion in Aberdeen a few months back. Rothienorman being a village close to his home at Drum of Wartle. If it is, that's a strange one and it's a small world, he thought.

The body of Arthur Summerskill arrived in the UK the day after it left Brazil. The same funeral director who had organised Annette's funeral took charge of Arthur's body at the airport and took care of the formalities relating to the death certificate.

Following DCI Sinclair advising Karen of her husband's death; Tom phoned Jim and advised him that Karen had been told of her husband's death and the shock had resulted in her being admitted to hospital where she remained. He also advised him that James' body was still in Rio waiting on the paperwork to be signed off to release it for shipment home. They agreed that Jim and his wife should come to Aberdeen and be there for Karen when she was released and to attend to the funeral arrangements if that was Karen's wish. Jim and Kathryn left that day to drive to Aberdeen.

The body of James Jackson arrived in the UK two days after it left Brazil. There had been some delay due to cargo space being in short supply on the Schiphol to Aberdeen flight. Tom

McLeod made the arrangements for the body to be collected from the airport, the Procurator Fiscal had been notified that the death had been certified in Brazil as accidental and he was content to accept that and allow the body to proceed for burial.

DCI Sinclair was anxious for the funeral to take place as quickly as possible so that it could be verified to the kidnapper and hopefully result in Molly's release.

Tom took the next metallic call the same day as James' body was arriving at Aberdeen.

'When is the funeral?' the voice asked.

'I don't have a date yet, very soon, his body arrives in Aberdeen today, why won't you accept he is dead and release Molly?'

'I will call in two days, have a funeral date'.

The call ended, again too short to trace.

DCI Sinclair, Tom Mcleod and Jim met at the farmhouse an hour after the kidnapper's call. It was decided that if Karen was well enough, they would rush the funeral arrangements. Jim went to the hospital with his wife and with Tom. Karen was coming to terms with James' death and the severe shock she had had when told was now just a dull pain in her heart. In consultation with her Doctor, it was agreed that Karen would be strong enough to face the funeral especially as it might result in her daughter's release. DCI Sinclair dealt with the detail, getting a funeral to take place in a few days as opposed to the normal ten-day delay. Everyone involved was made aware of the reason for the urgency and there were no objections. The national and local newspapers and TV were asked to make mention of the funeral taking place of a prominent Aberdeen businessman who, having narrowly escaped death in an explosion that killed many of his work colleagues last year, had died in a tragic accident in Brazil. They were asked not to make mention of the message broadcast on a local radio station. They all respected this request; their editors being advised of the hope that Molly would be released after the funeral. A story that would fill the news for several days.

CHAPTER 28

JAMES' burial service was well attended. Many of his oilfield friends attended. Karen was escorted by Jim; she had recovered enough to attend the service but the stress and trauma of the kidnapping and James' death had left her weak and her complexion was grey. She stood slumped, leaning on Jim for support. The presence of her relatives did nothing to console her and they like everyone else in attendance felt useless and helpless. DCI Sinclair stood on the other side of Karen, not from duty but out of respect for her. He felt that Karen had been extraordinarily strong throughout the ordeal and only now in this terrible grief had she showed any fragility. The police team scanned the faces at the church service and at the graveside putting names to faces and discreetly questioning any who they were unsure of. In all cases, there were only people who had a genuine reason for being there. It looked like the kidnapper had not attended.

Richard had read the papers and listened to the news. He watched through binoculars as the coffin was loaded into the hearse and the funeral party left in a line of highly polished black limousines. He was half a mile away on a hill overlooking the house. He had prepared his hide some weeks previously. He had seen grief enough times to know that the scene being played out before him was no play acting. He was convinced James Jackson was dead.

He waited two days. The routine in the cottage maintained. He had not told Molly about James' death. His relationship with her was very good now. More like father and daughter than kidnapper and hostage. He had felt a sexual attraction to her in the beginning but he knew that any involvement like that would jeopardise his chances of a clean escape; so he kept the thoughts locked up in the back of his mind. It was easier to be nice to her than to be mean to her. She had done nothing to upset him apart from trying to put a message on the tape some months ago; but she had been good since. Molly liked Richard, he had been good to her mostly, he smelt good, was strong and muscular and when he carried her to the shower she had tried several times to tease him by pressing her body against his. He had never responded, so she thought he hadn't noticed so stopped doing it. He fed her regularly, made sure she had clean clothes and batteries for her Walkman. He was not rough with her. She was fully aware that she was the captive and that he was the captor, doing a job. Why and what for she didn't know. She hoped that soon she could be back with Mum and James and this would just be a memory.

Richard walked through the woods and back tracked twice to make sure he wasn't being followed or watched. He walked quickly and quietly making his way towards Aberchirder. The village was quiet in the afternoon winter sunshine. The phone box was empty, he dialled taking the voice distorter from his pocket. The phone rang and rang, he counted twenty rings, twenty one, twenty two then it was answered.

He switched on the voice distorter.

'Let me talk to the police.'

'They're not here,' said Karen 'who is this?'

'Where is the senior policeman?'

'I have a number you can reach him on, his mother is ill' said Karen playing her part.

'Give me the number.'

'01224 178497.'

The phone line went dead.

Richard was not happy. His mind raced. Was this a trick? He leant on the side of the phone box not sure what to do. He saw a public house across the street, The New Inn. Have a drink and think about things he told himself.

'Grouse and water please' he said to the plump blonde behind the bar. He looked around, there were no other customers. He paid her and she pushed the water jug towards him so he could add water himself.

'Haven't seen you in here before' she said smiling.

'No' he replied moving away to a table near the window. Not wishing to get into conversation but also not wishing to draw attention to himself by appearing rude.

'No' he repeated, 'I am house hunting and have to meet my wife here. I'm a bit early'

'Not local are you' she said, it wasn't a question. 'Didn't hear your car, where did you leave it?'

'In the next road, near the house we are looking at.'

'Oh, you don't look dressed for a house viewing, most folk get dressed up, to create a good impression I expect' she said.

Richard was nervous. She hadn't recognised him as the panther hunter therefore to her he was a stranger. He looked into his glass, then out of the small window. He would not have been nervous if he had known Dorothy, for that was the barmaid's name; like her other customers knew her. She was just trying to make conversation. She could have five conversations going at once and not recall one of them minutes later. She was just a friendly, old school, barmaid. Richard didn't know this. His mind made up he stood and strode quickly to the bar, picked up a pint glass that she had just polished and smashed it over her head. She went down. He waited a few moments then checked her pulse, there was none. He opened the till and took what little money there was. He hadn't removed his gloves since entering so had left no fingerprints. With no remorse he left the pub, the village, and the area. It was still quiet in the afternoon sunshine. His grouse and water jug on the table, the only evidence that someone had been in the bar. It was fifteen minutes before the next customer entered the bar. He waited for Dorothy to appear but when she didn't, he went around the bar to pour his own drink. Dorothy was on the floor. At first, he thought she had fainted, and he knelt by her side, gently tapping her cheek and calling her name. He noticed some blood on the floor by her head, stopped patting and called the health centre. A doctor was there in a few minutes. He checked her pulse and looked at her head wound then dialled 999.

Richard was four miles away before the police arrived at The New Inn, another hour to cordon off the village then house to house enquiries. No witnesses, no strangers reported in the village, no one had seen anything. The only clue, a glass of whisky and a jug of water on the table and a pint mug with blood stains on it on the floor at the back of the bar and an open till.

Richard moved silently and unseen overland keeping to the fields, hedgerows and drystone dykes. He arrived at Turriff in the dark, the day still rain free and mild. Turriff was as quiet as Aberchirder had been and he found a phone box without being seen and dialled the number 01224-178497.

'Hello' said an elderly sounding woman's voice.

Richard turned on his voice changer.

'Detective Chief Inspector Sinclair please' the metallic voice said.

'Hello dear, I can't understand you, I am a bit deaf' said the woman.

'Detective Chief Inspector Sinclair please' Richard said again.

'Insect what, dear?' said the woman.

'Oh, fuck,' said Richard to himself, 'that's all I need the DCI has a geriatric mother.'

He turned off the voice box and said as clearly as he could.

'DCI Sinclair, please.'

'Oh, right one moment, dear' said the woman.

He heard her calling. 'John, John, call for you.'

After a wait of some twenty seconds DCI Sinclair came to the phone.

'Hello' he said.

With the voice box switched back on Richard said.

'DCI Sinclair, I wish to free the girl.'

'Oh. Yes, excellent. Sorry but my mother has not been well, have you been trying to get hold of me for a while?'

'Cut the bullshit, I will release the girl tomorrow afternoon and call you at the farmhouse to tell you where to find her.'

'Right at the Jackson's in the afternoon, excellent.'

The line went dead.

DCI Sinclair put down the phone.

'Did we get it?' he asked.

The intercept team leader was beaming.

'Yes, we did, a phone box in Turriff. Cars on their way there now.'

'Did we get his voice?'

'Yes, we did' said the female police sergeant who had acted the part of DCI Sinclair's mother.

'Great job Glenda, you will be leaving us for the stage' he said. 'Let's filter out the voice box distortion and see what we can find out about matey and where he comes from.'

His eyes swept the faces in the room many of whom had been on the team from day one of Molly's abduction.

'Great job everyone, now let's get Molly and this bastard.'

Richard was long gone from Turriff before any police car got to the phone box he had used; but he had heard them, sirens blaring and realised that this afternoon he had made several mistakes. One had cost a woman her life, the other might cost him his freedom. Tighten up he told himself.

It was past midnight when he got back to the cottage. Molly was sleeping. He asked her if she was hungry because he certainly was. She was. He barbequed sausages and hamburgers to perfection over the open fire in the front room and carried the food through to her, guided her hands to the food and she ate hungrily. He sat with her eating his own meal, something he rarely did.

'Molly, tomorrow I am going to release you. I make no excuses for keeping you captive. I have been well paid to do this. I have done a good job but tomorrow it will be over. I want you to behave tomorrow; we just need to get you back home now.'

'I will miss you' said Molly 'thank you for not hurting me and for taking care of me.'

'Okay, sleep tight, see you tomorrow.' Richard picked up the plates and left the room. Molly, excited now. had difficulty falling asleep and had to call him to go to the bathroom twice during the night.

Richard, despite a disturbed night woke early. The pleasant weather of yesterday had turned into pouring rain with low cloud which hung heavy over the ground. He had made his plans, the number one to be a long way away when they came to get Molly.

He spent an hour checking the detonators, gelignite and petrol cannisters that he had spent several hours rigging up in the cottage over the past week. Detonators and gelignite that he had stolen over the past months from various quarries, none of them within twenty miles of the cottage. He set the timer, rigged from a battery-operated alarm clock. One hour thirty minutes from now.

He woke Molly and gave her breakfast. She was excited. He gave her clean underwear and a new jogging suit and trainers along with a waterproof jacket. He told her they would leave the cottage in thirty minutes. He was sure that the explosion would erase all evidence of their stay but just to be on the safe side he gathered up anything that might be evidence and put it in the grate and set fire to it. Surplus food he scattered in the woods at the back of the cottage, for the animals to eat. When he was finished the only evidence of their stay was Molly's bedding and her dirty clothes.

He packed his own clothes into his rucksack to take with him. His cameras and outdoor gear he put into the Discovery and moved it as close to the back of the cottage as possible. He doused it in petrol. It would incinerate when the cottage blew. He was ready to go.

He came for her, he had his balaclava on, so she took off her blindfold when he told her to. He led her from the cottage into the rain. Forty minutes to detonation. The low cloud and heavy rain had soaked the trees and bushes and the puddles on the track were joining to form a stream of water that they trudged through. They were soaked within minutes of leaving the cottage.

They climbed the slope leading to the quarry. The large rock plateau from where he had set the Toyota pick-up on its final journey and which angled gently to the quarry lip was running with water which cascaded over the lip into the quarry. He sat her down in the running water. He secured her feet and hands with cable ties. He planned to leave her here and make his way to Huntly where he would make the call to the police advising of her location. He would take off across country and make his way to Inverness and then using train or bus to Glasgow, stay low for a few days then depart by air for South Africa. He knew he needed some luck but felt sure it was on his side.

'Okay Molly, this is where I leave you. You should be found within the hour.' With that he was gone.

Molly saw him disappearing down the track and he was lost in the mist. She wriggled to get comfortable but found herself slipping towards the quarry edge just three feet away. She shouted.

'HELP!'

Richard heard the cry, stupid girl he thought, no one here to hear her she is just going to have to wait.

Molly couldn't stop herself from slipping, her new shoes had no grip on the flat wet rock, she slipped over the quarry edge and screamed again, this time in absolute panic.

'HELP!' the shout cut off as she hit the water and went under.

Richard heard this cut off shout and he sensed it was more than a cry for general help, it was a panic cry for immediate help. He stopped, listened, he shouted.

'Molly, you okay?'

No answer. He raced back up the track to the ledge, there was no sign of Molly. He looked over the edge and saw disturbed water and then a glimpse of Molly struggling to stay afloat, she was silhouetted against the white of the Toyota.

'Oh shit!' he cried as he struggled out of his backpack and jumped feet first into the water. He hit the submerged bonnet of the Toyota, his legs buckling under him. He turned and reached for her, he got a hold of her and she struggled in his arms, his foot went through the windscreen and through the steering wheel catching in the spokes. He was struggling to free her hands. He pulled his knife from the sheath on his belt and cut the cable tie securing her hands. She reached for a small ledge above her and caught her breath. She looked for him, he was struggling under the water, struggling furiously to release his foot trapped by the steering wheel. She turned and swam down to him, she swam past him and tried to free his foot, but the wheel had deformed around it and she could not twist his foot or the wheel to free him. The water was dirty, and she could not see clearly. She felt his hand on the back of her jacket pulling her up and then pushing her towards the surface. Twice more she dived down trying to release his foot now slippery with his blood and only when his struggles stopped did she realise and accept that he had drowned. She clawed at the ledge with her hands, pulling her upper body up and then swinging her legs, still secured at the ankles, up and onto the ledge. She lay there, the water streaming from the lip above cascading onto her head, she looked down and saw his body under the water, lifeless.

Molly was cold and realised that she needed to get out of the quarry. She looked around to see any way that could enable her to climb. To her left, about thirty yards away, she saw an iron ladder that rose vertically out of the water and twenty feet or so up to a large ledge, that seemed to be the top of a huge block of stone, and from there it looked like she could climb further block to block. The only way to get to the ladder was to go back in the water and swim to it. She realised that if she didn't do it now, she would only get colder and not have the strength to do anything. She went back in the water and swam with difficulty to the ladder. She grabbed it and heaved herself up so that her feet were on a rung and her arms were holding the ladder above her head. The ladder was rusty but seemed solid enough so she pulled her body up with her arms and jumped with her feet so that, rung by rung, she managed to haul her way up the ladder to the flat ledge of the block above. Reaching the block, she lay exhausted getting her breath back. The ledge she was on was wide and flat and there was a lot of rubbish on it. A broken bottle was near the back of the block and she crawled over to it and used it to saw through the tie wrap that secured her ankles. She cut her hand and her foot in the process but felt no pain. Cold and shivering but now with the full use of her legs she climbed and scrambled block by block to the quarry lip. She got her bearings and ran back towards the track that led to the cottage. Stopping at the T-junction she wondered if it were best to go back to the cottage where at least she could shelter or follow the track the other way to see where it led. Deciding on the cottage she summoned up the last of her energy and ran towards it. She was forty yards away when the cottage erupted in a ball of orange flame, and she was knocked unconscious by a flying slate.

On the main A96 a police sergeant had finished writing a speeding ticket and turned from the errant motorist back to his patrol car when he heard the dull thud of an explosion. He looked north towards where he thought the noise had come from. The rain was very heavy and the mist still reducing visibility. He saw no smoke and no fire.

'Funny,' he said to the police constable who was already in the vehicle, 'sounded like an explosion, the only thing over there is an old quarry and I'm sure it's been some years since they blasted.'

'Let's have a look at the map Sarge,' said the constable unfolding the large scale map that they carried. 'Yea, there's the quarry, there's a cottage as well and a track from the quarry. Should we go look?'

'No way, we won't get this car up there in this weather, let's call it in and see if there is a four by four available.'

It was nearly an hour before the police Range Rover arrived at the track. They cleared the boulders and bushes from the track and the acrid smell of burning was in the air. They arrived at the remains of the cottage, a smouldering heap of stone and charred wood with what looked like the frame of a burnt out vehicle in the middle of it. Stone and slate scattered over a wide area.

'Good God some powerful explosion, call control first, tell them we will have a look around' said the senior policeman to his partner.

They passed within twenty yards of Molly twice and didn't

see her. It was only when the rain eased a little and the mist cleared that the sergeant noticed what looked like an orange coat on the ground. Out of interest he walked to it, he was feet away when he realised there was a body inside the coat.

'She's breathing!' he shouted to his partner who was running towards the Range Rover. 'Very weak pulse, we need an ambulance, medivac chopper, if we can get it in here, she's in a bad way.'

They made her as comfortable as they could, using everything they had in the vehicle to try to get her warm. The police sergeant lay next to her under the coats and blankets they brought from the Range Rover, trying to get some warmth into her cold body. The blood from her head wound seeped through the first aid bandage they applied. The sergeant noticed the cuts and raw skin on her wrists and ankles and his instinct told him they had found Molly. That was the next call the constable made to control.

The ambulance was still thirty minutes away when the helicopter touched down in a clearing some three hundred yards from the remains of the cottage. Within an hour of being found Molly was on her way by air to Aberdeen Royal Infirmary.

DCI Sinclair had been waiting at the Jackson's farmhouse for the telephone call that the kidnapper had told him to expect. The clock showed three and he had heard nothing. At three thirty he heard news of what was thought to be an explosion at a cottage. It was an hour later before he heard that, pending a positive ID, Molly had been found and was on her way to hospital with a serious head wound.

CHAPTER 29

A full forensics team was sent to the cottage along with military bomb disposal personnel who ensured that the area was safe for the forensics team to start their investigation. Early on, forensics came to the conclusion that whoever had set the explosives had done a professional job. Getting the information from the burnt and distorted frame of the vehicle was easy, the VIN plate was still in place and intact and that led to it being traced to the Land Rover dealer in Aberdeen. This in turn led to the Skean Dhu Hotel and that, along with the interview of the owner of the cottage, formed a reasonably complete picture of the kidnapper and his recent history. An all ports warning was issued within a couple of hours of Molly being found but it was too vague to be of much use. It was a forensics officer who the next day, a sunny day, decided he would go and eat his sandwiches up at the quarry. He discovered the back pack on the ledge and the Toyota with the body still firmly trapped by the leg. The underwater team were called in and the body and the Toyota were retrieved.

Molly was unconscious and critical for forty-eight hours after she was admitted to hospital. The nursing team were anxious that she did not become stressed or agitated. They monitored her every few minutes, allowing her to regain consciousness slowly, as her body temperature returned to normal. Karen sat with her the whole time and reassured her that she was safe. Karen was holding Molly's hand and they were both dozing in the warmth of the hospital room when Molly began to cry and woke Karen with the sound of her sobbing.

'It's Ok darling, you're safe. No one is going to hurt you,' said Karen

'I'm sorry Mum, I couldn't save him. He pushed me to safety, I tried to save him but I couldn't, he was trapped. I watched him die. He saved me and it cost him his life. I'm sorry Mum.'

'Don't think about it, they found his body a few days ago, it wasn't your fault, you have nothing to feel sorry about. If he hadn't taken you, he wouldn't have died.' Karen said comforting Molly.

The doctors did not allow the police to talk to Molly for a further twenty-four hours. Molly told her story to DCI Sinclair and Tom McLeod which confirmed that the body retrieved from the quarry was that of the kidnapper.

Over the course of the next few weeks, after Richard's picture had been given to the press and published in the national and local newspapers there were many reports about him and his movements over the prior months. Most of the people he had spoken to in his guise as a panther hunter, writer and photographer spoke well of him. They had found him polite and interesting and had difficulty in imagining him as a ruthless kidnapper. A photography studio in Inverness where Richard had taken many rolls of film to be developed still had three developed rolls which were waiting on his collection. These were released to the police and there were some excellent wildlife photographs including some extraordinary ones of a family of black panthers; two large adults with three cubs. There were several others including close ups of adult panthers singly and in pairs. These photographs were given to the newspapers and news of black panthers in North East Scotland went around the world.

Molly remained in hospital for several weeks, her physical injuries healing well but her mental health was another matter. Not only the trauma of being held captive but also being told that her stepfather had sacrificed himself for her. Karen was mentally extraordinarily strong. Supporting her daughter and carefully reintroducing her to life, holding nothing back, telling her of James' previous marriage and the car accident and as much as she herself knew about his trip to Brazil and subsequent 'accident'. Slowly but steadily life for Molly and Karen returned to some normality. Molly returned to school and her studies.

Jim kept his promise to James, and Karen and Molly wanted for nothing. Jim set up an education fund for Molly to ensure that, should she wish to go to university, lack of money would not prevent her. Cut and Pull Inc were marvellous; as James had not officially resigned, they classed his death as a death in service and the lump sum payment and monthly pension payment to Karen more than covered outgoings. As James' death had been officially declared an accident by the Brazilian authorities, several insurance policies paid out in full. Karen was a wealthy woman but would have traded it all for one more day with James.

The investigation into the deaths caused by the explosion at Cut and Pull had continued during the kidnap but was getting nowhere. The team investigated to see if there was any connection between Richard or Arthur and the explosion, but no connection was found. As the lead investigator was retiring DCI Sinclair took control of this investigation.

The murder of Dorothy the barmaid at The New Inn, Aberchirder remained unsolved, the only clue the whisky tumbler and the water jug. No fingerprints, no persons seen. While the case remained open it was commonly thought in police circles that Richard was the killer as he had made a telephone call that same afternoon from a phone box only seven miles away. Why he had killed her was an unknown.

With the kidnap over, Tom McLeod was seconded to the British Government Foreign and Commonwealth Office who loaned him out to various friendly foreign governments who used his expertise as a negotiator mainly in Somalia, Yemen and Afghanistan.

Phillip and Mary Stephenson were packing up the contents of the quarry cottage in Backwell getting ready for retirement and a move back to Cornwall. They had asked friends and neighbours to save newspapers so they could use them to safely pack their glasses and ornaments. Phillip had a pile of newspapers in front of him and was wrapping the wine glasses. Mary heard breaking glass and turned to see Phillip, staring down at the newspaper in front of him.

'Be careful Phillip, we've had those glasses for a long time they were a wedding present' shouted Mary leaving the kitchen and walking through to the lounge where Phillip was working.

Phillip didn't respond to her but concentrated on the newspaper he was reading. He didn't acknowledge her for a couple of minutes.

'Mary, I can't believe this, look at this picture, do you recognise this man?'

Mary looked at the picture that Phillip was pointing to. She studied the picture, a man's face stared back at her.

'That's George Thomas, or it looks like him, the one who came to see us, he knew our Jane, they went to college together, why is he in the paper?'

'That's what I thought but this says he is not George Thomas. He is someone called Richard Watt and he has died but this story says he kidnapped a young girl who is the stepdaughter of James Jackson who, this says, died in an accident in Brazil and, listen to this, another man involved in the accident, Arthur Summerskill, also dead. I need to sit down and read this. Have a look, and see if this story is in any of the other newspapers.'

Mary set to looking through the pile of newspapers and soon had several of them to one side and was reading the stories they contained.

'It says that the police would like to speak to anyone who has had contact with this Richard Watt, we should tell them he was George Thomas when he came to see us. Will you call them, or should I do it?' Mary asked.

Phillip became agitated 'No we aren't going to tell them anything, we don't want Jane's name being dragged into this mess. This George or Richard, whoever he is, is dead, and so is that James Jackson who killed our Jane, good riddance to him, at last he has got his comeuppance and we have the justice that has been denied to us for so long. We do nothing to help them.. I mean it, do not contact them and don't go talking about this to anyone. Do you hear me?'

Mary was shocked, she hadn't seen Phillip, who was normally mild mannered and not at all aggressive, this angry and determined.

'I think we should Phillip, we don't know if this man has done anything else that the police are trying to investigate, there might be other girls he has kidnapped, if we have information, we should help them' said Mary trying to reason with him.

'Mary, I'm serious do not defy me on this, you will open a can of worms that you have no idea about. It's over, I live with it, you live with it. End of story Mary now let's get on with our packing.'

Mary turned on her heel and walked back to the kitchen and returned to her packing but left off every now and again to read and re-read the newspaper that she had taken with her. Mary walked back into the lounge; Phillip stood looking out of the window his face full of emotion.

'Phillip, you have to rethink this, we have a duty to tell the police he was here. We have nothing to hide, what's this nonsense about opening a can of worms, that's just silly, please have a think about it. I think we need to call them.'

Phillip looked at her, 'I'm telling you leave it be, you have no idea what you are talking about, you have no idea at all. I'm very serious Mary I don't need the police knocking on our door. Trust me on this.'

Mary stormed out of the kitchen. This was not like Phillip at all, it was very out of character. They had nothing to hide from the police. This was just nonsense, she didn't know why he was being like this but she was concerned that George or Richard or whatever his real name was could have kidnapped someone else, or hurt someone, or worse, and maybe if the police were told it would help them. She thought she would wait a few days and ask Phillip again to reconsider.

A week went by before she thought it was the right time to bring up the subject again, but she soon discovered it wasn't the right time. He would have none of it and was angry with her for mentioning it again. Mary was angry too; she was an independent woman and the more she thought about telling the police the more she thought it was the right thing to do. The move from the cottage was imminent and their bungalow in Padstow was ready, so Mary decided to get the move over with before making the phone call to the police. She put the newspaper report with the contact details into her handbag and prepared for the move. The move to Padstow and settling into the new bungalow took a little longer than she expected. Mary concentrated on getting the bungalow in order and Phillip on putting his work tools and gardening equipment in to the old two-storey netting shed that had really sold him on the property. Phillip wasn't taking to retirement very well and was not very helpful. Mary feared that he was showing early signs of dementia, his mood had definitely changed and his unreasonable anger with her over her wish to call the police had worried her. It was some three months after the move when Mary took the newspaper report from her handbag and re-read it, once more. Convinced that telling the police was the right thing to do she decided to talk to Phillip about it and see if his opinion had changed. It hadn't. He was furious with her for bringing it up and so angry with her that she was frightened that he might become aggressive. Her worries about his health increased. Mary had no one to talk to about Phillip's health or whether she should call the police. Her life had always been in support of Phillip, all their time at the quarry in Backwell she had washed, cooked and cleaned so that he could go to work, there was never time for herself or to make real friends and now here in Cornwall, a move that he had insisted they make, she had no friends and no support. Mary was angry with Phillip and angry with herself, so she made the call.

It was a week before her name, phone number and address got to the desk of DCI Sinclair. He called the number. A man answered.

'Mrs Stephenson please, Mrs Mary Stephenson' he said.

'Whose calling?' asked Phillip.

'Detective Chief Inspector Sinclair from Aberdeen Police in Scotland.'

There was silence. DCI Sinclair waited. The silence went on for too long.

'Hello, hello, you still there?' DCI Sinclair asked.

There was no reply, longer silence, then the line was cut.

That was strange DCI Sinclair thought, he wondered if he should call again or get one of his colleagues in Cornwall to pay a visit. He called Devon and Cornwall police and asked them to visit and get back to him.

Phillip put the phone down, he was angry, shocked, and scared. 'Mary, what have you done, the police just called. Did you call them? I told you not to, you have no idea, why didn't you listen to me?' he stormed out of the house and went to his shed.

It was several days later before the local police visited the bungalow. Phillip answered the door to them, and immediately they were aware of his aggressive demeaner and his reluctance to let them talk to his wife, but Mary, hearing an argument starting at the door, went through from the kitchen and spoke to the police officers.

'It's okay Phillip, I will deal with this,' she said. 'How can I help you?'

Phillip walked away muttering, and the police officer spoke to Mary.

'Are you Mary Stephenson?' he asked.

'Yes, I am' she replied.

"Did you make a call to Aberdeen police relating to a Richard Watt and also mentioned a George Thomas?'

'Yes. I did, that was a few days ago, they never called me back' she said

'Well Madam they did call, a gentleman answered the phone and when they asked to speak to you the phone line went dead, that's why they asked us to call around and make sure everything is okay and to tell you they would very much like to speak to you. They have given us a direct line number to the DCI in charge. Would you please call them?' the policeman asked.

'Yes of course, one moment.' Turning away from the policeman, 'Phillip did you have the police on the phone a few days ago asking to speak to me?' she shouted through to her husband.

There was no answer.

'I'm sorry he has been acting very strangely recently, would you like to come in and I will make the call while you are here' she asked.

The two policemen entered the house, gave Mary the phone number for DCI Sinclair and she made the call. Phillip hovered nearby saying nothing but looking worried.

Mary explained to DCI Sinclair all about the visit and the man who visited. She explained to him about seeing a newspaper report about the man and James Jackson and how it was their late daughter Jane who was married to Jackson and who died in a car crash. This information stunned the DCI he had never given Janes' parents a thought and it appeared that no one else on his team had either. She wasn't one hundred percent sure of the date of the visit but knew within a day or so of when it took place. DCI Sinclair asked Mary why her husband had cut off his call of a few days previous. Mary didn't have a good explanation but told him that her husband had been very much against them getting involved and had even told her that she was opening a can of worms. Phillip was stood next to Mary and was tutting and shaking his head, he pushed past the two policemen and went out to his shed. Once he was gone Mary opened up about her concerns for his health and how it was not like him to act in this way.

'It's really since he retired and we moved. He always hated James Jackson for what he did to Jane and this newspaper story has brought it all back to him. I don't know what it is, but he isn't the man he was' she said.

'What did he retire from?' asked DCI Sinclair.

'He managed a quarry, was at the last one for twenty odd years but we have been all over the country' Mary replied.

'Thank you, Mary, you have been most helpful, if I need to call you again is that okay or if you think of anything please feel free to call me on this number.'

DCI Sinclair put down the phone, he held his head in his hands and looking down at his notes, said aloud

'For fucks sake.'

He called an urgent meeting of his team. The eight of them gathered an hour later.

'Gents, I had a conversation today with Mary Stephenson, does that name mean anything to any of you?' he waited, no response. 'Okay what about Phillip Stephenson, does that name ring a bell?' he waited again, no response. 'No, the names meant nothing to me either but by God they should have done, we have failed badly, and I hope it's not going to bite us in the arse.'

His team shuffled and looked bemused wondering what it was they should have known or done. There was no doubt the boss was angry.

'Right guys, a bit of history. You should. No. We should. We should all know this, but I will go over it for those who may have forgotten. James Jackson was married years ago and his wife Jane died on the day after their wedding in a car crash. James Jackson was taken to court and charged with causing her death and that of Arthur Summerskill's children, he was the driver, or maybe wasn't, of the other car involved. James was found not guilty, basically it could not be proven that he was the driver of the vehicle and he had a genuine loss of memory relating to the accident. You with me so far?' he looked around the room he had their attention. 'Now we were not aware of James' marriage to Jane or the car crash because a certain police officer did not perform the task he was ordered to do and compounded his negligence by lying about it. If we had known we might have got to Arthur Summerskill before James did and we might have averted the tragedy that it became and freed Molly, but we didn't because we were negligent. Now it seems to me we have been negligent again. Ladies and Gents. Jane's maiden name was Stephenson; Mary and Phillip Stephenson her parents. Mary told me on the phone that Phillip had a hatred for James Jackson, blamed him for his daughter's death. Oh, and guess what, Phillip has managed quarries all over the UK. Quarries means explosives. We didn't even know about Phillip, but we should have known. Why we didn't is for another day but for now we need to see if he has any connection to our investigation of the Cut and Pull murders.'

None of the team looked him in the eye. They daren't. They realised that the ball had been dropped and their boss was angry. The senior Detective Sergeant on the team, Gus Evans, had been seconded in when the original senior sergeant suffered a heart attack. Gus didn't feel responsible for the negligent oversight, he hadn't been a team member then.

'Okay Guv, how do you want to handle this? Will we let the local boys in Cornwall talk to them or do you want to go down.'

'Yes. We need to do it Gus, you and I will make plans to go down in the next couple of days, are you clear to go?'

'Yes Guv, do you want me to make the arrangements, will you call the Stephenson's?'

'Yes I'll call them, let's see if we can make it for the day after tomorrow.'

DCI Sinclair picked up the phone and called Cornwall. It was answered by Phillip.

'Mr Stephenson, this is Detective Chief Inspector Sinclair in Aberdeen, Scotland. I spoke with your wife yesterday. Did she tell you that we spoke?'

Phillip paused before replying 'Yes she did, and I have to tell you that I think she made a terrible mistake getting us involved in something that's nothing to do with us, I told her we shouldn't get involved.'

'Mr Stephenson, Richard Watt meeting with you and asking about your late daughter is one thing, and we would certainly like to ask you a few questions about that; but I'm not sure if you are aware that James Jackson's company building was destroyed in an explosion some weeks before his stepdaughter was kidnapped, unfortunately there were multiple fatalities and this is a multi-murder investigation. We would like to have an informal interview with you regarding this so that we may rule you out of our investigation. Would tomorrow afternoon be suitable for you at your house or you could come into the Padstow police station if that would be easier?'

There was a long silence before Phillip replied,

'At the police station. Do I need a lawyer?' he asked.

That will be your decision, as I said I want an informal interview so we can rule you out of our enquiries. Shall we say two thirty tomorrow afternoon? asked DCI Sinclair wondering now why Phillip would think he needed a lawyer.

'Yes Ok, do you want my wife to be there as well?' asked Phillip.

'It may help. Yes, that would be good.'

DCI Sinclair and DS Gus Evans got the red eye flight Aberdeen to Newquay then took a taxi to Padstow. They were at the police station within forty-five minutes of landing.

The interview room was set up and they awaited the arrival of Phillip and Mary Stephenson. Two thirty came and went. At two forty-five a police car was despatched to the Stephenson's bungalow. All hell broke loose in the ten minutes it took the police car to drive from the station to the Stephensons'. Minutes after the police car had left the station a 999 call was received requesting an ambulance; the address was the Stephensons'; the caller Mary Stephenson.

The police car and the ambulance arrived within moments of each other. The front door was open, and the police, followed by the ambulance crew, rushed in. There was no one in the house but the back door was open and at the end of the garden sitting on a bench outside of the netting shed was Mary. Her head in her hands and she was sobbing, heart breaking tears

'Are you hurt?' asked the policeman as he reached her.

'No. He's in the shed' she pointed towards the closed door.

The policeman pushed the door open. No one there. The wooden stairs to the upper floor of the shed were on the back wall of the building and he climbed them. Before he got to the top, he could see trousered legs dangling in space. He shouted to his colleague.

'One male hanging. Let's get him down, hurry. Get those medics up here!'

Phillip was hanging, a rope around the main roof beam hung taut down to and around his neck. A step ladder he had used to get height lay on its side below his feet. The two policemen took his weight while one of the ambulance crew untied the rope from the beam and between them, they lowered him to the ground. Releasing the rope from around his neck they started with mouth to mouth and cardiopulmonary resuscitation. They kept this up for fifteen minutes until the emergency doctor arrived and declared Phillip dead. DCI Sinclair and DS Evans arrived shortly after the doctor and were able to speak with the two police constables who were first on scene. Mary was in dreadful shock and the ambulance took her to hospital where she was sedated. Phillip's body was moved to the police mortuary. The two detectives returned to Aberdeen stunned and shocked by the turn of events their visit had caused.

It was almost two months later before they returned to Cornwall. Phillip had been buried and Mary discharged from hospital. She agreed that the two detectives could come to the house and speak with her. They found her nervous but in good spirits. DCI Sinclair led the conversation firstly by offering his condolences. He asked her what happened on the day when she and her husband were supposed to be at the police station for informal interview. Mary explained how she had got ready in good time. At about one Phillip had told her he was going to the shop to buy a paper; he rarely did this, so she thought it was a little odd. She remembered telling him not to be long and to make sure he was back in good time to get to the meeting. She was ready and waiting to go at two, but he hadn't come home. She waited, wondering where he could have been all this time. At two thirty she became very worried and decided to give him another ten minutes and if he still wasn't home, she would call the police station. She said that she went through to the kitchen to make a cup of tea and looking down the garden she noticed the netting shed door was open. That needs to be closed if were going out, she thought, and she went to the shed. She didn't know why she looked inside and called Phillips's name, there was no answer, but she felt his presence. She climbed the stairs and saw his body hanging. She felt sure he was dead by the way his head was hanging. She ran back to the house called 999 and that is about all she could remember before waking up in hospital.

DCI Sinclair thanked her for telling the story. It must have been an awful experience.

'Did he tell you why we were coming to interview him Mary?'

'Yes, he said you wanted to go over the visit by Richard or George whatever he was called' she answered.

'Did he not mention that we wanted to clear him from our enquiries regarding an explosion which resulted in multiple deaths at James Jackson's workplace back in September of last year? I was very clear to him that this was the reason for the interview. You know he even asked me if he needed a lawyer to attend. Why do you think he asked that?'

'No, he never mentioned it, how awful. I really have no idea. He just said it was about Richard's visit. He has been a different man lately. His retirement, I thought it was, he has always been so active. I thought maybe dementia but then I took a peek at his diaries, he always kept immaculate diaries and up until his death they were still immaculate with every detail written down. I never looked at them normally and haven't since he's gone, they were his secrets, but I think maybe I will have a look at them and see if there is a reason for his taking his own life.' Mary wiped a tear and then offered tea and cake.

'Nice cup of tea Mary and lovely cake, thank you. How long did he keep a diary?'

'Oh, from before we were married, every night he would spend some time writing it up. He had lovely handwriting.'

'Do you have them Mary, are they away somewhere?' asked DCI Sinclair.

'Oh no, we have them, they are in several boxes in the loft and the most recent is in the cutlery drawer, that's where he kept them.'

'Mary, would you mind if I took a look at them? I promise you that you will get them back. It's just that I would like to examine them to see if they would help me eliminate Phillip from our enquiries. It would really help us, I'm sure, if they are as detailed as you say.'

'Yes,' said Mary, 'you can go up in the loft now. I know where the boxes are and there is the one in the cutlery drawer. Would you like to get them now?'

'That would be great Mary, thank you.' Turning to Gus he said 'Guess you know who's going into the loft?'

'I'm ahead of you there, Guv. Right Mary, lead on; where's the loft hatch. Do I need a ladder?'

Gus didn't need a ladder, there was a fitted loft ladder in place and several electric lights which made finding the boxes an easy task. Gus wrote Mary a receipt for the two boxes of diaries and the single. DCI Sinclair assured her they would work on them as quickly as possible and get them back to her. He also told her that if she needed to speak to him about anything then just pick up the phone and call; and thanking her for her cooperation and for the cake and tea, they wished her a good afternoon.

DCI Sinclair was amazed when he examined the diaries. They covered nearly fifty years of Phillip's life. In the early years the diaries were from various manufacturers and weren't matching but for at least forty years the diaries were identical, dark blue with gold embossed lettering with the year. Philip's writing had changed little, maybe just smaller in the later years. The entries were incredibly detailed, events, times, names, addresses, the weather, conversations with strangers. He set his small team on reading.

They found the diary entries for the period covering Jane's death and the detail of the grief and distress was so moving that several of the officers who read it were moved to tears. The time leading up to the trial was disturbing as Phillip came to detest and hate James Jackson. There were many references to getting even and doing harm to James. The trial itself was incredibly detailed and the not guilty verdict was a shock to the Stephenson's. Phillip could not believe the verdict and was convinced it was a complete miscarriage of justice. Some months later there was reference to a visit to Jane's grave and seeing James Jackson at the graveside and a troubled story of how Mary had persuaded him not to approach James as she knew how angry Phillip was and what the consequences of a meeting could be. Phillip had written that he would have killed James Jackson that day.

Much of the diary content was routine and uninteresting, the daily humdrum of his life and relationships with work colleagues and with Mary but now and again Phillip's anger and grief at losing his daughter was clearly detailed. Every anniversary of her death was a special day for Phillip, he chose his words carefully and to read of his sadness and feeling of desolation was painful. The diaries clearly showed that Phillip was very much a loving family man who was unable to understand why his daughter had been taken from him. The team spent nearly two weeks going through the diaries; dates and entries that might relate to the explosion at

Cut and Pull in Aberdeen were found and passed to DCI Sinclair. There were several references to a private detective and details of James Jackson's house and work locations. This covered many years, and appeared to be an annual check and confirmation and included James' work and home in Great Yarmouth and his later move to Aberdeen. The latest confirmation of James' location was one year ago, some months before the explosion. A call to the private detective confirmed that Phillip would call every year for an update, he never told the investigator why and the investigator had not asked, just providing the information and billing Phillip for it. What he read disturbed DCI Sinclair in its simplicity. Phillip wrote that he had been on a Quarry Manager's Health and Safety Course in Perth, Scotland the week before the explosion. Leading up to this course, Phillip had written how he would like to make a visit to James Jackson and get even. He detailed in the diary how on one day there had been an explosives demonstration and lecture followed by a practical afternoon. (Investigation showed that Phillip had a lifetime's experience in quarry explosives and was well versed in the strict rules applying to the use and accounting for explosives and detonators used.) Phillip noticed that the 'expert' delivering the course was lax in his explosives accounting and Phillip, seizing the moment, managed to steal a quantity of gelignite and detonators. He wrote that he had no plan but that the opportunity had presented itself, so he took it. For several days his diary notes were clear in that he was thinking about James and blowing him up, but he hadn't thought it through. A day later (a Friday) his diary confirmed that his mind was made up. He had called his wife and told her he was staying on a few days as he had invitations from several quarry managers to look at their quarries in Scotland (a call to Mary confirmed this conversation). There were no quarry visits recorded in his diary. He had stayed on at the hotel where the course was based. He had rented a car, checked out of the hotel early Monday morning and driven to Aberdeen. He drove to Cut and Pull's warehouse arriving at six thirty and his diary said that he parked and waited in the car park until an employee came and opened the warehouse door and went in. Between then and eight several other employees entered. He took his chance and sneaked into the warehouse, placed the explosives, inserted the detonator and attached a 13 amp plug timer, set the timer for ten plugged the timer into a 13-amp socket, and switched on the socket. It took him less than five minutes; he wasn't disturbed and was driving out of Aberdeen by eight thirty. He drove back to Perth. On the way, he heard on the radio that there had been an explosion in Aberdeen. He returned the hire car at eleven thirty and was driving his own car back to Somerset before midday. It was the following day's diary entry that was the most shocking. He heard on the radio that his intended victim was being called Mr Lucky and had escaped the blast because of an emergency dental appointment. The other deaths he termed as unfortunate, but he felt that they would at least hurt James Jackson. He seemed to have no remorse or feelings of guilt. For several weeks he was worried that he would be caught if they identified the explosive but after that it appeared he had put it in the back of his mind and didn't mention it in his diary entries again.

DCI Sinclair kept examination of the most recent diary for himself. The diary detailed his last telephone conversation and the reference to the explosion in Aberdeen had clearly sent Phillip into a disturbed state of mind. His entry on the day prior to his suicide and his interview clearly laid out how he intended to kill himself and when. The last words in the diary were simply… 'goodbye Mary, thank you'.

The team were gathered, the Procurator Fiscal in attendance as well as the Deputy Chief Constable. DCI Sinclair addressed the team.

'Ma'am, Procurator, ladies, gents, it is my conclusion that the explosion in September at Cut and Pull was the work of Phillip Stephenson. We have his diary entries and written admission that he was responsible and we know why. That is all well and good, but we now must prove beyond reasonable doubt that he did it. We might assume the diaries are a figment of his imagination, farfetched; I agree, but we must turn over every stone to try to prove what he has told us in writing. We have a responsibility to the deceased, the relatives and loved ones of the deceased and the citizens of Aberdeen. There will be an official enquiry and we will be part of that enquiry. We still have not found the timer he refers to and we haven't found any of the gelignite or the detonators identification. We need to redouble our efforts. In the days following the explosion the debris that was blocking the main road was cleared and taken to the warehouse we rented at Altens along with all the debris from the site, we need to go through all that debris again. We also need to check roofs, gullies, drains, waste ground, on all areas and buildings within a 500-yard radius of the explosion site. I know, I know, settle down; I know we have already done it, but we are going to do it again. We have got some painful interviews to do. We need to interview Mary Stephenson under caution to determine if she knew about any of this. We need to interview the private detective, the quarry health and safety expert, the car hire company. There will be others but right now that is enough to be getting on with. This is high profile, it's costing the force a lot of money to keep this team together so the work needs to be done quickly but thoroughly and we need to come to the right conclusion. Ma'am do you wish to add anything?'

The Deputy Chief Constable shook her head 'No thank you, I think you have covered everything, keep me updated.'

'Yes Ma'am. Procurator do you have anything to add?'

'No Detective Chief Inspector, thank you, as you said its high profile, so accuracy is critical, I'm available anytime, as per the DCC keep me in the loop.'

The DCC and the Procurator Fiscal left the meeting.

'Right boys and girls let's get on it,' DCI Sinclair mingled with the group as they stood up, 'let's keep up the energy, thanks everyone.'

His formal interview with Mary Stephenson left no doubt in DCI Sinclair's mind that she knew nothing about her husband's plans and had not helped her husband or colluded in any way. She did know, of course, about his hatred of James Jackson and how he had spent the years after Jane's death hating him, but she was shocked to learn that her husband was suspected of killing innocent people in a failed attempt to kill Jackson. She found it hard to believe that Phillip had committed suicide. DCI Sinclair genuinely felt sorry for this woman, she had lost a daughter, a husband and now she would have to live with the knowledge of her husband's heinous crime. The enquiry would be a dreadful strain on her.

The real breakthrough came three months after the team meeting. A building several hundred yards along the road from the Cut and Pull building was undergoing some upgrading and modernisation. The rainwater drainage system was being torn off to be replaced, when an observant labourer noticed a piece of plastic like an electric plug fall from the bottom of one of the pipes as it was being lowered to the ground. He was more than observant, he was also a close relative of one of the victims of the Cut and Pull explosion and had heard the police appeal some months previously for any information or unusual objects found in the area. He immediately stopped the job and called the police. After examination, the object was found to be part of the timer assembly that had triggered the detonator, a minute length of detonator wire was still attached to it. This detonator wire was traced back to a batch match to the detonators still held by the Quarry Health and Safety Directorate and was the same as had been used in the September demonstration at Perth. Just a few days later the fingertip debris search at the police warehouse uncovered a one-inch circle of hard green cardboard with a seven digit number on it. This was identified as a gelignite end cap and this too batch matched the gelignite that had been used in Perth. The rental car records, the mileage driven that Monday by Phillip from Perth to Aberdeen and back and his credit card record for the rental of the vehicle put him in the right place and confirmed his diary entry.

CHAPTER 30

EUAN Sinclair drove from town into the autumn countryside. More than a year had passed since the explosion and Molly's kidnap. For Euan it was a time of reflection. The kidnap and the explosion had certainly not done his career any harm. He was now one of the most high-profile officers on the force. The upcoming enquiry would explore every aspect of the deaths caused by the explosion and would no doubt highlight the time that was lost when a certain sergeant, now retired on mental health grounds, had failed to do his job and worse had said that he had done it. Check, double check and check again, that was the lesson that all police officers must learn. Any one of us is only a small cog in a big wheel and what we do on any day can have a big impact on tomorrow, he thought. He turned left in Rothienorman village, the small village now no longer the centre of media attention. The short drive to Karen's farmhouse in the sunshine was very pleasant and he thought of the times he had driven the same road when Molly was still held hostage. He had liked James; James was someone who had got himself together after a traumatic event and had carved out a successful career. A loss, but what a selfless man he was. Molly was sitting on the swing below the big elm tree and waved as she saw him drive in. She walked over smiling, pleased to see him.

'Hello Molly, lovely to see you, you are looking well, are you okay?' he asked.

'Oh yes, Mr Euan thank you, all good. I am well and school is great. How are you?' she smiled, pleased to see him.

'I'm well Molly thanks. Looks like we have tied up all the loose ends on the explosion and the enquiry will be held soon, that's what I came to tell your Mum, is she around?'

'Yes. Mum's down near the stable, rounding up the ducks, I'll call her' Molly ran off calling for her Mum.

A few minutes later Karen appeared looking relaxed and happy, Molly by her side.

'Hello Euan, what a nice surprise. How are you? I hear you have been very busy, come in let's get some tea.'

Euan turned to follow her across the yard into the house when another figure appeared from the direction of the stable.

'Good afternoon Sir, been a while, how are you?'

Euan smiled, amused, but not surprised to see Sergeant McLeod.

'I'm well Tom thank you, how are you? How's life at the foreign office? You must have some stories to tell.'

Together, with Molly between them and Kettles yapping around their feet they followed Karen into the farmhouse.

Where are they now? 2021.

Karen still lives in the farmhouse at Rothienorman tending her ducks and other livestock.

Molly went to university and graduated with first class honours in History. She is a television producer with STV and lives in Glasgow.

Tom retired from the police force but still does some consulting for the foreign office. He has stayed very close to Karen and Molly and is often to be found at the farmhouse where he has his own bedroom.

Euan retired from the police; he made Detective Chief Superintendent. He now lives in Cleethorpes. He married last year to a childhood sweetheart. He has a productive allotment and a thirty-foot sailing yacht, both of which keep him fit and active. He and Tom remain friends.

Mary Stephenson never recovered from her husband's suicide and found it very difficult to accept that he was responsible for multiple murders. She is living in sheltered housing in Padstow and is very frail in her late eighties.

Cut and Pull was bought a year or so after the explosion and is now part of a multinational oilfield service company its name no longer used.

The remains of the cottage where Molly was held can still be seen but nature is relentlessly taking over the site and the track leading to it. The quarry is still flooded and is a haven for wildlife.

Jim Seager and his wife are still living in Great Yarmouth and are still close friends with Karen and Molly.

Large black cats are still occasionally seen in the north east of Scotland but no photographs to compare with Richard's have ever been taken. Richard's photographs are on display at Aberdeen Art Gallery.

END

About the Author

Robert (Bob) Harper worked in the oil industry for 40 years, travelling around the world. He has also worked in the whisky industry and prior to his retirement was a crab and lobster fisherman on the Moray Firth Coast. Some of these jobs he was particularly good at, others not so good! He lives with his Wife, Jenny and spends time on their allotment or his yacht (not super!).